AN AWARD WINNING SCOTTISH ROMANCE

THE MACAULAY BRIDE

NANCY PIRRI

To Steve, who brings out the best in me.

The MacAulay Bride definitely has its moments of greatness and its moments of not so good, but it is not in the way the book is written. It is in the story that is told with great finesse and skill. You are swept along on the tide of emotion, and it is a very difficult book to put down. For anyone who likes to see the strong male meet an equally strong female, and laugh and cry and rejoice with them as they meet head to head, Nancy has written the story for you. I found the characters strong and well-rounded and the story memorable. The MacAulay Bride should definitely be on your buy list. You will find yourself enjoying the clash and the joy to be found in the lives of Brianna and Harrison MacAulay.

— *ROMANCE AT HEART, ROSE BRUNGARD*

Rating: 9/10

The setting was fantastic. Vivid scenes allowed readers to be right on scene and in the essence permeating the aura floating off the page. As it is, Harrison is a man worth having. But first, Brianna needs to tame his desires. Pirri does a fine job. This is a unique idea that worked.

— *THE BLETHER BOOK REVIEW, BRENDA RAMSBACHER*

PROLOGUE

June 1, 1888
Winterhaven Manor, Edinburgh, Scotland

"My God, Raleigh," Harrison MacAulay said, "I feel as though I've just awakened from a bad dream, and none of what you have told me is true. Och! You are saying I must produce an heir or lose my home?"

"That's precisely what I'm saying," his solicitor replied. "It's right here, in your father's will, which he drafted when he was healthy and of sound mind, in case you have doubts."

Raleigh McKenna smoothed the parchment on the desk and read the old laird's words aloud. "My elder son, Harrison James McKenna, shall produce an heir by his thirty-first birthday. Otherwise, the MacAulay estates, including the ancestral home, Winterhaven Manor, shall accede to my second son, Payton Edward."

Harrison paced the green and gold Aubusson carpet,

from one end of the walnut-paneled library to the other, a scowl firmly planted on his face. After a while, he paused and leveled his gaze on Raleigh. "Must I abide by this?"

Raleigh folded his hands on the desk and leaned forward. "If you expect to keep possession of your home and wealth."

"What in the world was the old man thinking, other than the fact he held a deep obsession at the prospect of becoming a grandfather?" Harrison raged. "Did you know Payton had contacted Father from America years ago and told him about his own two sons? Payton wrote to me and said he never received an acknowledgement from Father."

"You're not surprised by the lack of response from your father, are you? Your brother fought a duel, killed a man and left the country, never to be seen again. Not to mention leaving the family name tarnished."

"Not surprised at all. I was the one who took the brunt of my father's fury with Payton's leaving." Harrison would never forget that fateful day ten years ago. Payton had killed the husband of his latest mistress. In order to avoid repercussions from the law, and to save his own life, he was forced to flee Scotland.

"You do earn a decent living from your work as a physician. Would it be devastating to give up the home and lands to your brother?"

Harrison shrugged. "Not at all. I spend more time at my townhouse in Edinburgh than at Winterhaven, anyway, since my clinic is nearby. But have you any doubt that Payton would run the place into the ground?"

"I see your point." Raleigh grimaced. "That younger brother of yours has been undeniably irresponsible at times."

Harrison snorted in disgust. "And what about all the cousins who reside here? I took on the responsibility of supporting and raising the young ones when their families couldn't, not to mention my duty caring for our tenant families. Payton wasn't raised for the job. So, it appears I must marry, hmm?"

A frown creased Raleigh's forehead as he perused the document. "Don't see marriage mentioned at all."

That gave Harrison pause. "But would my heir be legal if I weren't married?"

"Of course! This is Scotland, man, not England!" Harrison's lips twitched at the irritable look on his solicitor's face as he continued, Hell, you could run off in an instant to Gretna Green and handfast, instead, for the required year and a day, then end the relationship."

Harrison scoffed, "Handfasting is an old tradition, but hardly legal."

"Yes, 'tis legal. Scotland's laws still recognize the tradition."

"If my handfasted wife provided me with an heir, would I be obligated to remain with her—to marry her officially after the fact?"

"No, not at all, which is likely why so many men have encouraged their lovers over the years to handfast instead of marry, I would imagine. Have you anyone particular in mind?"

"Perhaps."

"Connie MacPhearson?" he suggested.

Harrison heard the stiff tone in Raleigh's voice as he sank into a chair across from his friend. "Not even remotely."

Raleigh growled, "Och, are ye saying she's not good enough for ye?"

"Hell, no, certainly not," Harrison said, laughter in his voice. "Watch it, Englishman. You're starting to sound like a

Scot. She would not have me because she's in love with you."

Sputtering, Raleigh jumped from his chair. "Now, see here... that is preposterous!"

"A moment ago you were ready to blow my head off at my response," Harrison drawled. "Thank God you hadn't a gun in your hand. When are you going to admit you're in love with the woman? You must know she's in love with you. The two of you are too stubborn for your own good, do you know that?"

"Enough," Raleigh snapped. "As your solicitor, I advise you to find a woman. Quickly. In eighteen months, you will be thirty-one. I'm leaving now. Do you require anything else?"

"No." Harrison rose and followed Raleigh to the door. "My thanks," he said, shaking his friend's hand. "I'll be making my decision soon."

After Raleigh left, Harrison stared out a long, narrow window, his hands folded behind his back. He watched his solicitor and long-time friend mount his horse and gallop away, all the while contemplating his choice of available womanhood.

Other than one particular woman who was always on his mind, none was appropriate. Brianna MacAulay was the only woman he'd thought about on a daily basis for the past ten years. The only woman he'd ever truly wanted yet had never met her—from the moment he'd seen her in the wedding picture Payton had sent to him.

It was truly unfortunate she was his brother's wife.

CHAPTER 1

November 1888
Stillwater, Minnesota

$\mathcal{B}$rianna MacAulay stood inside the train depot for the third afternoon in a row, watching passengers disembark from the last train of the day. She peered at the people swarming through the doorway, worried that some mishap might have befallen her husband's brother since she found no sign of the man.

There was nothing she could do now but go home and hope he would arrive tomorrow. She presumed it would then be a simple matter for him to settle her late husband's will. She frowned as she thought about the money she hadn't been allowed to withdraw from Payton's bank account. It was hers! She needed that money—every single penny—in order to furnish two more bedchambers in her home by spring. More lumberjacks would be arriving to work for the town's sawmills by then, and they would be in need of a place to stay.

Squaring her shoulders and hitching up her black taffeta skirt and petticoats, she walked toward the door and opened it. Huge drops of cold autumn rain splashed against her face and she squinted against the onslaught. For the little good it did, she held the umbrella over her head, bracing herself against the wind and rain. She sighed, wishing it were snow instead of rain. Snow wouldn't ruin the hat she wore. It was her favorite, with a bird's nest perched on top, its cloth occupant having long since flown away.

She dodged puddles on the deserted boardwalk before gingerly stepping into the muddy street, then rushed to her wagon. Upon reaching it, she held the umbrella in one hand as she placed a foot upon the running board, ready to board, when she heard a deep masculine voice shouting.

"Madam! A moment, please."

A big man wearing a top hat approached her. She lowered her foot and the umbrella just as he arrived at her side. He swept his cloak off his shoulders, held an edge of it high above her head, gallantly shielding her from the rain.

"I must speak with you," he said in a deep, accented voice.

As she peered up at him, she thought him familiar, but could not place him.

He took her elbow and nodded at Francis Marshall's Dry Goods. "Let us find protection."

Before she could dig in her heels, he fairly propelled her across the street, where they ducked beneath Marshall's dark green and white striped awning. Lord knew she should never have gone willingly with this stranger, yet she could not help but wonder why he had approached her. She tilted her head back to meet his eyes, but discovered them concealed behind a pair of rain-spattered, wire-rimmed spectacles.

Then he removed his hat and she recognized him—
Harrison MacAulay, her brother-in-law. She'd never seen a
picture of him, but the pleasant curve of his lips was very
similar to her husband's, yet, with his smile the similarity
ended. Where Payton had been fair-haired, blue-eyed and
fine of build, Harrison was tall and broad-shouldered, his
complexion darker.

Brianna's cheeks grew warm under his intent look and
she gasped, "*You* are Harrison MacAulay?" From the
moment he spoke, she should have guessed his identity
because of his Scottish dialect.

"I am, dear sister-in-law," he said, inclining his head,
"and at your beck and call for as long as you need me." He
lifted her hand and brushed it with a gentle kiss.

She shivered. Her heart raced at his warm touch that she
felt through the thin fabric of her glove. She pulled her hand
away, not at all happy about the way his kiss caused a funny
feeling inside of her. Of course, many women would have
difficulty ignoring a handsome man of such extraordinary
height, lean yet powerful build, black, wavy hair and deep
brown eyes.

"I... I worried that something had happened to you." A
sudden bolt of lightning splitting the sky startled her, and
she added, "I suggest we leave for home before the roads
become impassable."

He looked around, then met her eyes with a frown. "And
where are your sons?"

"My neighbor, Mrs. Crane, offered to stay with them on
the condition I return shortly."

"I apologize for my lateness. Two days ago, I boarded a
train in Chicago. That was shortly after I sent the wire
notifying you of my arrival. Alas, the train derailed and I
was forced to wait for another that did not leave until this
morning. I sent you a second wire."

"I never received it."

For some reason, she trusted his word, though she had long ago given up believing a single word from her husband. Payton had been a gambler and tippler, until he drowned a month ago in the St. Croix River. During the last two years of their marriage, she had learned to depend upon herself for her livelihood. Which was fine with her. She'd never been the sort of woman to sit idle day after day. Running the boarding house gave her something worthwhile to do, and she earned a fair living besides. The money she'd saved from her boarders was dwindling, though, and the next season's lumberjacks wouldn't be arriving for four long months.

"I suppose it could not be helped. Now, we must get out of this rain, although it doesn't matter since we are both thoroughly drenched."

He replaced his hat, took her arm and escorted her to her wagon, which luckily had a bonnet of sorts over the seats. "I must fetch my bags," he said, assisting her into the driver's seat. Within moments, he returned with two leather bags and tossed them into the back of the wagon. "Have you any suggestions regarding accommodations in town?"

"I wouldn't hear of you staying at a hotel. I've a room at home ready for you."

He raised his brow. "For propriety's sake, that may not be a good idea."

"My friends and neighbors wouldn't think poorly of me for offering a family member a place to stay." She saw the hesitant look on his face and she flushed, chiding herself for being so forward. She wanted him to stay with her, yet he appeared ready to decline. If he did, it would greatly disappoint her sons. They missed a man's presence in their young lives. As much as she hated to admit it, as much as she enjoyed her freedom, she missed a man in the house.

"Verra well. Then I shall see you later," he said and whacked Winney's hindquarters.

Brianna held onto the reins as the horse started moving forward and she shouted over her shoulder, "Aren't you coming?"

"I have business to tend to first."

"But you have no idea where I live!"

In the dimming light, she caught a flash of white and bristled when she realized he was smiling. "I'm certain I will have no trouble finding you."

As she headed for home, she couldn't help but wonder what business a stranger from Scotland could have in town with the approach of evening. From past experience where her husband was concerned, there were only a few reasons why a man went to town after dark. She shook her head and heaved a sigh, chagrined at her wayward thoughts. "All right, Brianna MacAulay," she muttered. "That will be enough of that sort of thinking."

Brianna stood in her parlor, satisfied that the cherry wood tables still glowed from her most recent polishing. The white lace curtains covering the windows were fresh and clean. The red, green and gold floral carpeting held nary a speck of lint. Her boys had their noses jammed against the parlor window as they anxiously awaited the arrival of their uncle.

"You will smear the glass, and after I just cleaned it," she scolded. "Now, come back to the kitchen and finish your supper."

"Not hungry, Ma," said seven-year-old Jamie.

"Me neither," announced Harry. The nine year old stared at her over his shoulder. "When did Uncle Harrison say he'd be here?"

She sighed and tried to count how many times they'd asked that same question since she arrived home more than an hour ago. "He didn't say. There will be no dessert if you don't eat the rest of your stew."

The boys turned to her, disappointment stamped on their faces. She crossed her arms and waited, fighting the urge to give into them. Admittedly, she indulged her boys— even understood her reasons for doing so. With the loss of their father, they seemed so sad much of the time, Harry, in particular.

Harry asked, "What's for dessert?"

"Do you not recognize the scent?"

Jamie inhaled and grinned. "Apple pie!"

She headed down the hallway, slowing at the sound of someone knocking on her door. She retraced her steps, but by the time she arrived at the door her sons had already opened it. They surveyed their uncle, small faces filled with suspicion, awe and curiosity.

Harrison's cloak hung over one arm. His black jacket fit his wide shoulders to perfection. A matching waistcoat, white shirt with crisp starched collar and gray tie completed his attire. He looked handsome, authoritative and wealthy.

Her younger son stuck out his hand. "I'm Jamie."

Brianna noted the pleased but melancholic expression crossing Harrison's face when he replied, "Jamie," and took his nephew's hand in his own. "You look remarkably like your father."

Brianna saw tears glistening in his eyes and thought how dreadful he must feel at the loss of his only brother he hadn't seen in ten years. She smiled when he reached down and swept Jamie into his arms, held him close. He closed his eyes and took a deep breath. He appeared to be inhaling the essence of her son's innocence, as one would inhale the sweet scent of a newly opened rose. Jamie allowed the affectionate embrace until Harrison lowered him to the floor.

She frowned when Jamie clung to his leg. "Your uncle cannot walk with you attached to him."

"He is fine where he is." He settled his big hand on Jamie's blonde thatch of hair, then turned to Harry, who stood by in silence.

"Greet your uncle, Harry," Brianna gently ordered.

"You don't look much like Pa," Harry blurted out, tilting his head to the side. "Except for your smile."

"Verra astute, my boy. I favor your grandfather, while your father took after your grandmother."

"I must also look like grandfather since I look like you."

From the moment Brianna had met Harrison at the train depot, she'd realized her eldest son's strong resemblance to his uncle. Until now, she'd always thought Harry resembled her.

Harrison opened his arms to welcome him, but Harry reached out, grabbed his hand and shook it, instead. Brianna saw fleeting disappointment cross Harrison's face before veiling it. "You know that your father named you after me, don't you?"

Harry shook his head. "Nope. I didn't." He grinned. "We were just going to the kitchen for dessert. Want some?"

"Depends on what it is."

"Oh, well, does it matter?" Harry asked, looking his uncle over carefully. "You look like you eat everything."

"Harry!" Brianna exclaimed, shocked.

Harrison threw back his head and laughed.

Harry's wide-eyed gaze never left his uncle. "But, Ma, he's big as old Farmer Jorgenson's ox!"

Brianna sighed, gave Harrison an apologetic smile. "Have you eaten supper yet?"

"Haven't had a bite since noon."

"How does beef stew, apple pie and coffee sound?"

He nodded. "Wonderful."

After the boys ate their pie and Harrison had finished his meal, the conversation was lively, interspersed with bouts of boisterous shouts and laughter. Brianna hated ending the evening. It had been a while since she'd seen her sons so happy. She hated doing it but at ten o'clock, she announced, "It's past bedtime, boys."

"Oh, but Ma, we don't have school tomorrow, and we want to talk more with Uncle!" Jamie protested.

"It is late," Harrison inserted. "I'll still be here come morning."

Brianna settled them down for the night and quietly made her way to her bedchamber. With a critical look, she examined herself in the oval mirror positioned over the cherry wood bureau, tucking a stray lock of black hair into the bun atop her head. While her sapphire-colored eyes were pretty and her short, straight nose was rather ordinary, she thought her high, wide cheekbones attractive. Enough, Brianna MacAulay! Whom are you trying to impress, anyway? Still, she pinched her cheeks before joining Harrison in the parlor.

He sat in a gold velvet gentleman's chair, which happened to be large enough to accommodate his bulk, one leg crossed over his knee, arms draped over the chair's arms. He rose upon her entrance and she took a seat on the threadbare crimson divan. He sat down again then. Brianna welcomed the heat from the fire he had stoked. Just the thought of kicking off her shoes and tucking her toes beneath her warm woolen blanket prompted her to close her weary eyes.

"Tell me about my brother. What caused his death?"

"If I could have kept him here with me he would not

have died," she said, opening her eyes. "You received my letter, didn't you?"

"Aye, but you offered no explanation as to how Payton drowned, which I couldn't understand at all since he'd been an excellent swimmer."

"Drunk on spirits was the mortician's findings. He had difficulty controlling himself in that way."

"You mentioned if you could have kept him here with you, he wouldn't be dead. What did you mean?"

"He lived..." She hung her head, too embarrassed to continue.

"Go on," he prompted. Behind the spectacles, his eyes were kind.

"Your brother kept a mistress for the past two years. He spent little time at home."

"Ah, now why doesn't that surprise me?" he said dryly.

She raised her brow. "Are you telling me he had a history of womanizing?"

"Aye. But it is not all that uncommon in Scotland for a man to keep a mistress—discreetly, of course. This doesn't mean he doesn't love his wife. It's just that a wife is a lady, and a lady cannot always provide her husband... well... with what he needs."

The man was dreadfully serious. My Lord, he hadn't lived through the pain and agony of losing a loved one as she had. Not Payton's dying, but his leaving her for another woman. "Is that a fact?" she murmured. "May I assume a wife has the same privilege?"

He stared at her a long moment, confusion on his face, before asking, "What privilege would that be?"

"Why, to have affairs."

"Hardly," he snapped, rising to his feet.

She watched him pace the floor, tears filling her eyes even as her voice quivered. "I gave your brother my unequivocal devotion. I kept his home tidy and served him fine meals—that is, when he chose to bless us with his presence. But even that wasn't enough for him."

He paused in his pacing and stared at her. "How long have you been shouldering the burden for your family, Brianna?"

"For quite some time." She swallowed the lump in her throat and swiped at a tear running down her cheek. "Your brother had grand dreams of forging a fortune, and was well on his way to fulfilling them when he purchased stock in Mayor's Lumber Company. He grew fascinated with the every-day workings of that enterprise. In fact, he spent entire winters up north in the logging camps, working as a lumberjack. He loved being outdoors. But it meant him being away from home for so long. We all missed him terribly during those months, but he was working the work he loved. How could I deny him?"

Harrison frowned. "Payton didn't establish a solicitor's practice when he arrived in America?"

She raised her brow. "Payton was a lawyer?"

"Yes, a very successful one in Scotland, until he was forced to... until he decided to move to America. I had thought he'd start up his business here."

Payton had been educated? While his manners were exceptional, he always possessed a physically hard working man body. He'd never mentioned a word to her. Just thinking about his pay as a logger compared with what an attorney earned caused her to seethe.

Harrison encouraged her, "Continue, please."

"He would come home in the spring, as all the lumberjacks did, and stay until October when he'd leave again."

Harrison shoved back the edges of his jacket and jammed his hands deep into his pockets. "Are ye telling me that my brother left ye alone for more than half a year at a time?"

Ah, there was that burr again. She nodded.

"However did you manage?"

She lifted her chin and met his gaze straight on. "With difficulty."

After Payton's death, she had approached his solicitor, Reginald Nielsen. He'd told her everything had been taken care of, and that she need not worry her pretty little head about a thing. He'd also explained that until Harrison MacAulay arrived he couldn't release so much as a single cent to her.

"We shall call upon my solicitor first thing Monday morning," she announced, thinking of the money she required to purchase bed frames and mattresses from Sears Roebuck. A monthly charge of seven dollars per month, including board, was reasonable rent for a lumberjack. And renting five bedchambers would give her all the money she required to keep her home, and to feed and clothe her children.

"That will not be necessary since Mr. Nielsen and I have met, this very evening, in fact. We've straightened out Payton's financial affairs, and everything is in order."

Brianna frowned. "But Mr. Nielsen never conducts business past five o'clock, and never on Saturday or Sunday."

Harrison inclined his head. "He was willing to oblige me."

She clapped her hands in delight. "Well, that's wonderful news! Now you may return home to Scotland, and I may get on with my life."

He sat down beside her and gave her a gentle smile. "You seem to be an intelligent woman, and so I believe you will understand me when I say your financial situation is far from good." He reached inside his pocket and withdrew a small packet of money. "This is all that is left of Payton's estate, once Nielson paid off his considerable debts." He pressed the bills into her hand. "I'm sorry, but it will be necessary to sell your home. I've requested Mr. Nielsen to immediately begin seeking a buyer."

Staring in wide-eyed dismay at the paltry sum, Brianna rose from the divan. Clenching the money in her fist, she felt a fury unlike any she'd ever felt before threaten to ignite. "How could Payton do this to us?"

She thought how she'd tolerated her husband's drinking and gambling for the sake of their children, and because she loved him. In hindsight, she realized she had known little of love when she married Payton at sixteen. Recognizing her own shortcomings, she knew she was not as easy on the eyes as many other women. She had long ago come to terms with the fact that she would never be petite and pretty. Still, Payton's taking a mistress had hurt her. But then she also knew that she had been much more in love with Payton than he'd been with her. To this day, she still wondered why he'd requested her hand in marriage.

Sadly, the next time she saw him was after he'd drowned. She'd had him laid out in his blue serge suit, in a simple pine box. With tears rolling down her cheeks and her grieving sons on either side of her, she cursed him for having caused them all so much pain while he lived.

"I apologize for my brother's lack of responsibility for you and your sons. Payton never did possess one iota of common sense." He stared into the fire a moment before turning to her again. "A few years ago Payton sent me a letter regarding your welfare, if something were to happen to him. His desire was for you to return with me to Scotland."

"I am capable of taking care of myself and my sons. For

two years I've taken in boarders and have done just fine, thank you." She swept past him and took and took up a place opposite him, on a straight-backed chair, folding her hands in her lap. She had to keep her distance from him. He attracted her... too much.

"You mean to tell me you open your home to strangers?" he asked, rising to his feet once more and headed toward her.

"I was forced to do so," she said, lifting her chin, meeting the fiery look in his eyes head-on. "This is my home and I'm not leaving it."

"Hell and damnation!" he growled, stopping directly in front of her. "Do you think I want to do this to you?" He raked a hand through his hair. "I hate uprooting you and your sons, but we have no choice in the matter. You've been left penniless, left with nothing but your children and, I'm afraid even they aren't legally yours.

"We leave for Scotland as soon as I can make arrangements," he stated firmly.

CHAPTER 2

"*W*hat are you saying?" Brianna's hand fluttered to her breast as an insidious coldness seeped into her body.

"Your sons are under my guardianship."

Her face paled as she rose from her seat and backed away from him.

He stopped her backward motion by going after her, stopping her when he took her hands in his. "When Payton wrote, with the birth of each of his sons, he requested that if something were to happen to him, his sons be educated in Scotland and I'm responsible for them until they reach eighteen years of age."

Brianna yanked her hands from his. "They're my sons, too! Doesn't that count for anything?"

He shook his head. "I'm afraid not. Eventually, you will learn to love Scotland and accept it as your home."

"Tell me, if I lived in Scotland—mind you, I said *if*—what ever would I do there?"

Harrison raised his brow. "Well, I would imagine what women usually do."

"And what might that be?"

"Grandmother Mary hosts tea parties, pays calls and performs many charitable works. Grandmother Jean is involved in her... causes."

"Causes?" she asked, unable to hide her curiosity.

Harrison gave her a lop-sided grin. "Aye. Her current passion is the saving of mankind."

She raised her brow. "Saving them from what?"

"Primarily the overindulgence of spirits. America isn't the only country involved in Women's Temperance."

"Your grandmothers live close by you then?"

"They reside with me."

"Both of them?"

He nodded. "Although my maternal grandmother spends many months in her own home on the Isle of Skye. When my grandfathers passed away a year apart, it was my responsibility to care for them. Now then, I know it's much too soon to contemplate marriage again, but..."

"I'll never again enter into that esteemed state. Once was quite enough," she said with as much authority as she could muster. "Allow me to relieve your conscience. I am not yours or anyone else's responsibility." It was difficult being strong with such a manly, vibrant presence as Harrison MacAulay, but she must. She couldn't give in to him and lose control of her life.

As much as she'd loved her parents, she had been their only child, and they'd worried about her safety and had severely hindered her from pursuing new endeavors. She recalled wanting to learn to ride a bicycle when she was young. But they'd been too fearful for her safety. They'd died when their carriage overturned on the way home from visiting friends in St. Paul shortly after her eighth birthday. Because she had no other relatives, she'd been placed at St. Benedict's orphanage, where she'd led a cloistered life until her sixteenth year. She'd met Payton while performing one of her chores, the daily shopping at the market. Not only had Payton been extremely handsome, which of course made him irresistible, he had offered her an opportunity to leave behind her restricted life, and gave her a home and children, which she'd wanted desperately.

Harrison scowled. "You must understand that I do not take my duty lightly."

"Duty?" She didn't want to be any man's duty. "Now, see here—"

"We will be leaving Friday morning, on the eight o'clock train."

Brianna swallowed the lump in her throat. "I believe a meeting with my solicitor is in order then. As I said earlier, I shall call on him first thing Monday."

"For what purpose, since I have already met with the man?" he asked, clearly exasperated.

"I'm questioning the terms of my husband's will. This isn't the dark ages, after all. I cannot believe I'm being denied the right to raise my own children, without the bother of a man."

Harrison sputtered, "Bother?"

She left him speechless as he thought how he had wanted Brianna from the first time he gazed upon her face ten long years ago. He'd received a letter from his brother, along with a wedding portrait of Brianna standing behind her husband, one hand on his shoulder. At the time, he had been disgusted with himself for coveting his brother's wife. But with the passage of time he had thanked God there had been an ocean between them, and recognized his desire for her for what it was. Pure lust.

His feelings for her hadn't changed, and with the demise of his brother, he would pursue her.

After Harrison had learned of Payton's death, there was nothing he could do but be the dutiful older brother he'd always been. He'd had no choice but to travel to America and fetch his sister-in-law. Once they married, she would, God willing, give him the son he needed. The idea of her not conceiving was unimaginable.

Once they reached Scotland, he would propose marriage. The thought gave him pause, though; why not now, he asked himself. Maybe she would be more receptive to moving to Scotland if he did. Then he looked at her again, saw the fury on her face and sighed. At the moment, he knew he could utter the most romantic of proposals and she wouldn't budge. She was that angry.

She turned to him. Meeting her troubled expression, he held out his hand, reasoning that if she took it she'd trust him, and accept him, and all he had to offer. He was disappointed when she shook her head and turned away. He moved closer. His hand ached to reach out and stroke the delicate curve of her neck above the starched collar of her dress.

She whirled around unaware he stood so close, and stumbled back. Swiftly, he reached out and grasped her forearms, preventing her from crashing into the windowpane. Once sure she had her balance, he released her and folded his arms across his chest. "Why must you see Payton's attorney when I have already done so?"

"I intend to challenge Payton's will and thought you could, perhaps, champion my cause in the courts. You can't possibly agree with the conditions of your brother's will, can you?"

He groaned. "Whether I agree or not is of little consequence. What's done is done, and I'm not a barrister,

Brianna." He swept his hair back from his forehead and straightened his spectacles. "Besides, even if I did help you, you haven't a remote chance of gaining custody of your sons."

"Can you not leave us here?" she pleaded. "Ignore your brother's wishes?

Harrison growled, "A woman alone, with no man to protect her, is prey for any scheming, unconscionable man. I frankly can't believe you expect me to ignore my brother's wishes. And do you honestly believe I would dishonor myself by shirking my duty? That you would question my integrity is unthinkable."

Her voice shook in outrage. "I've built a good life for my sons and have raised them alone since Payton proved to be so undependable. I believe your brother cared for us in his own way, but he wasn't a strong man. I couldn't trust his word or believe he would be here for us when we needed him." She sighed, raised her hands, and massaged her temples. "I'm exhausted, so if you will excuse me, I'm retiring for the night."

"An excellent idea." He followed her out of the parlor and down the hallway. "This will all make perfect sense to you come morning. Now, would you kindly direct me to your guest room?"

She stopped and raised her brow. "Whatever for?"

"You offered me a room. Remember?"

She shook her head and lifted her chin. "It wouldn't be proper if you stayed here. No, it wouldn't do at all." Plucking up her skirts, she continued down the hallway leaving Harrison standing there, dumbfounded. He swore under his breath, snatched up his satchel and chased after her.

"But you informed me not to take accommodations elsewhere," he protested.

"That was before you tried to take charge of my life, and before I knew my husband considered me incapable of caring for our children." She reached the front door, swung it open and stepped aside.

He stopped in front of her. "Being a woman, I realize it's difficult for you to be reasonable, but—"

"Not reasonable, you say?"

He cringed at the shrill tone in her voice.

"Since I'm an unprotected woman, I believe I'm being quite sensible in not allowing you to stay here. As for finding a place, thus far you've proven to be a resourceful man. I believe you'll have no problem, whatsoever."

"You truly are turning me out, aren't you?" he asked in astonishment.

She nodded and looked somewhere above his head. He was stunned when she looked away, unwilling to meet his eyes. After a long moment of horrid silence, she did finally look at him. He couldn't prevent glaring down at her, having used the same expression at home with his servants and peers, which usually got him exactly what he wanted. After some length, he sighed when he realized she wasn't afraid of him. Damn. He was used to having things his way... always. But not this time.

She maintained her stance, door open and hand on the knob. Harrison swore under his breath and strode outside.

From the open door, Brianna watched his long-legged strides carry him away until he was at the front gate. Then she called out, "Mister MacAulay!"

He came to an abrupt halt, turned stiffly. It was dark, but she saw how tall and straight he stood.

"If I choose not to leave with you on Friday next, what will you do?" she inquired. Oh, she didn't want to encourage his anger further, yet much depended upon his answer. Even in the dark, she saw his chest heaving and clenched her fists at her side, waiting for the ranting to begin.

She was surprised when he said rather mildly, "For your sake, Madam, and for the sake of your children, you will be packed and ready to leave, and you will not give me another moment's grief about it."

Her body shook at his threatening words. She watched him as he stalked away and disappeared into the night. The good Lord in His blessed wisdom had rid her of her philandering husband. Now He had sent her this headstrong male with whom to contend. She cursed her abysmal luck that she was saddled with another MacAulay, yet this one appeared to be dependable, honorable, and dreadfully dutiful.

With a heavy heart, she closed the door, trudged into the parlor and came to a decision. No man was going to get the better of her. As the good sisters at St. Benedict's Orphanage always said, crying never helped a blessed thing.

A plan came to mind then. While her children slept, she packed the bare necessities, determined to reach Clearwater, Wisconsin, by mid-morning. Her friend, Angela Miller, and her family had moved to the small town a year ago. She lived twelve miles away and across the St. Croix River. Far enough away that Harrison wouldn't know where to begin searching.

Then he couldn't force her to leave her home, leaving behind friends, her home and her means of livelihood. She'd return to her home after a while, knowing well he had duties to tend to back home and would eventually leave. Move to Scotland? What a ridiculous idea! However would she support herself? She'd never been east of the St. Croix, for heaven's sake!

An hour later, she stood beside her wagon and adjusted a trunk of clothing, a barrel of food and water, and other necessities for her journey. She returned to the kitchen where she snatched Payton's Winchester rifle from its usual place against the wall. Cradling the weapon against her chest, she made her way out the door. Her hands twitched as she held the gun, and she cursed Payton for refusing to instruct her in its proper use.

The scent of snow in the air prompted her to say a prayer that she would reach her destination before the first flakes fell. She reached the stall and opened the door. As she led Winney to the wagon, she said, "There, there, girl. Stand still and be the cooperative dear that you have always been."

Brianna laid the gun down on the ground. She'd bent down to her knee to harness Winney when she heard footsteps on the path alongside the house.

Her head darted up. She saw a huge shadow bearing down on her. She snatched up the rifle while on her knees and swung it into position. The shadow showed no sign of stopping at the threat of the gun. As the shadow drew closer, she realized she pointed the gun straight at Harrison MacAulay's dutiful, stubborn heart.

"You!" She rose and backed away, her fingers relaxing on the trigger.

He strode toward her, eyes ablaze, and halted in front her. He reached out and wound his hand around the gun's barrel, his eyes never leaving hers. Brianna released the rifle and he positioned it under his arm. "Don't ever point a gun at me."

She stumbled back, placing more distance between them. "I would never have shot you!"

"Of course you wouldn't," he said dryly. Now get back to the house," he ordered.

She watched him lead Winney back to her stall. Before locking the animal inside, he turned and pinned her with a look colder than the November night.

"Didn't I tell you to get inside?"

Brianna lifted her chin. "I'm not going to Scotland."

He glared at her a moment longer before he swiveled around to complete his task. Within moments, he left the stall and slammed the door shut.

Brianna backed away, panicked. Her neighbor's home was quiet and dark. Would the hard of hearing Mr. Feeney hear her if she screamed? She started running toward Feeney's house but wasn't fast enough.

Harrison caught up with her and smoothly bent down and hoisted her over one broad shoulder. In the next instant, she was stunned when he reached up and laid a firm hand upon her derriere.

Heat coursed through her body and she shouted, "Put me down this instant!"

"Stop that infernal screeching," he warned.

Brianna squeezed her eyes shut, humiliated by the touch of his hand on her buttocks. "How did you know I would try to leave?" she demanded.

"If you only knew how predictable you are, you would never open your pretty little mouth again."

"What are you talking about?" She braced her hands on his strong shoulders and pushed herself upright, to relieve the pressure on her stomach.

"I guessed when I left you earlier you would try something foolish. What? Do you believe I'm some sort of ogre because you must return to Scotland with me? Well, I'm not, and, I have come to realize you are more stubborn than any Scots lass I have ever known.

"For shame, Brianna, had you even considered the risk to your children by leaving like this? The weather is frigid and it will be snowing by morning. The roads are in poor condition from the heavy rainfall, not to mention the fact there could be rapists, robbers and sundry other criminals lurking along the way."

Brianna thought over his words as she held onto his shoulders. He made his way into the house, gently closing and locking the door behind them. As he strode up the stairs to the second floor, she silently admitted he was correct in his assessment of the situation. Harry and Jamie's safety should have been her primary consideration. Ever since Harrison's arrival a mere six hours ago, she had lost the ability to think clearly.

"Which is your room?"

"The last one on the right," she said, knowing she had no choice but to tell him. Then she bit her lip, guessing the mule-headed Scotsman wouldn't leave her alone this night. Unfortunately, there was nothing she could do now but offer him a room. He meant to take one, anyway, with or without her consent. She prayed he was a sound sleeper because she planned on leaving, if not this night, then another very soon.

He entered her bedchamber, kicked the door closed behind them and set her down on her feet. She couldn't see his face since the room was pitch black, but she had no doubt he was furious with her. She'd felt the tenseness in his body when he'd carried her up the stairs. Yet she was astonished when he spoke in a calm, gentle voice.

His soft voice came to her in the darkness. "Accept my sincere apology for handling you so roughly, but I needed to find a way to silence you before you woke up the neighborhood."

With her mouth gaping, she stood there, riveted by his unexpected words. She heard his footsteps, then the wooden floor creaking under his feet. The room brightened to a warm, sunny glow—he'd lit a kerosene lamp. The quilt on her bed, once a rich royal blue, had faded to gray; the matching curtains dulled from the southern exposure. One of her finest hand-embroidered doilies she'd set upon the washstand, topped by a white chamber set.

Her attention turned to his unbuttoned jacket that revealed a fine silk brocaded vest. She noted the silvery gray color of his eyes matched the vest. An exquisite mother-of-pearl pin glistened, like a drop of new fallen rain, on his lapel.

Gently, he took her hand, raised it to his lips and her heart raced from his hot, dry touch.

"A truce, Brianna. I do not relish battling with you the entire way to Scotland. Can I trust you not to run again?"

She shook her head. "You know I cannot make any promises."

He sighed. "I was afraid that might be your answer." He released her hand and strode across the room, pausing in front of an armoire. He opened the double doors and searched inside, then pulled one of Payton's snowy cravats off a shelf. She gasped when he turned to her with a determined look in his eyes. Then he snapped the cloth between his two hands.

"Oh, my Lord!" she gasped. "You wouldn't dare!"

CHAPTER 3

"No!" Brianna shouted as she hurled herself across the bed. Before she bounded off the other side, Harrison snagged one ankle. Then he hauled her to the bed's center and flipped her onto her back. She kicked out and made contact with his jaw.

He swore before sinking to the bed and straddling her hips.

"I enjoy wrestlin' as much as any man," he said, chuckling, "Particularly with a bonnie woman." Gripping her sides with his powerful thighs, he snatched up one of her flailing wrists. He wound the cravat around it, securing it to a heavy bedpost. Brianna screamed in frustration and dug at the knot with her free hand.

Harrison growled, "Be still or you'll hurt yourself." Then he hoisted himself off her body and sat down beside her.

"I promise I won't run away again!" she said, pulling at the knot.

"I'm sorry, Brianna. I very much doubt that."

She commenced kicking her legs, twisting and turning to no avail. "Damn you to hell, Harrison MacAulay!"

"Payton never enjoyed challenges," he said, "but if he were alive today, he'd tell you how I thrive on them. It will take more than a mere slip of a woman like you to best me. By the way, do other American women curse as proficiently as you?"

Her cheeks burned in humiliation when she recalled her language a moment ago. "You'll not be here long enough to find out," she retorted.

He laughed. "On the contrary, I have five days to enjoy myself, and I intend to make the most of them. Imagine my delight when I discovered you have an opera house in town. It's quite grand." Reaching for the woolen blanket at the foot of the bed, he pulled it up and covered her to her chin. "As I said earlier, sleep now. Things will look better in the morning." He sank down beside her.

She gasped, "You can't sleep here!"

One eyebrow shot up. His gaze swept her body, a twisted smile on his lips. "I don't believe you are in any position to stop me."

Brianna gasped when his body touched hers as he made himself comfortable. She shrank away from him but he rolled nearer. She opened her mouth to protest but choked on her words when he plucked a pin from her hair and released a curl, winding the tress around one finger.

"You have lovely hair." He brought the lock to his nostrils. "Lovely scent, as well. I must admit I'm quite hedonistic when it comes to a woman's crowning glory."

Hedonistic? Oh, my! His tender hold on her hair made it impossible to move away. His fingers delved into her locks and massaged her scalp as he released each and every single curl. Her eyes drifted shut as she gave into the intoxication his fingers provoked. She had no desire to think. She felt a thumping in her chest and it took her a moment to realize it was her heart racing. His touch reminded her only to feel; reminded her how long since Payton had touched her.

"I don't want you here," she whispered, a token protest.

"I know, but you have no choice in the matter."

She opened her eyes when she felt him shift at her side. Then he reached up and turned down the lamp, plunging the room into darkness.

"Sleep, sweetheart."

"I'm not your sweet anything, and I doubt I'll sleep a wink the entire night."

He didn't reply. Brianna was amazed a moment later when she felt a weight lift from the bed and footsteps crossing the floor. When she heard the door open, she asked in surprise, "You're leaving me?"

His low chuckle grated on her nerves. "Contrary to what you believe about me, sweet sister-in-law, I've always behaved as a perfect gentleman should. I will be nearby so just call out if you require anything."

After he left Brianna struggled with the knot, to no avail. Comfort came to mind when she realized she had the entire night to think of another escape plan.

By the next evening, Brianna knew Harrison meant to keep her in his sight every minute of the day. Wherever she went, he followed. She was amazed when he helped her clean up the kitchen and dried the dishes. She stifled her laughter when he tried to tie an apron around his waist but the ties were too short. Now she entered the parlor after sending the boys to bed and worked at the knot in her apron.

Harrison sat on her best velvet high-backed chair, smoking a cigar and reading the Stillwater Gazette. He appeared much too comfortable in her home and she didn't like it a bit.

"We need to talk," she said abruptly, stopping in front of him.

He folded the newspaper and set it aside without a word. Sitting forward he placed his hands at her waist and turned her around.

She stiffened and held her breath while he easily loosened the knotted strings. A tingling sensation traveled up and down her spine from his touch. She exhaled when he removed the apron and laid it over the back of a chair.

"I'm going to town in the morning to speak with Mr. Nielsen," she announced as she sat on the divan across from him. "I give you warning I haven't changed my mind about not leaving. Have you any idea how many years it's taken me to set up housekeeping and establish my vegetable garden, not to mention the rooms I furnished to let?"

"You may tear up all of Winterhaven's lawns if you wish to plant a garden," he said magnanimously. "We have a gardener who'd be delighted to engage in a new enterprise other than his current tending of the roses and such." He frowned. "You are giving me negligible excuses for staying."

"And you have yet to give me a plausible reason for returning with you," she said caustically.

"What better reason then for the welfare of your sons?" He eased back in his chair. "You don't seem to understand how important it is for me to fulfill my obligation to my brother."

"I know precisely how important your duty is," she retorted. "You may be considered nobility of sorts in your country, but not here. Here you are nothing but a...a mister, and you have no power over me!"

He shrugged. "It doesn't matter. I have the law on my

side. Believe me, Brianna, I will not hesitate to call upon the authorities for assistance, if I require it."

"I'm fairly certain Sheriff Johnson will not force me to leave my home," she said confidently.

"No, but a short stay in prison should change your mind, I would imagine."

"Prison!" She stared at him in shock as he rose from his chair and took a seat beside her.

"Um, yes. I've learned incarceration has been utilized on occasion to curb a willful woman's behavior in this progressive country of which you are so fond." He leaned forward, his eyes piercing hers. "Women who choose to ignore the law. In your case, Payton's lawful will."

She sputtered, "I'll appeal it and sit in jail until my case is heard. So you see you still won't have fulfilled your blasted duty."

"Have you any idea how ridiculous you are behaving? The outcome of your stubbornness would cause your sons irrevocable harm. And for what? Your selfish desire to maintain the freedom you have enjoyed due to my brother's hideous lack of responsibility?"

He rose and Brianna winced at his glowering look. "Let me inform you that I am surrounded by too much family. My home is literally bursting at the seams with them. So what, pray tell, makes you think I would cherish housing another relative? One who happens to be stubborn and self-centered?" He strode to the window, turned his back on her and clasped the framework.

Brianna bit her lip and blinked back tears as she thought over his words. In all truth, she had never thought herself selfish at all, though she couldn't quibble about her stubborn streak. He had made it crystal-clear he did not want her under his roof, that it was duty compelling him to offer her a home, and nothing more.

She gathered her pride, suppressing the undeniable urge to smash him over the head with something that would do him permanent damage. She rushed up behind him. Reaching out, she grasped his elbow and yanked on it until he turned to her.

"Selfish, you say? Allow me to inform you I wouldn't step foot inside your precious home if you paid me to do so. As a matter of fact, I expect you to provide me with a home of my own, preferably one in the country where the children may run and play to their hearts' content. Ponies for the boys and a carriage for our use would be other requirements."

"Of course," Harrison said with a mild smile. "Anything else?"

"That should be all for now, I believe."

"Then that settles things nicely."

Brianna noted the tender satisfaction in his voice and looked at him, confused. Hadn't he just moments ago accused her of being self-centered and stubborn? She narrowed her eyes on his smug countenance until it dawned on her what she had done.

"Oh, my Lord! Please tell me I did not agree to cooperate with you?" She groaned and rubbed her temples. "Tell me I didn't."

He grinned. "You most certainly did! If I had guessed you possessed even the slightest streak of greed, I would have attempted bribing you from the beginning. It certainly would have saved me all this aggravation."

"You have no sense of fair play, whatsoever," she spat.

Harrison chucked her chin with a fist. "It will be a cold day in hell before you best me, Mrs. MacAulay."

She narrowed her eyes. "You may have won this significant scrimmage, my lord, but it doesn't alter the fact I still intend to pursue having Payton's will changed."

"Why is it so important you stay here when I have so much to offer you? You've been on your own for so long, struggling. Why won't you allow me to care for you?"

"I'll not be under the authority of any man again. I was sixteen when I married your brother, shortly after leaving a cloistered life at St. Benedict's Orphanage. At that time, I knew nothing of men and the world. Your brother offered me an opportunity to see much of the excitement in life I'd been missing. Payton and I hardly knew each other, but within a short time after we married, I fell in love with him."

"Until he proved to be irresponsible," Harrison said.

She nodded. "For a long time I kept making excuses for his behavior. I kept telling myself he'd learn to love me enough to change. He never did."

His gray eyes bored into hers. "I'm nothing like my brother."

"From the little I've learned about you, I don't doubt that, still, being a man, you take your liberty for granted. Even though I'm a woman I will not give up my freedom without a fight."

Harrison sighed. "All right. On the morrow, I'll accompany you to Nielsen's."

"I'd rather go on my own."

"I'm sure you would, but I'm afraid you will have to suffer my escort. I've already explained that I'll not let you out of my sight until we reach Scotland's shores. Possibly, not even then."

The next day, Harrison managed to divert Brianna's attention from paying a visit to her solicitor in the one sure way he knew. He took her shopping. Normally, he abhorred the activity. But, after traipsing along with her from store to store, he decided that shopping with Brianna was fun, painless, and highly entertaining.

Harrison had driven them into town Monday morning to purchase supplies for their journey to Scotland. He smiled when he thought about her obvious delight in store-bought clothing for Harry and Jamie. She had told him the treat would relieve her of the arduous task of mending their old clothing again. By mid-afternoon, Brianna recalled her purpose for coming to town in the first place, and she made her way to Nielsen's doorstep. She was disappointed to discover only his secretary there, who informed her Nielsen had left on holiday for an undetermined time.

Harrison was satisfied Nielsen had followed his request to make himself scarce. He had no desire for Brianna to discover their gentleman's agreement.

He'd convinced her she required new clothing as well as her boys. He stopped in front of J. Burke Clothier's and secured the reins. Brianna tapped her foot impatiently, scowling when Harrison reached inside a pocket and gave Harry and Jamie each a penny.

"Across the street is the sweet shop. Come straight back here when you are through," he ordered. "Sit on the bench here and wait until we're through inside."

"Yes, sir!" the boys chorused.

Brianna cringed when they raced across the street with nary a care for the bustling horse and wagon traffic. She turned a jaundiced eye on Harrison. He smiled, reached around her and opened the door to Burke's.

She swept through the doorway ahead of him. "They never called their own father 'sir'. I must admit you've certainly made an impression on them." With a sniff, she added, "Of course, I'm fairly certain I would gain their cooperation and loyalty too, if I stooped to bribing them."

"A penny for a treat is hardly bribery, Brianna. Your sons

respect the voice of authority, something you have yet to learn."

"You'll never see me groveling at your feet," she informed him.

He gave her a devilish grin. "That remains to be seen, doesn't it?" Harrison's gaze followed her as she meandered down one aisle, then another.

She paused beside an indigo gown—not black, thank God—and pulled it from the rack. "This one should do nicely as a day gown."

"Whatever you like, it's yours," he said magnanimously. "And choose an evening gown or two, as well."

She raised her brow. "I hardly think I'll be going out into society, since I'm in mourning, my lord."

He ignored her and went on his own search for gowns. He pulled a rose silk one from a hanger. "How about this?"

She turned to him and he saw the delight in her eyes. Just as quickly, it vanished. "I don't think so. It's not practical. Where would I wear it?"

Harrison opened his mouth to say, anywhere you want, but had second thoughts. He reached the end of the row and found several day dresses to his liking. Selecting what he thought was her size he strode to her side. Her arms were filled with pants and shirts.

He frowned. "More for the boys?"

"They have so few things."

He nodded. "Fine, but I'd like you try these on."

She dumped the pants and shirts into his arms, took the dresses and hurried across the store. The storekeeper caught Harrison's eye and nodded. Harrison gave a miniscule nod in return.

While he waited for Brianna, he saw a mannequin clad in a gray worsted woolen coat. Recalling Brianna's threadbare brown coat, he checked the label, saw it was her size, then snatched the gray off the mannequin and carried it to the counter, along with the articles of clothing for the boys, including new jackets as well.

In a far corner of the shop, he stared at a gown on a mannequin. It was far more sophisticated than anything he'd expect to find in this provincial town. He imagined Brianna settling the deep colored wine satin over her womanly hips, the daringly low, rounded neckline embellished with beads of the same color

"Harrison?"

He looked at Brianna, disappointed to find her still wearing her black widow's weeds. He pointed at the gown on the mannequin. "This would be perfect for you. Try it on."

She raised her brow. "I've already told you that I won't be going out into society since I'm in mourning." She looked at the gown then and narrowed her eyes. "If I didn't know better, I'd say you'd tipped a pint too many."

He chuckled. "It's magnificent."

"Do you believe me to be a woman of loose morals?" she snapped.

His smile slipped. "Och, what are you talking about?"

"You expect me to be happy to don a garment of such a garish color when only a woman of the—well, you know precisely what I mean!" she said indignantly.

Harrison wasn't the least bit surprised when she turned on her heel and stormed from the shop.

He paid for the clothing, including the red gown, and tossed Brianna's threadbare coat to Burke. "Get rid of it," he said, then headed toward the door. He noticed another coat, a full-length chocolate-colored fur. He turned to Burke. "What animal is this?"

The older man beamed. "Why, the finest beaver this side

of the Mississippi, Sir. It's warm enough a lady would roast, even on the coldest winter day."

Harrison pondered the brisk cold winds that blew incessantly across Scotland's hills and valleys during the winter months. He pulled the coat from the model and and as luck would have it, it was her size and it beneath his arm. Once he'd paid for his purchases he followed Brianna down the street, enjoying the sight of her skirts twitching fetchingly as she headed for the wagon. He grimaced when she settled down in the driver's seat with the reins in hand.

He went to the back of the wagon, gave Brianna a wry look in passing. While he straightened and shifted packages, he winked at Harry, who sat beside Jamie in the wagon bed.

"What did you say to Ma? She looks real mad, Uncle Harry."

Harrison chose his words carefully. "Your mother is having a difficult time adjusting to someone taking care of her. I could use your help. It's my responsibility to care for you boys, and your mother. We are a family now. I've spoken to you about moving to Scotland, and I believe you will enjoy the adventure, don't you?"

They nodded in unison.

"Then help me convince your mother that moving is the right thing to do."

"What are you three whispering about back there?" Brianna asked impatiently. "If you expect supper tonight we had better head home soon."

Harrison vaulted into the seat beside her and stretched out his legs in a seemingly nonchalant manner. Though his male pride shuddered at the very idea of her driving, he didn't want to upset her more. He hoped to heaven she was competent.

Brianna spared him a sour glance before clicking her

tongue and gently snapping the reins. He soon discovered that she was an excellent driver, and he relaxed. He'd vexed her plenty today by pressuring her into accepting the dresses.

Hopefully, she'd include him at her supper table.

As far as Brianna was concerned, Friday arrived much too soon. She glanced up from her packing and found Harrison lounging in her bedchamber doorway.

"I know you would like nothing better than to miss the train, but it won't matter. There will always be another one along."

Brianna raised her brow. "Are you accusing me of delaying our departure?"

"You have arranged and rearranged that particular trunk three times in the last hour," he said gently. "The boys and I have been sitting in the wagon for twenty minutes. Are you ready?"

She banged the lid shut. "As ready as I'll ever be, I guess."

He strode to her side, bent down and easily hoisted the trunk to his shoulder. Brianna admired the fine fit of his wool coat stretching across his broad back and shoulders. It appeared that the head of the MacAulays was as strong as an ox. Of course, she had challenged his masculinity when she suggested earlier that they hire some strong young men to help them load up the wagon. He'd tersely told her he would handle the job and went on to prove himself more than capable.

She sighed, thinking how her sons had even turned traitor on her. Harrison had gained their devotion and unequivocal loyalty once he'd purchased everything their yearning, greedy little hearts desired.

Harrison entered the bedchamber again as she closed the lid on another trunk. "This is the last one."

"Amen." He strode to the trunk, hefted it to his shoulder and left the room once more.

Brianna trudged down the stairs behind him, pausing in the entrance to the parlor. She gazed at her worn red divan and chair and, with a melancholy smile, recalled Payton's initial reaction to the furnishings she had purchased after they married. His words, even now, years later, brought a smile to her lips.

"Good God! The parlor looks like a bloody brothel," he'd exclaimed before suggesting she exchange the furnishings for items a bit more sedate. Brianna held fast to her choice, though, and the furniture had stayed. Having spent many years in St. Benedict's Orphanage, where the furnishings had little comfort and style, the red divan and chair had suited her perfectly. Tears filled her eyes at both the bitter and joyous memories of their years together. Her eyes stung when they lit upon the old wooden rocker where she had rocked and fed her babies.

"Just once more," she whispered as she sat down and closed her eyes.

Harry scrambled from the wagon when Harrison said, "Go and see what is keeping your mother."

The boy scampered up the path to the house. Harrison smiled when he heard him shout in an astonishingly adult fashion, "Aw, come on, Ma. We'll miss the train!" Brianna might deny the allegation, but Harrison knew she had not resigned herself to leaving her home.

Within moments, Harry appeared, bounded down the sidewalk and came to a screeching stop by the wagon.

"Ma said she's not coming, Uncle Harry!"

Harrison uncrossed his arms, his heart pounding in his chest. "Do tell?"

Harry nodded. "She said the only way she's leaving is if you make her."

"I see." Harrison shoved his spectacles into position, then jumped down from the wagon. "Wait here. I'll be back shortly." He strode up the path and entered the house, where he found Brianna sitting in her rocking chair with her eyes closed.

"Confound it, Brianna," he began irritably, pausing when he saw that the front of her dress was soaking wet. Tears were slipping slowly down her cheeks. His heart sank at her bleak look and he squatted down beside her. Reaching up, he stroked her cheek, catching a tear on one finger.

Not sparing him so much as a glance, she spoke softly, her hands clenched in her lap. "I remember the day Payton purchased this house. It's hard to believe that was ten years ago. At the time, I felt it much too pretentious, much too fine. Payton laughed at first, then explained why he'd chosen it. The house reminded him a bit of his family's home, Winterhaven, on a smaller scale, of course. When I said it was too costly, he'd only laughed and said he could afford it."

She stopped rocking and turned sad blue eyes on him. "And now you tell me I must leave my home. I'm afraid I'm not strong enough to do so. It would be like admitting I want to go when all I want is to stay here, inside these familiar walls."

Harrison covered her hand with his, realizing she was frightened—more than she would ever admit, he guessed—more than he expected.

"You have a new home and family," he reminded her. "And remember, your furnishings will be transported on another ship shortly. Once your possessions arrive in Scotland, you'll feel at home. Now, then, we'll have plenty of time to talk about things, and sort all of this out during our journey. It's past time we left."

She continued rocking and didn't reply.

"You will not leave on your own then, is that it?"

She clenched her eyes tight. "I cannot."

Harrison gritted his teeth. "So be it, Madam." He came to his feet, bent and scooped her up easily from the chair. As he strode out of the house, he fully expected her to show some resistance so he tightened his grip on her. She took him completely by surprise when she went limp in his arms and laid her head upon his chest. He swallowed the lump in his throat.

When they reached the wagon, she lifted her arms and wound them around his neck. Her long delicate fingers sent shivers up his spine. He stifled a delighted groan when her breasts brushed against his chest. He looked up and noticed Harry and Jamie's wide-eyed looks from where they sat in the back of the wagon.

"Ma didn't faint, did she?" Harry whispered.

"No, but she is very sad about leaving. She will be fine once we board the train." He reached out and grasped the side of the wagon. He pulled himself up with one hand, keeping Brianna securely locked against his chest with the other, then he settled her down on the seat beside him.

Harry scooted forward and handed his mother's coat to Harrison. He draped it around her shoulders, eased her limp arms into the armholes and buttoned it up to her chin. She looked at him then and Harrison saw the sad, bewildered look in her eyes.

"I give you my solemn vow, Brianna, everything will be fine."

Tears filled her eyes and she bit her lip. After a moment,

she said, "Please, don't make promises you cannot possibly keep." She turned away and focused her eyes on the road.

Harrison heaved a deep sigh and snapped the reins against Winney's back. For ten long years, he'd wanted this woman. Now that he had her in his possession, he vowed nothing would separate them.

CHAPTER 4

December 5, 1888
Somewhere in the middle of the Atlantic Ocean

*B*rianna paced the promenade deck of the steamship Atlantis, a scowl on her face. "Why the devil hasn't he come out of his cabin yet?"

Harry and Jack sat side by side upon wooden deck chairs, shuffling decks of cards. Her brow knitted thoughtfully as she watched their small hands practice the shuffling movements Harrison had taught them on the train. He'd also given them instructions in poker and how to place wagers.

"Who, Ma?" Harry asked.

"Your uncle. He made such haste to sell our home and hustle us on board this monstrous, heaving ship, and now he completely ignores us."

"But the captain told us not to worry," Harry said. "Uncle Harrison's just decapitated."

Brianna gently corrected him. "Incapacitated, darling." She smiled at the thought of cutting off the head of this fine laird from Scotland. "I cannot imagine that man having an ill bone in his big body. I do not for a single minute believe he's sick. He just doesn't give a whit about us, now he's fulfilled his wretched duty."

"So, Uncle Harrison's not gonna get me a pony?" Jamie looked at her woefully.

She reached down and tousled his hair. "Don't worry. You'll get your pony." Along with everything else she had managed to wheedle out of him. She frowned. All right, so she hadn't found it necessary to sweet-talk him out of a blessed thing. He'd given his word he would meet all her demands, if she would cooperate with the move to Scotland. Hopefully, her moment of weakness when he had to carry her out of her home, he wouldn't remember.

Seven days ago, they had boarded the Atlantis in New York City's Harbor. The train trip had been smooth and uneventful, once she and Harrison had reached a truce of sorts. Now, she found herself in the middle of the Atlantic Ocean, and he had deserted them.

She leaned against the ship's railing and stared out to sea, marveling at how her life had changed in such a short time. Suddenly she gasped, "Boys, come look at the whale. Oh, how magnificent!"

They scampered off their chairs and ran to her. Following the direction of her finger pointing out to sea they crowed when they caught a glimpse of the fluke of a whale as it disappeared beneath the cold, churning water.

Several others gathered at the railing to watch in awe.

"Incredible, aren't they?" asked a man, his cultured voice a bit high-pitched.

Brianna whirled around in surprise and met the unwavering blue eyes of a stranger standing close beside her.

He was inches taller than she, as tall as Harrison, with a narrow and elegant build, and he appeared close to her age. Since his furry coat was open, she could see his frock coat and trousers were made of lightweight wool in a brilliant green color, the vest fashioned in gold silk, unlike Harrison's preferred subdued-colored clothing.

She examined him and wondered if perhaps his nature was geared toward some other persuasion, even though she hadn't had first-hand experience of such men. After a moment, she dismissed the notion. There was something intrinsically masculine about him, even though his clothing and voice indicated otherwise. She flushed when his gaze casually roved down her body and lingered on her breasts.

When he returned his gaze to her face he gave her a benign smile. "Their numbers have dwindled over the years. It is predicted that within the next century some of the species will be extinct."

"How sad," she murmured.

"The whaling industry is a profitable enterprise." He looked at Harry and Jamie who stood with their small hands wrapped around the ship's railing. Their eyes were wide with excitement as they waited for the appearance of another whale. "Are they yours?"

"Yes," Brianna replied levelly, realizing the man's accent was similar to Harrison's.

"You are exceedingly lucky, and your husband as well."

"Thank you." She started backing away from him.

He gently took her elbow, preventing her from escaping. "Don't leave yet, pretty lady. I can share my knowledge with you. About the whales."

Brianna extracted her arm from his grasp and lifted her chin. "No, I do not believe so." She turned to her sons. "It is time for luncheon, children." She placed her hands on their shoulders and guided them down the ship's deck.

The man followed them. "I would be honored if you would consent to join me at my table. Especially since your husband does not appear to be traveling with you."

Lord, but he is persistent! "He is here, but in our cabin, convalescing from an illness."

He grasped her arm and brought her to a complete halt. "Please allow me to introduce myself."

"Ma don't care who you are!" Harry shouted.

The dandy laughed at Harry. He turned amused eyes on Brianna. "This youngster could use some manners."

"The boy's correct," a low, furious voice said from behind them. "My wife doesn't give a bloody damn what your name is."

Brianna breathed a sigh of relief at Harrison's unexpected intervention. At this moment, she understood perfectly why he'd insisted they pose as a married couple.

"Remove yer hand, MacPhearson, or ye will be very, very sorry."

The man's face paled as he slowly released Brianna.

Brianna knew Harrison was furious because his Scots burr was so evident. She was stunned to realize he knew this man! She stared at him as he swayed in the hallway that led to his cabin. His legs were spread wide, his spectacles sat crookedly on the bridge of his nose. He hadn't buttoned his white shirt, and in his haste had strung a black tie around his neck but didn't tie it. His inky thatch of hair was standing on end. Even in his disheveled condition, he was a splendid example of masculinity.

"Well, this is a surprise." The man's voice was smooth and droll. "Ye do get around, old man. And surprisingly well fer someone who cannot abide sea travel," he said with a laugh.

Harrison closed the distance between them. "What in bloody hell are ye doing here, MacPhearson?"

MacPhearson backed up a few paces and stared at Brianna with a gleam in his eye. "Wife, ye say? Ye have been holding out on us!" He backed up further and added, "To answer yer question, my sister and I decided to take the grand tour again, only this time we included America in our schedule. Ah, New York City is magnificent, isn't it?" He sighed. "Alas, it is truly unfortunate Americans have no breeding."

"Connie is here?"

"No. I left her in New York. She developed a fondness for the place. So, you have taken a wife, have ye? Connie will be shocked, and disappointed." MacPhearson gave Brianna another appreciative look. "She is delightful, MacAulay—for an American, that is—and quite beautiful."

Brianna grew uneasy when she saw the fury in Harrison's expression. Unwisely, the foolish man dared to speak again. "Obviously, yer wife is a wonderful breeder, which is a necessary requirement for ye, isn't it? And I must say ye have found her just in the nick of time!"

She couldn't believe the man's audacity when he chuckled again. Harrison appeared on the verge of committing murder.

Harrison's gaze remained riveted on the man, yet he directed his words to Brianna. "I will meet you in the dining room when I'm through here."

"Through?" She did not like the sound of that at all, having no desire for him to get into fisticuffs with the man. She proceeded to button up Harrison's shirt, as she would perform the small task for her sons. Only this wasn't a child she tended, she thought, her eyes gazing upon his broad, furred chest. By the time she reached the top button, her cheeks felt decidedly warm. "Darling," she said gently, "I'll fetch your coat and you may join us for dinner."

49

He turned to Harry, ignoring her. "Son? Escort your mother to the dining room, please."

"You bet, Uncle Harrison!"

Harry and Jamie each grabbed one of Brianna's hands and for the first time she noticed their anxious expressions. She left with them, all the while hoping Harrison wouldn't get into a brawl.

Half an hour later Brianna and her boys had finished eating a supper of Boston baked beans, brown bread and butter, and fried chicken. She glanced at the pin watch on her bodice as she rose from her seat. "I'm going to check on your uncle, boys. As soon as you finish your cherry pie, return to your cabin. Understand?"

Leaving the boys at the table, Brianna made her way to Harrison's suite. She stood in the hallway, her hand poised to knock when the door swung open and a steward emerged. "Is...is my husband all right?"

The young man shook his head. "Never have I seen a worse case of seasickness in all my bloody days, Ma'am." He nodded at the door. "Never seen a gentleman still upchucking his food, even when his belly's empty. If I was you, Mrs. MacAulay, I'd be worried he ain't keeping even water down."

He strode away, leaving Harrison's cabin unguarded, which surprised her. She had tried entering the suite on numerous occasions in the last few days, but had been turned away by one of the crewmembers. Carefully, she opened the door and slipped inside.

Harrison stood beside his rumpled bed, leaning over a chamber pot on a small table attached to the decking. His naked back was broad and tanned, his waist lean. He shivered. Brianna saw that his splendid torso was covered in a fine sheen of moisture. She searched the cabin for a pitcher of water. When she didn't find one, she scowled and slipped out the door.

Catching another steward passing by, she said, "Would you please fetch me a cold pitcher of water and deliver it to the top deck, at the bow of the ship? Oh, and a large mug of beef stock. Also, there's a well-padded chair in my husband's cabin. I'd like it carried up to the top deck as well."

"Sure thing, Madam," the steward replied.

"Thank you."

He strode off to do her bidding. She chewed her lip and wondered how she was going to coerce Harrison into going up to the top deck. She understood why he'd incarcerated himself in his cabin. He had no desire for anyone to see him in such a weak condition.

She walked down a set of stairs to the captain's door and rapped on it.

A gray-haired man opened the door and smiled. "Ah, Mrs. MacAulay. How is your husband? Has he perhaps found his 'sea stomach' yet?" He laughed, apparently amused by his little quip.

"He is not doing well at all. I would like to enlist your help in getting him to the top deck. He is much too large for me to manage on my own."

"What have you in mind?" he asked, narrowing his eyes suspiciously.

"Fresh air. I know he won't leave his cabin, since I suspect he doesn't want others seeing him in this condition."

"A man's got his pride," the captain replied.

"Well, his foolish pride will kill him!" she retorted. "He is going to die if he doesn't keep down some fluids, but first we must settle his stomach. Won't you please help me?"

Captain Wilkinson sighed. "Just tell me where you want him."

Harrison seethed, furious at Brianna, and at the men who'd helped her, against his wishes. He wouldn't look at her. If he did, there was no telling what he'd do to her. He thought tossing her overboard would give him great satisfaction.

"Mark my words," Brianna said, tucking a blanket around him. "You'll feel ever so much better once you take in a bit of fresh air."

By God, this was, by far, the most humiliating day of his entire existence. He still couldn't believe it when a quarter of an hour ago his cabin had been invaded by his interfering sister-in-law and six burly sailors. Before he could even think to protest, they had snatched him up from his bed and carried him up the stairs sprawled among them. Then they plunked him down in the large chair they'd dragged from his cabin.

The sailors had quickly departed. Now he and Brianna were alone on the top deck. She knelt beside him and reached for a pitcher, from which she filled a glass. He rolled his eyes. Heaven help the man in the hands of a woman on a mission.

"Here, now. I want you to drink some water."

He growled and knocked the glass from her hand.

She gasped and watched it disappear over the ship's side. She scolded, "You are behaving worse than your nephews in a snit, and they are children! Can't you see I'm trying to help you get through the days ahead in a healthy fashion? Why did you not inform me sea travel doesn't agree with you?"

"Damn it, woman," he snarled. "I do not require your help!"

Brianna reached for his spectacles but he stopped her and gripped her wrist. "Leave the bloody things alone!"

She rose to her feet. "Why can't you accept my help? You've been so ill..."

"Because I'm a man, and a physician, and able to care for myself."

She widened her eyes. "You are a medical doctor?"

He nodded curtly. "Payton never told you?"

"No, he didn't."

"The eldest born MacAulay in every generation has been male, and educated to become a doctor."

She nodded. "All right, I can see where you may have more knowledge than I with regards to healing, but what in the world has gender to do with anything?"

"Men are stronger than women," he said, his voice low. "It is a man's responsibility to care for his woman and children."

"Stop being ridiculous."

Harrison groaned and shook his head. Now she was calling him ridiculous. "Leave me the hell alone."

"I am tired of your arrogance, and your damnable duty!" she shouted in exasperation. "Who do you think you are? Some omnipotent being who never gets ill? Who never errs?" She laughed mirthlessly. "I'm sorry to disappoint you, but you are made of flesh and blood, same as all humans, and until you can accept my help, I will not take anything from you."

She tore off her fur coat and flung it at him. It sailed through the air and landed on his head. He reached up and yanked it down, uncovering his face and spitting a mouth full of fur. He gaped at the beautiful virago making a hasty retreat, realizing she was serious about leaving him

"Damn it, woman!" he roared. "Ye can't leave me out here!" When she ignored him, he shouted again, "Get back here, ye little witch!"

She disappeared around the corner. Harrison threw his

head against the back of the chair and justified his anger. A man had his pride, after all. She should have discussed her idea with him first, before raiding his cabin with those sailors in tow, leaving him little dignity.

The rays of the winter sun beat down on his head, warming him. Shortly it dawned on him, as he gazed out to sea, that he felt better. Even with the cold winds from the north blowing. He followed Brianna's directions and focused his eyes straight ahead. He was amazed to discover that as long as he remained very still, for the first time in days his stomach didn't feel the least bit queasy.

He covered himself with Brianna's coat and sank lower in his chair. A drowsy languor came over him, which wasn't surprising. He hadn't slept well since the day he boarded the ship. Unfortunately, he still hadn't recovered from his journey to America in the first place, which didn't help matters. Oh, Lord, but the breeze felt wonderful! He couldn't stay out past dark, he knew, since the temperature would plummet with the setting sun. But for now he'd take advantage of the warmth, so he closed his eyes and slept.

CHAPTER 5

*H*arrison shivered as a chill crept up his spine. He'd opened his eyes a moment ago and had been surprised to see night had fallen, which meant he'd slept for two hours, possibly more. From behind him, and down the stairs, he could see the lights from the modern electric light fixtures installed outside each cabin. He lay back in his chair and shifted his position, easing the stiffness in his body. He was near to freezing, but damn it if he didn't feel spectacular.

"Harrison! You will catch your death out here!"

He looked up and saw Brianna rushing toward him, skirts lifted, revealing her pretty ankles. He smiled and slid his gaze up her body until he met her eyes

"Heavens, I thought you had returned to your cabin ages ago. Come along now. I'll help you inside."

She fell to her knees beside him and placed a hand on his shoulder. He drew his hand out from beneath the blanket and cupped her chin, claimed her mouth, his lips slanting across hers. Oh, my Lord, she was sweet. The scent of her skin tantalized him, tempting him to do much more then take one measly kiss.

He raised his head and smiled at the stunned look on her face. "Your cure worked, Brianna. You have no idea what you have done for me, and how this remedy of yours will forever change my life. I've never been able to travel by sea, due to this hateful, debilitating illness. Do you know how many places I've never seen? How cheated I've felt?" He tilted back his head and gazed at the clear, starry night. "Can you even begin to imagine how much I've missed my brother? For ten long years I longed to see Payton, but knew there was the very real possibility I wouldn't survive the journey."

Brianna frowned. "But you came for me and my sons."

"You were an obligation. A responsibility. If I'd ignored Payton's wishes and left you in America, I wouldn't have been able to live with myself."

She sighed. "Sometimes, it seems things we cannot have are ones we desire the most. If you hadn't been able to ride a horse, you would have felt cheated. If you were unable to tolerate a particular food, believe me, that food would be the one you desire more than any other." She gave him a dimpled smile and shrugged. "It seems to be the way of things."

"Brianna MacAulay, you are a very perceptive woman."

"No, I'm not, but I have acquired an awful lot of common sense in twenty-six years of living. Of course, I believe I was blessed with this gift when I became a mother. Birthing a child does convince a girl to grow up rather quickly. By the way, I would like my coat back, thank you."

He watched her in mesmerized fascination as she donned the coat, pulled up the collar and snuggled her chin down inside its warmth. He would give away all his wealth to be that coat, to embrace her, to hold her close, his body hot with desire for her. To touch her as a man touches his woman.

Why not take a chance and tell her his feelings? He would, damn it. "I want you very much," he admitted. He ignored the voice inside warning him it was too soon to make any declarations, yet he did. "From the first moment I saw you at the train depot with rain dripping off your nose, I wanted you."

Brianna scowled at him as she rose, her cheeks burning. "Stop speaking such nonsense. What you need is some nourishing food in your belly, another glass of water, and a good night's rest. Can you walk, or shall I call the crew again?"

"You are what I need," he insisted.

"Stand and I will assist you," she said in her usual no-nonsense manner.

He folded his arms across his chest and sank lower in his chair. "I'm not returning to my cabin until you tell me whether you reciprocate my feelings or not."

Brianna whirled away and proceeded to pace the deck. After a time, she turned to him, eyes ablaze. "How do you expect me to answer? We all want something, do we not? But, we cannot always have what we want."

He grinned. "Not true, Brianna. Sea travel aside, I've earned, taken, or been given everything I've ever desired in life."

"Then you are an exception. You think you want me, yet I guarantee, if by any remote chance you did acquire me, it wouldn't be long before you would lose interest."

"The way my brother did?" Harrison asked, his voice low and gentle.

She turned away, but not before he glimpsed the hurt in her eyes.

He went to her side and took her hand. "You must

understand, at this moment, you are the most important thing in my life. I want you more than I've ever wanted any woman. That means something."

She stared at him with tear-filled eyes. "Why? Because you now feel well enough to..."

"Yes?" Harrison asked, smiling innocently.

She scowled. "You know well what I mean."

He leaned back and draped his arms over the rail on either side of him. "Perfectly." Lord, she was beautiful and honest. The most provocative woman he'd ever met.

"Your arrogance is unfathomable."

"Not arrogance. Confidence."

She sputtered in reply.

As long as he'd confessed this much, he may as well say it all. "I want you in my bed. I want to view and touch your glorious hair cascading across my pillows." His gaze caressed her body. "I want to make you mine, your delectable, naked body cushioned upon the coat you are wearing at this very moment."

He raised his brow at Brianna's shocked expression. "You cannot be all that surprised about my wanting you, for I am certain you have felt this attraction between us. We are like magnets, drawn to each other. I know you feel the same way. Do not deny it."

She narrowed her eyes. "There is more to all this, is there not?"

Damn! Could the woman read minds? He was not at all prepared to delve too deeply into his true reasons for coming for her, aside from duty. But perhaps it would be better to tell her the truth of the matter, portions of it, at least.

"Yes, there's more." He took a deep breath. "If I do not produce an heir by my thirty-first birthday, I will be forced to forfeit the MacAulay estate and all its holdings."

Shock crossed her face. "When is this birthday?"

"In fourteen months time."

She pressed a hand against her heart. "Why me?"

"Due to the short amount of time I've been given to find a wife, I believe a woman who has already conceived and birthed children will have a better chance of providing me an heir. You meet the criteria since you have birthed sons for my brother."

"Perhaps that is the true reason you came to fetch me," she said. "Perhaps it had nothing to do with duty."

He hoped it would be a long time before she discovered the truth of the matter—that he'd coveted his brother's wife, sight unseen, for ten long years.

"Harrison?"

He looked up, chagrined that she had caught him deep in thought.

"This situation could not be more perfect for you, could it?"

He frowned. "Contrary to what you may think, I never before contemplated marrying a woman, sight unseen. Especially when I have had the cream of the crop of beautiful, tractable ladies at home, willing to do my bidding."

"So, when did you conceive this incredible notion that I'm the woman for you?" she inquired.

"Recently." He said no more, deciding it prudent to keep his mouth shut. She'd never believe him if he told her the truth; that he'd fallen in lust with her, from a portrait, ten years ago.

"I may regret it, but for some reason, I believe you. I've also felt this attraction between us, but it isn't love. I will not marry again, and I cannot be...intimate with a man without benefit of marriage. So you see, your proposition would never work. A woman needs to feel she is in love, and is loved in return before entering an intimate relationship with a man," she said. "And that can only happen in the sanctity of marriage."

Harrison heard the trembling in her voice and regretted his impatience. He took her hand and smiled into her eyes. "We will marry then."

She wrenched her hand away. "I've told you I will not marry again. Besides, even if we were to exchange vows, would you be content with me for more than a fortnight?"

Her words gave him pause. Thus far, he'd been fortunate to have many women in his life, but not one for very long. But then that was because not a one of them was perfect for him. He believed Brianna was perfection, but wasn't at all sure about being truly in love with her—infatuated, for certain—but love?

"I cannot say how long these feelings I have for you will last since I've seen many more unhappy marriages than happy ones." He tightened his jaw. "But I desire you more than I have ever desired anyone else. When we mate, it will be very, very good between us."

Brianna sighed. "I'm afraid this is all impossible."

She paced the deck. Harrison stared at her profile, struggling to maintain his composure. What he wanted to do was take her in his arms and kiss her into submission. Never would he have believed that begetting a son could be so difficult!

"I gather matrimony is not a requirement?" she asked.

"No, just the heir." He thought about how often he'd taken his privileged life for granted. His entire existence had been turned upside down with the revelations in his father's will. The requirements placed the MacAulay clan's future in jeopardy. He was still reeling from the loss of his father and brother, within a short span of each other. Initially, upon hearing of Payton's demise, he'd thought that would void the will. Not the case, he quickly learned from his solicitor.

The provision in the will stated if Harrison provided no heir by the age of 31, and if Payton were to die, the estate would be sold, the wealth of the estate given to St. Mary's Convent in Edinburgh.

"Let's get you out of the cold," Brianna said.

She led him across the decking and down the stairs. When they reached his cabin, she stopped just inside the door. "I will leave you to a good night's rest. Sleep with two pillows propping you up and you should be fine."

An elusive thought lingered at the back of Harrison's mind as he thought over her words. She needed to feel married in order to be intimate with a man, but had no desire to be married. And then the answer to their dilemma was right in front of him, especially when he recalled Raleigh's words months ago when he'd read Harrison his father's will.

She turned to leave but he wound an arm around her narrow waist and hauled her inside the cabin, slamming the door behind them. Then he twirled her around in a madcap dance, laughing the entire time.

"Have you lost your mind?" she asked when he paused with his arms around her. She stared at him as though he were stark-raving mad. "What is wrong with you?"

"Hand in fist! Why the hell had I not thought of it earlier? Thanks to your chattering I remembered Raleigh's advice."

"I have never chattered in my life, and who is Raleigh?" She pressed her hands against his chest for release.

He tightened his grasp and grinned into her scowling face. "You do chatter and I adore it. Allow me to explain. You object to marriage, but would consent to another arrangement, if you had something to gain from it I'm guessing. Raleigh is my solicitor and offered a solution."

"Let me go. I'm exhausted, and do not understand you at all."

He released her and she headed for the door, but her steps slowed with his next words.

"Handfasting. It is an old Scottish custom. A cohabitation agreement made between a man and a woman who declare themselves to each other in a public place. The couple is considered married for a year and a day."

"And then?" she asked.

"The couple would know after that time passed whether or not they desired to remain together. If they do, they may then legally marry. This would be a perfect solution for us, Brianna."

Harrison decided it expedient not to mention that handfasting was not as socially acceptable in Scotland today as it had been in years past. That did not stop a number of men and women from still partaking of the ceremony.

"So, according to Scots law, we would not be married?"

He nodded. "Yet in the eyes of the law and society, the relationship would be considered as valid as any marriage. And if our union produced a son, he would acquire my name and be recognized as my heir."

After a long moment of thought, she replied, "Maybe you are right."

"I promise, Brianna, you will not regret this."

She jammed her hands on her hips and frowned. "Taking into consideration we have not seen eye to eye on one blessed thing since the day we met, we shall see. You did mention I would gain something from this arrangement."

"What would you like?" he asked, generosity enveloping him now that he was certain she would agree to become his handfasted wife.

Brianna sank down on the bed, deep in thought. After a

while, she tilted her head back and leveled her eyes on him. "I want sole custody of my sons, and to return to America."

He groaned, "Not that again."

"I know you have the resources and power at hand to help me."

"There is no question that monetarily I could secure the best solicitors. However, that does not mean the courts will give you custody of your sons. They may very well decide the boys should remain with me."

"I require your word of honor that you will help me when the time comes."

"What is the point of rebelling against my brother's will?"

Brianna pierced him with a hard look. "If Payton had been a good husband, do you think for one minute I would be fighting you at all? For two years, I raised my sons alone. I do not wish for society to condone Payton's horrid behavior. And tell me, why is it unacceptable for a woman to raise her children without a man?"

"Because society has drummed it into the male species that women are the weaker sex. A fact which I have of late discovered is erroneous," he said, his voice filled with irony. "I'm afraid it will take another generation or two to change things. Now then, I have one more question to ask before we seal our bargain. Once we handfast, will you come to my bed? Willingly?"

Brianna met his eyes with a hesitant look but nodded, her cheeks reddening. "If I come to that decision, I will."

Harrison nodded in satisfaction. "Excellent. And if you do gain custody of your children, and birth my heir, will you be able to turn him over to me when it comes time for you to return to America?" Her face paled and her eyes widened as he continued, "Will you be able to turn your back on him?

If you cannot, believe me when I say you do not want to fight me for custodial proprietorship in Scotland's courts."

Brianna rose and paced the floor, hugging her body. She turned and met his eyes. "Must I give you an answer now?"

He nodded. "Due to the element of time, I need to know as soon as possible."

"You promise me you will do all you can to help me obtain custody of my sons?"

"Aye."

"Then perhaps I shall agree to the arrangement."

Harrison frowned. "So, are you saying yes?"

"No. I'm saying I will think on it very hard."

Harrison's heart filled with such incredible joy he wanted to shout out to the world that she would soon be his. Perhaps. He frowned again as apprehension set in. Thus far, Brianna had proved to be independent and contrary. And there was the possibility that, in the end, she could decide against the arrangement.

"Harrison? What would happen if we did handfast and I birthed a daughter?"

He sighed. "Wouldn't count. I don't suppose there is any chance you would be willing to begin this procreation before we handfast, is there?"

Brianna swung around and headed for the door. There she paused and gave him a dimpled smile. "Do not worry. If I do agree to the arrangement, I'll have no problem conceiving."

He gave her an incredulous look. "How can you be certain?"

"As you have said—my sons are proof enough." She left the cabin.

Harrison sank onto the bed. Lacing his hands behind his head, he stared at the ceiling, his grin slipping at the uncomfortable thought of his trickery. No one could have forced Brianna, an American citizen, to leave her home. No one could take her children from her, no matter Payton's death wish. It was a damned good thing her attorney had eagerly taken the bribe Harrison had offered him, and made himself unavailable to Brianna before leaving America.

CHAPTER 6

January, 1889
Edinburgh, Scotland

A cheer rose from the passengers aboard the steamship Atlantis when it slid alongside one of several long docks rimming Edinburgh's shoreline. Brianna stood at the railing huddled inside her beaver fur coat. Snowflakes drifted down from the cloud-filled sky as she turned to Harrison, who leaned against the railing beside her. He appeared comfortable and warm, although he wore no overcoat, just a wool serge jacket over a white shirt and waistcoat.

"Now then, that wasn't such a bad journey, was it?" Even though his complexion was pale, Brianna knew he hadn't been ill in over a week. His dark hair had grown longer over their weeks of travel so he'd brushed it back and secured it at the nape of his neck with a narrow band of soft leather.

"It's bloody well about time we arrived," he grumbled, taking her hand.

She sighed at the welcome warmth of his hand, then turned her eyes to the magnificent city before her. Harrison's description of his homeland had not prepared her for the incredible beauty that greeted her. Tall buildings dotted the land. As she looked closer, she saw that one of them was an enormous, gray stone castle with several turrets and spires. She was struck by the strong contrast of vibrant-colored hues; from the magnificent brown and gray snow-capped mountains in the distance, to the nearer lush green valleys sprinkled with purple heather.

"I will find the boys while you stay here and rest."

"Woman, I am cross-eyed from all of the rest I've taken of late. The seasickness has passed, thank God."

"You are certain?"

"Quite. Of course, it helps that we have come to a standstill," he said dryly.

She turned away and had taken just a few steps when Harrison asked, "Have I been so awful?"

She scowled at him over her shoulder. "Positively beastly." Her expression softened. "But with good reason."

He followed her as she lifted her skirts in order to clear the ship's wet decking. He caught a glimpse of fine white lace edging the silk pantalets she wore beneath her mourning gown. He'd managed to convince her that she could wear some of the fripperies he had purchased for her.

Brianna was tall and full bosomed, a perfect match for him. She wore her dark brown hair pulled up into a soft style, twisted into a bun at the back of her head. Her sapphire eyes were her best feature. Her nose was short and tipped on the end, but did not detract from her unique beauty. She is so fine. The weeks he'd spent with her he'd cherish always. But tomorrow could not come soon enough.

Arranging their handfasting once they arrived at Winterhaven was paramount to anything else.

He frowned, bemused by her rejection of his marriage proposal. She desired no permanent ties to him, or to any man. Furthermore, she'd added, they did not love each other. He'd scoffed and told her he knew of many couples that had not loved each other before marrying, but had learned to abide one another over time.

Brianna and his nephews appeared on deck. They waited with the other passengers to leave the ship, and Harrison joined them.

She threaded one arm through his. "Who will be meeting us?"

"My coachman, Stanton, and Wesley, my valet. He will see to our trunks."

"How far away is your home?"

"Seven miles to the northwest." He pulled her along when he saw her grimacing, likely from the stench of the seamen's sweat, and the distinct odor of fish. "I feel an urge to burn off some energy now that I'm on solid ground. Stanton will have brought my steed along. I intend to ride ahead to the manor while you and the boys travel by coach."

They stepped off the ship. Jamie and Harry ran down the wharf, weaving through the crowd. Harrison called out, "Boys! Not too far."

"Yes, sir!" they chimed over their shoulders. They ran along the wharf toward the docked fishing boats. They stopped beside one fisherman who had rolled a large barrel down the ramp from a ship and set it upright.

Harrison grinned when the boys leaned down and watched the man pry off the lid, knowing well it was filled with fish. He turned to Brianna. "Would you care to ride ahead with me? There are a number of stables here in Edinburgh. I could find you a gentle mount."

"I couldn't leave Harry and Jamie alone."

"Wesley and Stanton will be with them. Ride with me," he demanded, his eyes telling her he wouldn't take no for an answer.

"I'm afraid I wouldn't feel comfortable riding a horse with which I'm not familiar."

He studied her thoughtfully a moment and said, "You may share my seat on Challenger."

"Laird MacAulay! Over here."

Harrison looked to the right and saw his valet waving his hand as he made his way through the crowd. He was a small man, tidily dressed.

"He...he is wearing a dress!" Brianna whispered, obviously shocked.

"It's a kilt. Even I wear them upon occasion," he said with a smile.

"Och, we have missed ye, Laird!" Wesley said, bowing deferentially. "Thank the Lord ye managed to survive both directions of yer journey."

"It is good to be home." Harrison grasped Wesley's hand. He wasn't just an employee, but a friend. He pulled Brianna forward. "Allow me to introduce you to Mrs. MacAulay. Brianna, I would like you to meet Wesley, who cares for my appearance more than I ever will."

The valet gallantly swept his billed cap off his balding head and bowed. "Happy I am to be makin' the acquaintance of poor Payton's widow. Welcome to Scotland, m'lady."

Brianna replied, "It is a pleasure to meet you, Mister...?"

"It has always been just Wesley." He glanced around and asked, "And where are your sons?"

Harrison pointed down the wharf. "There. Would you escort them to the coach? I assume Stanton is here?"

"Around the corner."

"And Challenger?"

Wesley snorted. "He's here all right. The beast has missed ye sorely, since ye are the only one he'll allow on his back."

"Attend to our trunks then, and settle the boys in the carriage. Mrs. MacAulay will be riding ahead with me."

"Aye, laird," Wesley said, then turned and headed down the wharf.

Harrison stared at Brianna and noticed her complexion had paled. He frowned. "What is the matter? Are you ill?"

"I'm fine. But I believe I will be more comfortable in the carriage with Harry and Jamie."

"Nonsense! You were cooped up on board that ship as long as I and need to stretch your legs."

Brianna lifted one eyebrow. "Stretch, you say? I believe a nice long walk would be just the thing, then."

Harrison stroked her cheek. "You will be safe. Trust me." He released her and folded his arms across his chest. "Of course, I can understand if you are fearful of riding."

"I beg your pardon," she said indignantly. "I am not frightened of a stupid animal."

He inclined his head. "Wonderful. Then you will join me."

Brianna gave him a frosty look and a curt nod. He grinned, snatched up her hand and pulled her across the street. They turned a corner and stopped beside an elegant black coach. The MacAulay clan's heraldic arms were emblazoned on the door in gold.

Ahead of the coach, and off to one side, a red-faced man struggled to hold the reins of an enormous tawny horse. The animal kicked and bucked in agitation at being restrained, but calmed somewhat at Harrison's approach.

Harrison noted the coach horses had been tied securely

to a post. "Thank you, Stanton. I see that devil horse of mine must have been giving you a difficult time."

Stanton rolled his eyes. "Nothing unusual about that, is there? I will have ye know he tried his hardest to pass yer coach to get here, and he was tied up to the back of it, mind ye!"

Harrison laughed. "Good job, my man. I'll take him now." He took the reins from his eager employee and added, "I would like you to meet Mrs. MacAulay. Brianna, this is my coachman, Stanton."

The man ducked his head shyly as he passed an apple to Harrison. "Pleased to meet ye, m'lady." He backed away and scrambled into the coach's driver seat.

Harrison tugged on his horse's reins. "Settle down, you brute," he said, holding out the fruit. The horse snatched the apple from Harrison. Brianna gasped and backed away. Harrison allowed him one bite, took the apple away and tucked it inside his pocket. "You may have the entire treat once we arrive home." He looked up and saw Stanton settling Harry and Jamie inside the coach. "As soon as Wesley returns with our bags, head for home. We will be just ahead of you."

"Right away, Laird!"

Brianna rushed to the coach and peered in the window. "Now, boys, behave yourselves. Misters Stanton and Wesley will be caring for you while I ride with your uncle on his horse."

Harry thrust his head out the window and stared at Challenger with wide eyes, then looked at his mother. "But Ma, you don't know how to ride!"

"Shhh!" Brianna glanced over her shoulder, and saw Harrison easing into the saddle, relieved he hadn't heard Harry. "Yes, well, there is always a first time for everything, dear."

She squared her shoulders and marched back to Harrison. He sat atop the animal, one hand holding the reins, the other extended and ready to assist her into the saddle.

"Come up," he ordered.

She eyed the horse again, then Harrison's thighs, noticing how they were widely spread due to the animal's broad back.

"What kind of horse is he?" she asked, noting Challenger's shaggy legs. "He has fur on his feet, and he is very large. I don't believe I will be able to mount him."

"Challenger is a Clydesdale, a descendent of the war horses that carried armored knights into battle centuries ago. We breed and raise them here in Scotland, and they are used primarily as workhorses. When gelded, though, they make wonderful mounts. Challenger is a stallion and I lend him out to stud, which accounts for his somewhat restless demeanor. He is my first choice of mount, however, and he carries my size splendidly, though he is small for a Clydesdale, he is suitable for my needs. Now then, I would like to arrive home before my coach."

Harrison removed his spectacles and pocketed them inside his jacket. He reached back and opened a pack behind his saddle, pulled out a pair of leather gloves and yanked them on. Reaching down he clasped her forearms and easily hoisted her up to sit in front of him. She gasped in surprise when he wound his arm around her waist, holding her in place, with her shoulder jammed against his chest and her limbs draped across one of his thighs. If he removed his arm, she'd slide off the horse.

He drew her close, and her body made contact with his heated core. "Much better," he murmured. Then he clicked his tongue and Challenger shot off into a jaw-breaking trot.

With further encouragement, the beast lengthened his stride into a gallop.

Soon Winterhaven loomed directly ahead, a red brick Georgian-style house of three stories. Harrison turned left and steered Challenger down the long cobblestone road. He brought the beast to a skidding halt in front of the manor house, lowered Brianna carefully to the road, then vaulted from the saddle to join her. Just then the massive double doors to the home opened.

Brianna smoothed her skirts with a trembling hand and narrowed her eyes on him. "Have you lost your mind, Harrison MacAulay?"

He jammed his hands on his hips. "Why the devil did you not tell me you never sat a horse before?"

"However did you guess?"

He snorted and held up his injured hand. "Once we go inside you may tend to my wounds, woman."

She saw the nail marks there and grew defensive. "It serves you right for riding like the devil was chasing you. I cannot believe you normally ride at such a breakneck speed."

"No harm was done. You were never in danger."

Laughter and shouts drew Brianna's attention then. She turned a wide-eyed look upon the horde of young people hurtling down the steps toward her. The crowd hemmed her in and she emitted a panicked shriek of protest.

"Step back, damn it all," Harrison thundered. "Give us some room here!"

Astonishingly, they did precisely as he ordered. They lined up in two rows, facing each other like obedient soldiers taking orders from their commander. "Now then," Harrison said severely as he paced the aisle. "Never have I allowed this undisciplined conduct in my home, and I have no intentions of doing so now. What ails all of ye?"

A pretty girl with long black braids entwined in a crown upon her head bravely stepped forward. "Ye have never been gone for such a long time, and we're happy ye're home, cousin."

Harrison favored the girl with a genuine smile. "Have you been a good girl and kept up with your studies, Alice?"

"Oh, yes! Just ask Master Thornton."

Harrison growled, "I recall you had some catching up to do. I will be meeting with him tomorrow and hope to hear good news."

"Aye, ye will," Alice said, her cheeks turning pink as she returned to her place in line.

Harrison looked toward the front door where a handful of servants stood hesitantly upon the steps, waiting to perform their laird's bidding. He said to his cousins, "I would like to introduce you to Payton's widow, Mrs. MacAulay," he said, drawing her forward. "Make her welcome."

One by one, the MacAulay clan members stepped forward and welcomed her with lovely regard.

After Harrison dismissed them, Brianna asked, "They are all related to you?"

He nodded. "Nine cousins live here on a permanent basis, in addition to my grandmothers. And on any given day of the week sundry other relatives call."

Harrison went on to introduce her to the household staff, and afterwards, a sweet, lyrical woman's voice said, "And let us not forget your one and only devoted baby sister."

Brianna looked up at the manor's entrance to see a petite young woman framed in the doorway. She was clad in a shawl of the MacAulay plaid, of red and green, worn over a bright red woolen skirt and white shirtwaist. Brianna admired the girl's auburn-colored hair and her gray eyes gleaming with laughter. They were remarkably similar to Harrison's eyes. Her nose was perfectly shaped and slightly tilted, her chin small, but determined, her lips full and turned up in a vivacious smile.

"Tess," Harrison said softly, swiftly taking the stairs. She raced down to meet him and launched herself into his arms. He pulled her to one side of the stairs to allow the household staff to enter the manor, his eyes never leaving the pretty young woman.

Brianna watched the loving scene unfold with a tearful smile. They separated then and Tess, who stood a step higher than Harrison, met her brother's eyes. They spoke softly to each other, smiling the entire time and holding hands.

After a few moments, Tess pulled away, darted around him and made her way down the stairs. She stopped in front of Brianna and caught hold of her hands. "Oh, you have no idea how much I have longed for a sister. Welcome home."

Brianna smiled at Tess's candid overture. "Thank you."

Tess turned to her brother. "You must give Brianna the suite of rooms next to mine in the west wing."

Harrison raised his brow. "Your rooms? I believe once you married last year I gave them to Grandmother Jean."

"Grandmother and I switched things around a bit now that I'm home," she replied.

Harrison scowled. "What do you mean you're home? You mean for a visit, don't you? And where is your husband?"

"In London, of course."

Tess sidled closer to Brianna and grasped her hand.

"And why are you not in London with him?"

"Because I've decided I do not wish to be married to Max any longer." Tess tilted up her chin.

"Your solicitor is looking into an annulment for me as we speak. I want the deed done as expeditiously as possible."

"Hell," Harrison growled. "Explain why ye have left Max. Then ye will pack yer trunks and return to England immediately."

"I won't go! I abhor the man and regret marrying him." She shrugged. "Besides, I'm too young to be married."

Harrison appeared on the verge of exploding, so Brianna intervened, hoping to diffuse the situation. "Yes, well, why do we not step inside and have this discussion over a nice hot cup of tea?"

"Tea," Harrison said, sending Brianna a blank look. "Wonderful idea." He swept his hand toward the stairs. "Ladies."

Brianna lifted her skirts and took the stairs beside Tess and Harrison followed. Inside the foyer, walls had been painted pale yellow. She gasped in delight when she saw a lavish flower garden through the doors of the drawing room. It took her a moment to realize it wasn't real. The lush Eden surrounding a pond where graceful swans floated was a mural painted on the wall!

Stunned, she sank down upon a green velvet divan, her eyes focused on the magnificent painting. Her hands slid over the carved rosewood arms of the chair just as an ancient, gray-haired woman appeared in the doorway.

Maeve from the kitchen stepped up and waited for orders from Harrison, which he gave. "Tea for the ladies, Maeve."

Harrison opened the doors of a beautifully carved cupboard. He pulled out a glass, lifted a tall brown bottle and poured himself a drink. Within moments, Maeve returned, pushing a teacart ahead of her.

Brianna gave Maeve a grateful smile when she was handed a steaming cup of tea. She clutched the dainty floral cup and saucer in her lap and sighed, readying herself for the impending discussion between brother and sister, which would likely turn into an argument.

Harrison sat on the sofa beside her and the cushion sank under his weight, jostling her. She caught her cup just before it slid off its saucer.

"Now, Tess, what has Max done to prompt you to seek an annulment, which I will remind you, is impossible?" Harrison asked.

"I'm not contemplating it at all. I'm certain of it," Tess replied.

"And I'm certain you will not," he shot back in a soft, dangerous voice.

Brianna had heard that warning tone in his voice before, and brother and sister stared at each other with matching fury in their eyes.

"What has caused you to leave your husband?" Brianna asked. "Has he harmed you in some way."

Harrison scoffed. "Max, harmful? Hardly! The man is hopelessly besotted with her."

"That's not true," Tess said. "At least, not always. And now he wants me to..."

Brianna saw the young woman was mortified when her cheeks turned red.

"He likely wants what any husband wants from his wife —her compliance in the marriage bed."

"Really, Harrison." Brianna turned a jaundiced eye on him

Tess sighed. "I'm afraid he is dreadfully right. Max wants...he expects me to conceive a babe for him soon."

There seems to be a lot of that sentiment going around these days, Brianna smoothly said under her breath, but Harrison heard and scowled at her.

"Correct me if I'm wrong here, but were you not the one

who begged me to allow you to marry the Englishman in the first place?" Harrison pointed his finger at her. "You, my girl, just need to grow up, and rather quickly. You've been married over six months! Besides, the marriage has been consummated so you cannot file for an annulment. Tomorrow morning I expect you to be packed and ready to return to London."

Tess lowered her eyes and mumbled something under her breath.

Harrison leaned forward and pierced her with a hard look. "Speak up, Tess."

"We haven't," she replied.

He looked at her in confusion. "Haven't what?"

"Your marriage hasn't been consummated, has it?" Brianna asked.

Tess shook her head.

"By, God, are ye telling me ye have not slept with yer own husband?" Harrison roared as he rose, then stalked toward Tess, halting to tower over her.

Brianna rose from the divan, touched his arm, warning him to maintain control. Tess sat in abject silence, her eyes downcast, refusing to meet his eyes.

"Of course we have," Tess replied.

Brianna heard Harrison expel a relieved sigh.

"We just have not done *it*, yet."

"Damn," Harrison swore under his breath.

Brianna winced, then met Tess's pleading expression.

"I cannot bring myself to..."

Brianna patted her hand. "We understand, dear. It isn't necessary you tell us anymore." She gave Harrison a pointed look before turning back to Tess. "We shall talk more after breakfast in the morning. You must be exhausted."

Harrison scowled at his sister. Brianna was right. Why

browbeat Tess now when she was obviously tired and feeling low. Tomorrow would be soon enough.

"In my study, directly after breakfast tomorrow, Tess," he ordered. "Is that understood?"

Tess sighed. "Certainly, brother dearest."

CHAPTER 7

Supper that evening was a lively event, once Jamie and Harry arrived in the coach. They were welcomed and fawned over and all Brianna could think of was how they'd surely be spoiled. She mentioned it to Harrison and he'd merely shrugged. "They deserve a bit of attention."

After an hour of lively conversation, the boys were allowed to follow one of the stable boys to the barns to view the animals, Harrison promising soon they would have their own mounts.

Harrison rose and extended his hand to Brianna, who was seated at his side. "Come, we've much to discuss this evening. We'll have privacy in the library." He looked to the others. "Excuse us."

Harrison's grandmother, Mary, protested, "But the poor woman is bone tired, grandson. She still hasn't recovered from her travels. Let her find her bed early this night."

"Och, it's true," chimed in Grandmother Jean. "You've days ahead to talk."

Tess said, "Just because you've been a brute to me all evening doesn't mean Brianna must suffer, too."

Brianna had just finished eating a dinner fit for a queen, surrounded by the MacAulay clan. They'd thrown questions at her unmercifully, until Harrison ordered them to stop. A talk in the library would be a welcome reprieve. She looked at Harrison. "I'll be in shortly, after I've finished this delicious pudding."

He nodded and bowed over her hand. Then he raised his head, and her heart started racing when she met the intent look in his eyes. She pulled her hand away and watched him saunter from the dining room. She turned back to her pudding. When she raised a spoonful to her lips, she realized no one was speaking.

She looked up at Grandmother Jean's surprised expression. "I'm impressed, Brianna. You handled him rather well, for a newcomer."

After Brianna finished her pudding, she left the table. She found Harrison slouched down on one end of the divan, an empty glass dangling by its stem from his fingertips. As she drew near, she wrinkled her nose, recognizing the pungent order of alcohol. His gaze was riveted on the fire, but soon he turned and met her censorious expression. His lips twitched. Reaching up, he clasped her wrist and pulled her down to sit beside him.

She sighed and rearranged her skirts.

"Would you like tea, or a sherry, perhaps?"

"Nothing, thank you," she said coolly. "Let's have the discussion you insisted upon having, shall we?"

Harrison moved to the teacart in the corner of the room. He poured her a cup of tea, ignoring her negative response. He held the cup under her nose and she sniffed and identified the inviting scent of saffron, one of her favorites. Grudgingly, she accepted the tea. He headed back to the corner. There he snatched up a bottle and poured himself a large draught of Scotch whisky before returning to her.

"Thank you for obliging me at such a late hour," he said, settling down beside her. "I know how tired you must be, but this is too important to wait. Why do you think Tess hasn't allowed her husband into her bed? Bear in mind the chit's been in love with him since she was a child of nine."

Brianna frowned. "I've been thinking about this, and have reached the conclusion she's frightened of the intimate side of marriage. This is a rather embarrassing topic to be discussing but I must ask you, had anyone prepared Tess for marriage?"

He lifted one eyebrow. "Prepared?"

"For what happens between a man and a woman," Brianna said, her cheeks turning hot.

"Ah!" Harrison sighed. "I'm not certain."

She stared at him aghast. "No one told her what to expect?"

He scowled. "I thought of it, but couldn't find the appropriate words. She is, after all, my baby sister. I approached the grandmothers, but they shrugged it off and said she'll learn on her own, as they had."

"So you said nothing."

"We have livestock aplenty on the estate. Tess has seen them mate. I do recall pointing out the similarity between animals and humans on occasion."

"You are comparing a man and a woman making love to animals mating?"

"Well...yes. The specific comparison I made was to the equine breed."

"Oh, my God!" she whispered, her eyes widening at the very idea of Tess watching the powerful, crude mating between the huge animals.

"In the end, I decided who better to educate a wife than a husband, so I left the duty to Max." He scowled. "Never had I dreamed a man of his vast experience would botch the job."

"Tess is frightened to death! Comparing horses and people? Heavens, what ever were you thinking?"

Harrison grinned. "You're blushing."

Brianna's hands flew to her cheeks and she slammed her eyes shut.

"You know, Brianna," he said matter-of-factly, "horses and people mating are very similar."

She decided she shouldn't be having this sort of conversation with him. It was too embarrassing! She rose, took one step to leave when Harrison reached out and grasped the back of her skirt.

"Sit down," he cajoled. "I was only teasing. I'm sorry, but one would think you an untried virgin and not a married woman of ten years."

"How old was Tess when your mother passed away?" Brianna asked, desperate to change the topic.

"Mother died giving birth to Tess. I was twelve, Payton eight. My father and I, along with Maeve's help, raised Payton and Tess."

"There's your answer, then."

He frowned. "Enlighten me."

"Tess is fearful of dying as her mother did, in childbirth. Which, of course, is the reason she won't allow Max to touch her."

"I had not thought of that, and damn it, I should have," Harrison softly replied. He shoved his spectacles into position on his nose. Then he rose and poured himself another libation. He drank the potent liquor down in one gulp and said, "In approximately a week's time, we'll be traveling to England to speak to Max. You're coming with me."

Brianna rose gracefully and walked to the doorway. With her hand on the knob, she stared at him over her shoulder. "I've no intentions of traveling to London to sort out your family troubles."

"You did mention you would enjoy a trip to London. Remember?"

"Not under these circumstances."

She started turning the knob but stopped at Harrison's next words. "If I were to venture a guess, I would say you are frightened of forming any attachments to my family."

"I have no idea what you are talking about," she exclaimed, flinging a furious look at him.

He moved to her side and pulled at one loose curl in her otherwise, perfectly coifed hair. "What indeed?" he said softly. "You have never been a part of a family before. I'm not speaking of your ten-year marriage to my brother. I mean a family including cousins, aunts, uncles, parents and grandparents. And now that you are, you're uncertain of the accountability and responsibility of it. Frightened of sharing the sadness and joys of a family, and skittish of permanency in your life."

He grasped her shoulders. "Brianna, I want you to think of the MacAulay clan as an anchor, holding you forever in their hearts. Learn that you may depend on us. I desperately need your help. Tess needs a woman to help her deal with this fear of hers. You are the only one who may help her."

Brianna groaned, "Oh, why me, when you've a number of other female relatives about?"

"You have been married before and have successfully given birth to two children."

Heaving a deep sigh, she said, "If I refuse to help you, I will feel guilty for the rest of my days. All right, I'll go. but please provide me enough time. Harry and Jamie will be coming with us."

"They will not be making the journey."

"I'll not leave my sons behind with strangers." She yanked open the door, but paused at Harrison's next words.

"No, they will not be coming with us this time because once we leave Tess in London we'll be traveling north to Aberdeen."

She spun around. "Why?"

He drew closer. "Our handfasting will take place there." He gripped the edge of the door, preventing her from slipping out.

"I have yet to agree to the arrangement."

He grinned. "True, but you will."

She crossed her arms and tapped her foot. "That's right. You do require an heir rather quickly, don't you?" she asked, her voice laced with sarcasm.

He gently cupped her chin in his hand. "The sooner we finish this business, the sooner you will be able to pursue your dreams of freedom and return to America. That is what you want, is it not?"

She nodded, then stilled when he lowered his head and brushed his lips across hers. He lifted his head and gazed at her a moment, his sherry eyes clearly showing his intent. He took her lips again in a kiss she'd remember until she went to her grave. He crushed her against him and she felt the thumping vibration of his heart with his first kiss. She went limp in his arms. The feeling of his lips on hers, his tongue swirling inside, made her forget where she was and what she was doing.

When the fingers on one of his broad hands splayed across her bottom, she broke away then yanked the door open. Her body screamed in agony as she ran. Between sleeping in unfamiliar berths aboard the ship, and bouncing on the saddle in front of Harrison, her body ached from head to toe. She'd reached the long flight of steps that led to the second level of the mansion when Harrison's voice stopped her.

"You will need ligament rubbed into your limbs." He smiled at her intimately. "Likely in other places, as well."

Brianna's cheeks heated again at his words, but she tilted up her chin and sent him a blazing look. "I'm fine."

His smile widened.

"For truth," she retorted.

He shrugged and leaned against the banister. "Don't say I didn't warn you. By morning you will barely be able to rise from your bed."

Oh, I wouldn't relish that! "Tess will assist me."

"If you find her awake, which I highly doubt at this hour. By the way, many have told me that my hands work magic. Call if you change your mind."

She watched him make his way down the hall, all the while thinking how she'd never allow him to touch her in such an intimate fashion. Of course, within a matter of days, if she agreed to handfast, he would be touching her as intimately as a husband touches his wife. She trudged up the stairs. Upon reaching the landing, she rubbed her pain-laden thighs and sore posterior. She heard a chuckle and whirled around to find Harrison ascending the steps, smiling at her. He paused a few steps below her and extended his hand. Brianna frowned at the jar he held and read the label.

"Horse liniment?"

He nodded. "The smell is not terribly enticing, but it works as well on the human as it does on a horse. As I mentioned, I'd be delighted to assist you."

"Oh, I'm sure you would, but no thank you."

He sighed. "My rooms are on the opposite end of the corridor, in case you decide to be sensible."

She glared at his broad back as he ambled away until he disappeared from sight. Then she stepped into her room and closed the door. There wasn't a key to lock it so she made a mental note to request one in the morning.

Brianna sat up with a start and water splashed over the sides of the tub. Someone was pounding on the bathing room door and calling her name.

"Answer me, Brianna! Are you all right?"

Rising, she snatched up a drying cloth and wound it around her shivering body. The door burst open and smashed against the wall with a deafening crash. Brianna looked up in horror and saw Harrison looming in the doorway. He was clad in a deep blue, belted robe, which stopped at his knees. His hair stood on end and his wire-rimmed spectacles sat crookedly on his nose.

"Why in bloody hell didn't ye answer me when I called?"

Her eyes darted from his furious expression to the door hanging from the top hinge. "You...you broke the door." She secured the wrap tight across her breasts.

"If ye hadn't locked it, I wouldn't have had to smash it in. I repeat, why didn't ye answer me?"

"I was asleep."

"I left you well over an hour ago and you have been sleeping in the tub the entire time?"

She nodded and edged around him, wondering why he was so angry. Then she thought she heard him say something about 'damned foolish woman drowning in the tub'. In her bedchamber, she searched for her robe. Unfortunately, she discovered it at the same time he did. They tugged on the fabric, each in the opposite direction, until he pulled it from her grip.

His silver eyes caressed her from head to toe. "You haven't used the liniment yet, have you?"

She shook her head.

"Where is it?"

Brianna shrugged and turned away. When next she looked, she discovered him in the bathing room, her robe still clutched in his hand. She dug inside the armoire for a nightdress but stopped with a sigh when he returned, jar in hand.

He dropped the liniment on the bed, gently grasped her shoulders and pressed until she sat down. He leaned toward her. She tried avoiding him by flopping down flat on the bed. Never breaking eye contact, he unscrewed the jar's lid and delved his fingers inside. When he withdrew them, they were coated with an oily concoction.

She wrinkled her nose at the pungent odor wafting through the air.

He laughed. "So, it isn't rose-scented, but it will ease your discomfort."

Brianna closed her eyes at the wicked thought of his long fingers touching her intimately. Her eyes snapped open when he suggested, "I'll rub this into each limb. I won't even peek." He inclined his head, waiting for her permission, as though he knew she'd give it.

"I'm not the least bit sore," she lied. Even after a long soak in the tub, her legs throbbed with a dull pain.

She focused on his fingers smeared with the liniment and sighed, imagining those strong fingers working their magic on her. She met his eyes. "Will you douse the lights?"

He did as she requested, but pulled the curtains back at the window, allowing a sliver of moonlight into the room before sitting beside her again.

"Roll over," he said, his voice soft and low.

She followed his directions, careful to keep the cloth

wound tightly around her body. She emitted a small gasp when his hands tucked the drying cloth up to the tops of her thighs. Her cheeks turned hot as she thought about him staring at her limbs. All she could think was how thankful she was for the dim lighting.

She heard his quick intake of breath and groaned, "Just get on with it!"

Harrison proceeded to rub the liniment into the backs of her thighs, marveling at their firmness, yet they were soft. He found it difficult to control his breathing and he gulped as he delved his fingers into the jar again. As he massaged the liniment into her calf muscles, he inched his hands up her legs and eased them apart.

"What do you think you're doing?" She arched off the bed and scowled at him over her shoulder.

"The insides of your limbs also require my attention. Hold still," he growled. Damn! He was every bit as anxious to get the deed done as she, cursing himself for laying a finger on her. She was exquisite, tempting, and, damn it all, he couldn't have her yet.

The more his fingers worked on her muscles the more relaxed she grew. He kept his fingers well away from the apex of her thighs, even though his entire body ached at the thought of touching her there. He smiled. She'd be shocked if he did, yet he also knew he could please her, as she'd never been pleased before.

He'd always had more patience than his brother.

Beneath the soft lighting, he could make out the pale globes of her bottom beneath the thin cloth. Fleetingly, he thought how wonderful it would be to massage that enticing portion of her anatomy. He frowned as he decided her limbs he could handle, but her derriere was an entirely different matter.

"Done?" she inquired impatiently a moment later.

"Not quite," he said, unable to control the hitch in his voice.

He smiled when he heard her sigh. He continued rubbing her thighs and calves, his eyes still focused on her buttocks. And when she emitted a soft groan of contentment he struggled against the temptation to rip the cloth away and reveal her body in all its glory. Her breathing quickened when he kneaded her limbs firmly. He was so intent upon her reaction to his touch he ignored his own body's response —until it was too late.

My God! He groaned when his manhood unexpectedly betrayed him, as though he were a callow youth. Keeping his eyes shut he barely choked back a shout of pleasure at his release. Then he felt hot liquid sliding down one leg. He removed his hands from her, rose from the bed and stepped back. He squinted down at the floor. The moonlight streaking through the window glinted off the small puddle there between his bare feet.

He tightened his belt and straightened his spectacles. Then, with as much dignity as he could muster, he turned away and did the only thing he possibly could—he left without uttering another word.

Brianna didn't feel his touch any longer, so she raised her head and turned to thank him. He was nowhere in sight. The door was ajar. She scrambled to her feet and stepped in something wet. Probably just water from her bath, she decided. She returned to the bathing room and pulled a drying cloth off a hook. She didn't want to be responsible for ruining the wood floor so she bent down and swiped the wet spot. As soon as she stood, she frowned when she caught the scent of salt in the air. She bent down once more, rubbed her finger in the puddle and sniffed it.

A growing smiled crossed her lips as she straightened up, then she couldn't contain a small chuckle. By the time she reached the door and closed it, she couldn't prevent herself from laughing outright, and rather loudly. Then she tugged on her nightgown and settled into bed, pulling the quilt up around her shoulders. She grinned at the thought of besting the patriarch of Clan MacAulay. Bested him not with her wit, nor with any typical weapon, but with a feminine arsenal a man would have difficulty resisting—by just being a woman.

CHAPTER 8

*T*he next day the clouds finally departed, after a week of gloomy weather. Even with the sun's brilliant appearance, Harrison's heavy disposition hadn't lightened a bit. He'd spent the better part of the night tossing and turning as he tried to understand Tess and Max's predicament. Divorce was such a foreign concept, and impossible for Tess to pursue.

Now he sat behind his desk, his hands folded in front of him. Brianna and Tess sat beside each other in the chairs opposite him. Tess looked young and vivacious, although she was quite pale. Brianna appeared achingly lovely—even in her dull widow's weeds. She'd done something different with her hair. She still wore it up but sections of it across the front had been woven and braided with fine silver ribbons, the ends tucked neatly up inside her dark brown locks of hair.

"What do you think of Brianna's new hair style, Harrison?"

Harrison kept his gaze on Brianna's face, grinning when her cheeks turned pink. "It's lovely."

"Thank you," Brianna replied softly, looking all the while at Tess. "Your sister is quite talented, my lord."

"Brianna has the most wonderful hair to work with. Why, it's thick, luxurious and several inches longer than mine, even though I've been growing it all my..."

"Tess?"

She paused and gave Harrison a round-eyed look.

"We can't put this off any longer. Now I'd like you to finish telling us what happened between you and Max. As a matter of fact, I had plenty of time during the night to think about it and have reached my own conclusion."

Tess raised her brow. "Really? What might that be?"

Harrison stared at his sister. "You can't bring yourself to mate with your husband. Isn't that it?"

He cursed when tears leaked from her eyes and slid down her cheeks. Finally, she nodded and said, "I'm just not ready!" She wrung her hands and sent Brianna a pleading look.

"Oh, my dear, has he hurt you? Are you frightened of him?" Brianna asked.

"Yes...no! Oh, I haven't any idea," she wailed.

"So, you denied him his conjugal rights," Harrison snapped.

"Yes! In time, perhaps I'll be ready, but not now. Besides, I don't care to have a baby, not for a number of years, actually."

The ache in Brianna's heart increased when she saw the tears in Tess's eyes. My Lord, what this poor young woman had been through was unbelievable. She couldn't imagine being so frightened of loving her husband that she felt compelled to run away.

"I thought I was in love with Max, but I realize now I was mistaken."

"That is unfortunate for you. Now that you have the man you insisted upon having, you will stay married to him. Max must be a saint, or so besotted with you to allow you to have your way in this."

Brianna patted Tess's hand. "You know, it wasn't fair of you to just up and leave your husband. Did you discuss your feelings with him? Did you tell him you were frightened of...the intimacy of marriage."

Tess shook her head and sobbed, "No! Just as I've no idea how to even begin to tell you about it."

Brianna recalled being apprehensive on her wedding night, but not frightened. Payton had put her at ease with his gentle laughter and hot-eyed looks. The next morning, she decided she'd follow him to the ends of the earth if he asked! She guessed Tess wasn't feeling mere anxiety, but a deep-seated fear. In order for her to help the girl, Tess would need to reveal her true feelings regarding intimacy.

"Perhaps a good place to start would be at the beginning," Brianna said. "Are you capable of doing that?"

Tess gulped and nodded.

Brianna watched as she tried to compose herself, saw how she'd clasped her hands tightly in her lap. "Each time he—oh, my Lord, it's too embarrassing to speak of."

Brianna watched Tess bite her lips and clench her hands. She reached out, pulled the girl into her arms and held her as she sobbed. After a while, Brianna said, "Go on, when you are able."

"It...it all began on our wedding night," said Tess, her voice shaking. "He asked me to...to get undressed." She gave Brianna a wide-eyed look. "Why, he even offered to help me!"

Harrison slumped in his chair and murmured, "No doubt."

Brianna shot him a scathing look.

"He started touching me all over and kissing me."

With a smile, Brianna asked, "And did you like it?"

Tess smiled shyly. "Oh, yes. His kisses were very much the same before we married." She frowned and added, "Well, perhaps they were a bit more forceful after we married—but still they were quite lovely. Then he raised my gown and pulled it over my head. I began to think this wasn't quite as nice."

"Did you tell him to stop?" Brianna inquired.

"Not yet. I was uncertain at this point, and I fully trusted Max. I believed I was in love with him."

Harrison sat forward in his chair, planted his elbows on the desk. "Of course you were in love with him. You still are."

"No," Tess snapped. "I thought I was in love with him, until he started touching me in places I didn't want him to."

Brianna noted the growing look of horror on Tess's face when she continued her tale. "When he reached between my legs and started touching me there I jumped from the bed. I ran to the hearth. There I snatched up a poker and threatened to brain him if he didn't stop touching me that way. I told him I very much enjoyed his kisses, but that's all I wanted him to do."

"And did this anger him?" Brianna asked.

Tess frowned, then gave Brianna a puzzled look. "No, he appeared sad. He rose from the bed and left the room." Haughtily, she added, "I've no idea where he spent the night, but it wasn't with me."

Brianna asked, "Do you care where he spent the night?"

Tess's face turned pink and she stumbled over her words. "What a...a silly question to ask! Of course I didn't care. And I still don't. Of course, I've heard stories..."

Brianna turned to Harrison and raised her brow.

Harrison asked, "Do you think Max has taken a mistress, Tess?"

"It wouldn't surprise me if he did," she retorted. "Isn't that what most men do?"

"If they don't love their wives—perhaps. But Max loves you, Tess. Believe it. Trust him. He won't harm you. Now, continue."

"Over the months since we married he tried to seduce me several times, but I managed to turn him away, until two evenings ago. He told me he'd waited as long as he could. That I was denying him his marital rights."

Brianna tried easing Tess. "Of course you denied him. You were frightened." Brianna held Tess's hand as she waited for her to continue. She met Harrison's contemplative expression and gave him an imploring look.

With a long sigh, Harrison rose from the divan. Squatting down beside Tess's chair, he asked, "Once more I ask, what are you afraid of? Has Max hurt you?"

Tess wildly shook her head. "But he has every intention of taking by force what I won't willingly give him. Thank God I managed to escape him."

Brianna didn't like the sound of that. The silence in the room was deafening.

"How did you manage that?" Harrison inquired. When she gave no response, he added, "Did he just allow you to leave? I question the fact Max hasn't appeared on our doorstep to fetch you home. Or has he?"

"He hasn't. You see, he had a rather unfortunate accident, which prevented him from following me."

A chill crept up Brianna's spine at the simple reply. She had an awful feeling about this. She looked at Harrison, who was unnaturally still.

"What happened?" His voice utterly cold.

"I shot him."

"My God!"

Brianna gasped, "Oh, dear!"

"Just a little," Tess wailed.

"Ye either shot the man or ye didn't!" Harrison thundered.

Tess sniffled but didn't reply.

Harrison paced the length of the room again. After a time, he stopped and leveled a hard look on his sister. "How badly is he hurt?"

"Oh, it's just a small wound in his thigh."

"How did you determine that when you likely left him in a bloody hurry? And in a bloody mess, I'm guessing."

"Our neighbor, Madeline Benson, sent me word."

Harrison stared at Tess for a long time. Brianna wanted to speak, just to break the tension in the room. At last, he said, "Max could have you thrown in jail, you know. He has every right to."

Tess nodded as she stared at her hands clasped in her lap.

"But the damned fool's probably still besotted with you. Has been for years." He paced the length of the room, then came to stand before Tess and Brianna. "You're no proper wife to him, and if he's not made his way into your bed, he's not much of a man, to my way of thinking.

"You have a week to gain courage to face your husband, Tess. And when we arrive at Cresthaven Abbey, I will speak with Max. You had better say your prayers, dear sister. Pray that he will take you back."

He strode out of the parlor, leaving Brianna to console Tess.

Brianna knew there was nothing she or Tess could say to

change Harrison's mind. She sympathized with her young sister-in-law, but understood Harrison was correct to send her back to her husband. From Tess's confessions regarding the intimate side of marriage, Brianna had to agree with Harrison. Max had been patient. Brianna had a strong hunch Tess truly loved her husband, and that he wasn't precisely her problem. She wasn't afraid of him, but was definitely fearful of making love.

She couldn't believe Tess's nerve. My goodness, she shot him! It was a brave thing to do, but terribly stupid.

Three days later
The Angus Inn, Aberdeen, Scotland

Brianna worried her lower lip and stared at the bed she would be sharing with Harrison that night. An inviting fluffy white comforter was spread across it, and the brass headboard had been polished until it gleamed. The walls were painted pale green and white shutters covered the windows. With evening's arrival, the room glimmered with a golden hue from the kerosene lamps positioned on two lace-covered tables on either side of the bed.

Very soon, she and Harrison would be handfasted and she would be spending the first night of an undetermined number of nights with him, until she conceived his heir. Heavens! She felt like a virgin for the first time in ten years.

As luck would have it, they hadn't delivered Tess home to England. Over the past three days, she'd taken ill with influenza and had been too sick to travel. Harrison had given her the week at Winterhaven anyway, but, he hadn't changed his mind about their handfasting. Brianna agreed, albeit reluctantly, to go through with the ceremony sooner than later.

A knock on the door startled her and her voice cracked when she called out, "Yes?"

"It's me," Harrison replied, his voice husky and low.

She made her way to the door and peeked out. "Don't you know it's bad luck for the bride and groom to see each other before the ceremony?"

"Doesn't that rule apply to traditional marriages only?" he inquired. "I have a need to discuss something of great importance with you before we handfast."

Stepping back, she allowed him entrance, wondering at his stiffness. Greedily, she perused his wide shoulders clad in a flawless black jacket, the double-breasted fastenings left open. A stark white shirt with a starched collar enhanced his swarthy good looks, and he'd tied a ruffled ascot at his neck. And there, nestled within the folds, was the gray pearl stickpin he'd worn the day she met him. She recognized the rich MacAulay plaid of the kilt he wore with unquestionable male aplomb.

There was nothing humorous about Harrison MacAulay in a kilt. She envisioned his long muscular thighs beneath the pleated fabric. Never had she imagined a skirt could make a man appear so utterly masculine. She wondered if he wore anything beneath it. Oh, Lord, she was tempted to ask, but she managed to hold her tongue.

She was happy she'd relented to his demands that she not wear one of her hideous widow's gowns, thankful he'd purchased the fashionable deep blue satin gown she'd donned. After all, it wouldn't do for the groom to be prettier than the bride, now would it? She met his eyes and noted his serious expression. "Is something amiss?"

Her heart lurched when he darted a quick look at her, then looked away. He raked a hand through his hair and cleared his throat. "No," he said. "Everything will be perfect in about half an hour. But there is some unfinished business which requires our immediate attention."

He took her hand, led her to the bed and pulled her down to sit beside him. It was then she noticed a creamy parchment in his hands. He passed the document to her. "Read this and let me know when you are ready to sign it, as we will require a witness."

He rose and went to the window. It overlooked a splendid view of Aberdeen and the sharp, jagged Grampian Mountains. They were some distance away, yet one could easily see the purple heather scattered across them. He glanced over his shoulder and found her staring at him, a confused look on her face.

"Read it," he snapped. "Please."

Brianna's hands shook as she read. By the time she finished, tears filled her eyes. Her voice quivered. "I cannot sign this."

He turned to her. "You must."

"You expect me to just give up my child? How can you ask this of me? You are heartless!"

"My child, as well," he replied.

She rushed to the hearth, crumpling the document. When she raised her hand to cast it into the fire, Harrison grasped her fist in one hand and wound the other around her waist.

"Don't do this," he warned. He pulled her against him and spoke softly into her ear. "You must sign or it may be years before you return to America. Remember your goal?"

Her hand tightened on the paper, but he easily wrested it from her grip. He smoothed the parchment flat on the small table beside the bed. Brianna held her curled fist against her mouth.

"I can't do it. I won't!"

"My heir must remain in Scotland with me."

Brianna was unable to believe he'd force her to give up her babe. She recalled when they'd first discussed handfasting, even though he'd warned her about it, she hadn't believed him.

"I've changed my mind," she replied. "You'll have to look elsewhere for your brood mare." She picked up her reticule and rushed toward the door, but stopped with his next words.

"I gather you've decided to stay in Scotland, rather than return to America. Think about this, Brianna. It will be ten years before Harry reaches twenty-one, and twelve for Jamie. If that's what you want, so be it."

She stilled when he reached around her to open the door. She had to think quickly. After a moment, she decided in the final analysis, he couldn't possibly hold her to this heartless agreement. Could he?

"Wait." She faced him, her back against the door. "All right."

"You will sign?" His eyes blazed fiercely into hers.

She nodded, knowing she had no choice.

He left the room and returned shortly with the innkeeper. Mr. Drummond wore a quizzical expression, and Harrison an expectant look as they waited for her. Before she could think to change her mind she raced to the table, reached for the fountain pen and scribbled her signature.

There! It was done. Closing her eyes, she held onto the sides of the table, her head hanging, all the while unable to believe she'd signed the document. She heard the door open and close, then felt big, strong hands engulf her shoulders.

"Thank you, Brianna," Harrison whispered, his warm breath feathering her ear. "You'll be the saving of the MacAulays. The clan will be forever grateful, and I am in your debt."

She pulled away from him, turned and stared out the window, tears coursing down her cheeks.

He murmured, "I'll see you downstairs shortly."

She maintained her position at the window until she heard the door close. Then she sobbed, sank to the bed and buried her head in the pillow.

Oh, my Lord. What have I done?

CHAPTER 9

*S*omehow, Brianna found the fortitude to go through with the handfasting without bolting. She thought about it, but each time she tried drawing her hand from Harrison's grip, he kept firm possession of it. Drat it! Could the man read minds?

She glanced down at the ring on the third finger of her left hand, stunned by the exquisite sapphire encircled with small diamonds. It had been Harrison's mother's betrothal ring. Now she waited, donned in a simple white nightgown, shaking like the proverbial sacrificial lamb, for her husband to bed her. Not only was he her handfasted husband, but her forthcoming lover, as well, the man with whom she'd decided to breed. She would succeed, she knew, and then she'd receive her reward—freedom to return to America.

She reached out and doused the lamp, plunging the room into near-darkness. Only a bit of light filtered into the room from the street lamps outside. She frowned as she studied the room, thinking it appeared too intimate without the light. She reached out to light it, but decided against it. It would be easier facing him in the darkness.

She threw herself back on the bed, thoroughly enjoying the pleasant, dizzy sensation drifting through her body, and the fuzzy feeling in her head. She would have consumed more of the fine champagne during their wedding supper if Harrison hadn't stopped her, saying he had no intentions of bedding a besotted bride. His desire was for her to remember every moment of their joining the morning after.

Restlessly she rose and went to the window. It was midnight now. She pressed her nose against the glass, gasping in delight when she saw flakes of snow falling from the sky.

"Beautiful, isn't it?" Harrison asked.

She started, for she hadn't heard him enter. He held two long-stemmed glasses in one hand and a tall brown bottle in the other. Apparently, his plans had changed, if they were going to consume spirits. He placed them on the bedside table, before lighting the lamp.

His eyes swept greedily over her. "The snow doesn't hold a candle to your beauty."

Brianna had no idea how to reply to the rather clichéd compliment. She smiled, silently thanking him for trying to ease her nervousness. But when he focused his gaze on her, she shivered.

Harrison looked upon his handfasted wife. Mine! No one would take her from him. She wasn't classically beautiful, but pretty in her own unique way. Her dark hair, a mere shade lighter than his own, shimmered as it cascaded in waves around her shoulders. Her eyes, reminded him of the sapphire ring he'd placed on her finger earlier that evening. They were her best feature.

He saw her arms crossed over her breasts, already concealed behind a nightgown and whispered, "Don't be embarrassed."

Slowly she lowered her hands and clasped them tightly at her waist.

He shed his jacket and waistcoat as he approached her, dropping them carelessly to the floor. His eyes remained on hers the entire time he undressed. By the time he reached her, he wore only his kilt. He grinned when Brianna's gaze traversed his body from head to toe. *Let her look. Let her get to know me.* "Do you like what ye see?"

She tilted her head and nodded.

He laughed at her stunned expression, and her uncharacteristic silence. His smile slipped when she boldly reached out and traced an index fingernail over the veins in his chest, dipping lower until she reached his waistline. Finally, she raised her eyes to his.

"Aren't you going to finish undressing? You are...beautiful."

Stepping close he slipped a hand behind her head. "The feeling is mutual, my darling bride. And to answer your first question, I'll undress shortly, but first, my only desire is to pleasure you."

He lowered his head and before he touched her lips, she whispered woefully, "I'm not a true bride."

"You are," he insisted. "Never doubt it."

He feathered his lips across hers until he felt her go limp in his arms. Then he maneuvered her toward the bed. While he plundered her mouth, he removed her hairpins and dropped them carelessly to the floor.

She broke away and pushed against his chest, panting.

He smiled. "Do I take your breath away?"

"You know you do!"

His grin faded. "It is going to be very good between us. I plan on leaving you breathless this night, and every night to come."

"You may certainly try," she whispered, her lips curving into a coy smile.

He stilled when she pressed her body fully against him and raised her arms around his neck. Groaning aloud, he wound a fist around a mass of black curls, anchoring her against his shoulder as he lowered her to the bed. He followed her, continuing his sweet assault on her mouth and rolled her beneath him.

She pressed her hands against his shoulders. "Finish undressing."

Saying a silent prayer of thanks for this wonderful woman, he rose, though he was reluctant to leave her even for a moment. As he crossed the room, he snatched up his shirt and jacket from the floor. When he reached the armoire, he hung them up. Deliberately, he faced her and removed his kilt. He grinned when Brianna sat up, focused on his groin and her mouth gaped. He knew she was astonished that he hadn't worn any drawers, but no upright-standing Scotsman would think of wearing them beneath his kilt.

He strutted toward her. When he reached the bed, he leaned across it. She fell back, giggling. Feeling like giggling himself, Harrison grinned instead like the king's fool. He crawled onto the bed and nibbled her neck. After straddling her hips, he took both of her wrists in one hand and raised them above her head.

She writhed beneath him, laughing.

Between nibbles, he asked, "What in the world is so funny?"

"You!" She laughed even more and managed to pull her hands from his gentle grip.

"How so, my lady wife?"

Brianna reached up and stroked one black lock of hair off his forehead. "The way you walked over here, your 'jewels' were bobbing out in front of you. You reminded me of a prancing, fancy peacock!"

"It's part of the mating ritual," he murmured, pressing his lips against the top of one breast. "The male species tends to show himself off to his best advantage when trying to impress a lady."

"Yes, well, I believe your front side is quite remarkable," she said. Her eyes were focused on the area. She reached for his spectacles, but he grasped her wrist.

"I want to see you. It seems I've waited a lifetime to make love to you, and I intend to see your every expression." He lowered his head and gently bit the side of her neck. "You taste good enough to eat," he growled. He bit harder, eliciting a surprised gasp from her.

"You don't mean that literally, do you?"

He just smiled as he sat back on his haunches. He trailed his hands down her body, lightly fingering her breasts through the soft fabric, gauging her reaction. She trembled as he slid his hands down to her hips and dragged up her nightdress. Then he scooped her up with a hand beneath her back, pulled it over her head and tossed it carelessly to the floor. He laid her down gently then leaned to the side, snatching up the champagne bottle and a glass from the floor. He had wicked plans in mind for the wine. Drinking it was well down on the list.

"What are you doing?" She reached for the hand-pieced quilt he'd pulled to the foot of the bed, but he held her down.

"I'm parched." He smiled when he heard her faint sigh of disappointment. Yes, she wanted him, wanted what he could give her. He poured a full glass of liquor and drank, then offered her a taste.

Brianna placed her lips where his had been. Sipping carefully, she met his gaze over the edge of the glass. He tilted it up too far and the golden liquid spilled down her chin, dribbled past her neck, settling between the sweet valleys of her breasts. She gasped and started to sit up. He stayed her with his hand, then flicked one peach-tinted nipple with his tongue.

She arched her hips off the bed. "Oh, my!"

Harrison lapped up the champagne, his tongue trailing around the outer perimeter of one magnificent breast. Soon the circles he made grew smaller and smaller, until his lips and tongue rimmed the nipple. He bit down gently and rolled the turgid flesh between his teeth.

"Oh, God!" She lurched up.

"Be still, sweetheart," he ordered. He yanked off his spectacles and tossed them onto the bedside table. This close he could see her very well. "It's been a long time, hasn't it? Since you have made love." He placed the bottle on the table.

"Two years."

Harrison groaned inside at the thought of Brianna not having been with a man for so long. His manhood hardened and throbbed with a dull ache. He viewed her glowing skin, then lowered his head and continued torturing her aroused, moisture-slicked body. Soon she was gasping and panting, her body arching as she dug her heels into the mattress. Harrison raised his head and met her eyes once more, a grin upon his lips.

A small frown marred her brow. "Are you laughing at me?"

"Yes, I suppose I am. I don't believe I've ever seen you at a loss for words."

Before she could even think of a retort, Harrison slid off the end of the bed and knelt on the floor. He took her thighs in his hands, lifted and settled her long legs over his shoulders.

"Harrison, no-o-o!" she wailed, struggling in his grip.

His hands moved up and clasped her buttocks. Easily he tamed her struggles. Positioning her close to his parted lips, he rapidly flicked his tongue over her pink nub until her low moans increased in volume.

He placed a finger against her lips. "Hush, sweet. We don't want to wake the entire inn," he warned.

She dug her fingers into the mattress and clenched the muslin sheet. "Why are you doing this? I won't let you. I won't!"

Harrison held onto her squirming body and looked at her sternly. "Ah, but you will, Brianna. Do ye remember what you did to me the first night we arrived at Winterhaven?" he casually inquired.

She scowled. "I did nothing!"

He watched her in silence and grinned wickedly when her eyes widened in alarm. She remembered all right, and he planned on her remembering this night the rest of her life.

"You cannot mean to...oh, my God!"

"Ah, I see I've refreshed your memory. Have you any idea how you tormented me that evening? Any idea how difficult it was for me to keep my hands away from all the tempting places on your sweet body, knowing I didn't have the right to touch you?"

She shook her head and clenched her eyes shut.

"I've the right now, wife," he said. "And the only advice I have for you is to relax and enjoy it."

He focused on her sweet core, mercilessly taking her from the brink of one delicious plateau to the next, stopping and denying her release, time and time again. After a long while, he raised his head and was satisfied to see her face contorted in aroused frustration. She was beautiful and she was his to do with as he wished.

Her litany of words broke the silence. "Oh, please, oh, please. I want you to..."

"Go on," he encouraged, gently parting her, pressing down on her with his thumb. "Say it, Brianna." She didn't, so he released the pressure of his thumb, but his lips took her once more.

She thrashed her head from side to side and her breathing quickened. When she was on the verge of reaching fulfillment, he lifted his head. "Say it and you will receive what you desire."

Her eyes shot open and she stared at him. After a long, tense moment of silence, she whispered fiercely, "Damn you, I won't."

"Ah, sweet curses," he said, laughing. "I've missed your colorful swearing of late."

"You hate it!" Then she muffled her shriek behind her hand when his fingers took over where his lips had been and they moved in a quick rhythm once more.

He paused and smiled when she gave another shriek.

"My God," Harrison said, "Don't tell me you have actually been obeying me for a change?"

She didn't reply.

It was growing damned difficult to control his body's response to her. Finally, knowing she'd won by denying him the words he wanted to hear, Harrison said, "Since I cannot wait any longer, you win."

He aroused her again to unbearable heights of pleasure with his lips and tongue. He moved her to small gasps, then long, drawn out cries as her body reached a shuddering climax. Brianna was languid, barely lucid when he slid onto the bed and positioned himself between her thighs. She cried out in delight when he slid deep inside her. He drew her into his arms and held her close, then rolled her to one side, his lips bruising hers.

With agonizing slow strokes, he moved in and out of her body, watching her the entire time. Until he slipped one hand between them and stroked her until she convulsed around him. When he reached his own climax, she anchored him against her, holding him until his shuddering eased. Eventually, he rolled off her, but kept her in his arms. A tear dropped onto his naked chest, startling him. He tipped up her chin and met her eyes. "Did I hurt you, sweetheart?"

"Oh, no," she said wistfully.

"Then why are you crying?"

"It...it was just so wonderful."

He smiled and kissed her gently. "Yes, it was." He lowered his head to take another kiss but paused with her next words.

"It is rather sad, and bothersome that we aren't in love, nor are we legally wed. But, this is, after all, a business arrangement and sentiment shouldn't play any part in it."

He hugged her close. "We'll marry in the morning."

She sat up and glared at him, clutching the sheets to her breast. "But we don't love each other!"

"I'm willing to marry you, Brianna, if it will make you feel less..."

"Less what?"

"Doesn't matter." He sat up and poured another glass of champagne. Gulping it down, he coughed violently with her next whispered words.

"Less like your whore, you mean?"

"That's not at all what I think!" He scowled at her. "Though it is, I believe, what you feel about yourself."

"Hogwash!" she exclaimed.

"Then why are you upset?"

"Is it the truth you want?"

He nodded and she continued, "Moments ago, as we

made love, I felt helpless, and out of control. I hated the power you had over me." She kneaded the blanket against her breasts. "It was as if this love-making between us was some sort of spectacular sport and you were the spectator while I provided the entertainment. I felt you watching me until you decided not to hold yourself in check any longer." She flopped back down on the bed and draped an arm over her eyes. "I am so tired..."

He smiled at her and said, "Ah, but what sweet torment." He rose and moved to the window, uncaring of his state of undress.

"Perhaps, in time, I'll tell you about..." Harrison started, as he turned to her then stopped. He was amazed to see she had fallen sleep. This was a good thing because she was too perceptive. It bothered him that she'd learned him so well in such a short time. But, he was the Patriarch of Clan MacAulay, and it was important he remain in control of himself at all times. Which was the precise reason he'd been furious with himself that first night at Winterhaven.

Of course, he'd offered to rub the liniment into her sore muscles. He had, in fact, been eager to, since he'd waited years to touch her. It wasn't her fault that just the sight of her near naked beauty had caused him to find his fulfillment.

He'd possessed mistresses over the years, and had never felt cheated when he'd denied them pleasuring him with their hands and lips. Pumping away and controlling his climax was imperative to him. If Brianna wasn't happy about it, well, it wasn't important. She'd agreed to their arrangement. Her job was to birth him an heir. He sighed and decided an apology of sorts was in order. That should appease her, for he hated seeing her unhappy.

Long ago memories of his initiation into lovemaking at the hands of his father's mistress entered his mind. He'd been just fourteen. Even after all these years he still felt humiliated when he recalled how he'd so easily climaxed with the first laving of the woman's lips on his cock. She had come to him often after that, continuing to take him for months in that fashion.

He'd enjoyed the attention at first—had been helpless to stop her. With time, he learned to hate the power she held over him. With each subsequent encounter he'd felt less and less fulfilled. As he grew older, he had managed to slow his mounting pleasure. But to his immense humiliation, he couldn't hold back indefinitely. The woman had been a professional, and he was falling in love with her.

One day he finally blurted out he wanted to make love in the normal fashion. She'd laughed and told him they hadn't made love. They'd had sex. When he grew into manhood, she added, when he learned to control himself completely, she would be happy to oblige him. He'd never had relations with the woman again after that. With subsequent amorous liaisons, he never allowed any woman to have such control over him, and vowed to never wear his heart on his sleeve.

He'd make no exceptions. Even for Brianna.

CHAPTER 10

February 1889
Winterhaven Manor

For the first time in her life, Brianna led a life of leisure. As she settled into her new home, she made fast friends with Harrison's family, especially Tess and his grandmothers. She adored them, and the feeling seemed to be mutual. Harrison left for his clinic every morning before she even contemplated opening her eyes. But without fail, she rose early enough to enjoy breakfast with Harry and Jamie. Then they'd retire to the north wing, to the schoolroom where the schoolmaster, Mr. Jeremy Thornton presided. He was a gentle, quiet man whom her sons greatly admired, especially Harry. Brianna spent her mornings reading or visiting with the grandmothers. She tried at one point to help in the kitchen, but the staff scolded her and turned her away.

Many a woman would envy her leisurely existence, but Brianna was thoroughly, utterly, bored.

The time with Harrison, however, had been far from boring. She'd spent six hedonistic weeks with him, and looked forward to spending many more. Even though her initial reaction to his lovemaking had made her feel cheap, she decided she'd judged him wrong. She analyzed the man, and realized he likely felt he had to be in control at all times, likely thought it not masculine if he weren't. After all, he was the head of his clan and needed to be strong.

The idea of staying in Scotland permanently was growing more appealing by the day. Harrison's pervasive sexual expertise left her deeply satisfied and eager for more. But sex was one thing, and love quite another.

Now she sat in the quaint room off the kitchen, an appropriate space for an informal meal such as breakfast. The sunny yellow painted walls, and the matching chair cushions, curtains and tablecloth were soothing and appealing.

Harrison entered. He leaned down and pecked her cheek, then sat down in his chair across from her. Last evening he'd informed her he wouldn't be going to his office this morning, but had a few scheduled appointments at home in the library.

Maeve bustled in from the kitchen with a pot of coffee in hand, performing double duty since the kitchen maid was sick. She placed the coffee on the table. "Eat up now, m'lady. There'll be no dawdlin' with yer food this morning. I'll be watching ye," she warned.

"Breakfast has never been my favorite meal of the day." She smiled at the usually rosy-cheeked woman who looked a bit off color. "I noticed you have a bit of a sniffle, Maeve. Why don't you rest?"

"Laird MacAulay isn't paying me to rest," Maeve stoutly replied.

Harrison glanced up from his paper. "Maeve. If you are sick and need to rest, do so. That's an order. And I'll still be paying your wages."

"I'm doing fine," she muttered.

He pierced her with a long look, but she wouldn't meet his eyes. "Are you unwell?"

She bit her lower lip and nodded.

"Seek your bed, then," he ordered then returned to his newspaper.

Maeve sent a grateful look at Brianna. She removed her apron and left the room on wobbly legs.

Brianna covertly watched Harrison over her cup of coffee while he read the paper. She was trying to decide upon the best way to pose her request without gaining a negative response from him. Idly, she dawdled with a triangular piece of toast smothered in strawberry jam, then gave a deep sigh.

He looked up. "Did you say something, sweet?"

"I'm bored."

He looked at her blankly. "Um-hum," he murmured. He turned sideways in his chair and folded the paper along its crease, then resumed reading.

Brianna gawked at him. That's it? She couldn't resist snatching the paper from his hands and tossing it over her shoulder.

He raised his brow and said drolly, "I gather you wanted my undivided attention."

She gave him a curt nod. "I said I'm bored."

He smiled. "I see. What can I do to alleviate this problem?"

"The use of a carriage this afternoon would be helpful."

"For what purpose?"

Between gritted teeth, she said, "I'd like to go into the city to do some shopping." She crossed her fingers behind her back.

"Ye deplore shopping."

"I've changed my mind."

He stared at her and her cheeks heated. She couldn't very well tell him she was going to town to look for work, since he'd told her his feelings on the matter.

"Fine. John or Stanton will drive you."

"I prefer driving myself, thank you."

"Someone will drive you and wait until you're finished shopping."

She shoved back her chair, scrambled to her feet and jammed her hands on her hips. "You still don't trust me, do you? Where in the bloody world would I possibly go? You know I wouldn't leave my children behind. Besides, we made a bargain."

He rose as well. "Since you have brought up the interesting topic, I've been meaning to speak to you about that. Maeve is quite receptive with regards to your eating habits, isn't she?"

She swallowed the lump in her throat, guessing the direction of his question. Lord, she wasn't ready to tell him yet! It was too early to be certain.

"When were you going to tell me?" he asked gently, his sherry-colored eyes flickering over her body.

She sniffed. "What are you talking about?"

Moving around the table, he reached her side, studied her face a moment longer, then stared pointedly at her breasts.

"Your monthly course hasn't arrived yet, has it?"

"Is there no secret I can keep from you?" she spat, utterly mortified. "Have you no regard for my privacy?"

He gently cupped her chin in one palm and brushed her

lips. "There will never be secrets between us. Besides, it's quite easy to know a woman's cycle when one is sharing the same bed."

"I'm just a bit late," she said shakily. "We can't be certain yet."

"Your complexion glows with the health of a newly pregnant woman," he said, releasing her chin. He cupped one breast.

She gasped but didn't move away.

He grazed the nipple with his thumb. "Your breasts are fuller, as well. Have you been ill in the morning?"

Tears filled her eyes at his concerned tone. She nodded and pulled his hand away. As she was prone to doing during the early stages of pregnancy, she burst into tears. Without thinking, she collapsed against his broad, comforting chest.

"Why are you crying?" he asked, tucking her head beneath his chin.

She sighed. "If I knew, I wouldn't be." She pulled out of his arms. "I'll get over it shortly. I have before. It's just that when I'm pregnant every little thing makes me cry."

He stepped back and held her hands. As he looked her over, he grinned. "I can't believe how easily this all worked out for us. Is it possible so much happiness could be ours?"

She frowned. "I'm warning you now, Harrison MacAulay. This is the last child I'll be having."

"One will be enough," he murmured, thinking otherwise, but he kept his thoughts to himself.

Later that day, Brianna peered down the stairway and found the foyer vacant. She rushed down and took her fur coat from the armoire in the corner. Harrison had insisted she rest a bit before going to town, but she hadn't meant to fall asleep. She'd slept four hours and awakened with a pounding headache, which would not deter her from driving into town to apply for work. She pulled on her hat with little care for her coiffure.

Just then, Harrison opened the library door and stepped out.

Brianna looked up. Framed behind him were several tiers of books on shelves, a polished oak floor and heavy burgundy colored velvet draperies hanging from a window. The scent of leather and varnish was pleasant and Brianna felt drawn to the room. She took a step toward the doorway, toward Harrison, before she caught herself.

"Where are you off to at this late hour?" he inquired.

"Edinburgh."

He closed the door behind him.

Brianna warily watched his approach. He pulled out his pocket watch and noted the time. "It's gone half past three. The shops will be closing in two hours."

Which was precisely the reason she intended to leave as soon as possible. She would receive the complete attention of the shopkeepers when she applied for work at the end of the workday, without suffering interruptions from customers.

"I'm going to town, Harrison, and you shall not stop me."

"I've already explained that the shops will be closing soon. Damn it, Brianna, see reason for once," he said tightly.

"Darling? What's taking so long?"

Brianna heard the sweet feminine voice and peered around him. A petite woman with full lips, and perfect coiffure of auburn-colored hair, stood in the library doorway. Brianna studied the woman from head to toe.

"It appears I'm detaining you from...business," Brianna said coolly.

"We are through, but you and I have much to settle."

"Aren't you going to introduce me to your wife?" the woman asked as she drew nearer.

Brianna noted Harrison's impatient expression. Then she looked at the woman and said, "Well, we aren't married. Yet."

The woman's eyes narrowed before a gleam of what Brianna could only consider as satisfaction appeared in them.

"This is Constance MacPhearson, Brianna. I'm sure you recall meeting her brother aboard ship."

Yes, the popinjay who wouldn't leave her alone. She tried to recall MacPhearson's words the day he and Harrison had nearly fought. He'd said something about how Connie would be stunned once she learned of their marriage.

Connie sashayed around Harrison, a sickly sweet smile on her lips. She stopped directly in front of Brianna. "Crawford had said you'd married. Apparently, he was mistaken."

"Connie," Harrison warned.

Brianna's frown deepened, her curiosity warring with jealousy. Harrison knew this woman. Well. Connie turned to Harrison and hooked her arm through his. She rose onto the tips of her toes and whispered into his ear.

Brianna heard only whispering, couldn't make out Connie's words, but a red haze filled her vision. When Harrison smiled at the MacPhearson witch, Brianna's fingernails dug into her palms as she made fists. She was unable to move, or to speak for the rage that filled her. She'd only entered into the handfast arrangement in order to regain her freedom, and custody of her sons. How could she ever have thought she might fall in love with a perfidious man like Harrison?

Harrison escorted Connie to the door, returned to Brianna and took her arm.

She pulled her arm from his grasp. "John is ready and waiting for me." Before she could take another step, he clamped his hand around her wrist and dragged her toward the library.

"Damn you! I said no!" Brianna dug in her heels and shrieked when he hauled her into his arms, all to no avail. He strode into the library and slammed the door behind him. Brianna managed to dig an elbow into his ribs when he set her down on his desk.

He towered over her and said in a dangerous, soft voice, "You may be breeding, but don't think that will prevent me from chastising you."

Brianna gasped when he moved closer. She fell back on her elbows in order to place some distance between them, but it unfortunately gave him the advantage.

He planted his hands on the desk on either side of her. "Now then," he said softly, "Shall we continue our discussion from where we left off?"

She sent him a fiery look. "I have nothing further to say to you."

"I do. You will not be going into Edinburgh today. I will not remind you again, this isn't open for further discussion."

"Then why in the world did you carry me in here?"

"I've important things on my mind."

"Such as..."

"Our impending marriage."

"I'm not marrying you."

"Things have changed," he said, moving away from her.

She shot off the desk and sank into the deep leather chair behind it.

Harrison leaned across the desk. "Be reasonable, Brianna. We must marry now that you are carrying my child."

"Which was precisely what we intended," she retorted.

"I believe I forgot to mention a significant matter with regards to our handfasting."

She narrowed her eyes. "And what might that be?"

"If a handfasted wife were to become pregnant within the year, the couple would, by law, be required to marry." Harrison cringed at the lie but desperate measures called for it.

"What!" Brianna shot to her feet.

"On my way to the clinic tomorrow morning I'll stop by St. Andrew's Church and have the banns posted."

"You're not Catholic!"

"No, but you are. Once a priest has given you the Lord's blessing you will truly feel married."

"It's quite generous of you to be so considerate of me, but then, you can afford to be magnanimous, can't you? You lied to me!"

"By omission only," he said softly. He headed for the door but paused and looked at her over his shoulder when she spoke.

"You knew from the very beginning, didn't you? Knew I wouldn't consent to this handfast if I knew the ramifications of it in its entirety."

"I believe your knowledge of these laws wouldn't have changed a thing. You still would have had to live here until your boys reached their majority. As I said earlier, that was my duty."

Brianna's eyes filled with tears. "But you see there's no point in my securing a solicitor any longer since I'll be obliged to remain here, forever, once we marry."

"I won't apologize for that, Brianna. I've wanted you from the moment...for a long time. Now that you are mine, I can't give you up. However, I can give you a measure of the independence you crave. As much as society will allow, that is."

"But you don't love me!" she protested.

"I never said that," he replied.

"But you never said you did."

The tension in the room was palpable as Harrison treaded softly across the floor until he stood before her. He stared down at her, a small smile on his lips. "Possibly, I do."

Her eyes widened. "What sort of answer is that? You either love me or you don't."

"It means it's more than likely that I do love you. But love isn't the only important thing between us, Brianna. Know this. I desire you more than I've ever desired any woman. I think of you each and every moment of a day." He moved to the window and stared down at his coachman, who, at the moment, was unhitching a horse from a carriage on the cobblestone drive. He glanced at her over his shoulder. "Perhaps that is what love is, this unflagging longing to enter your sweet body at any given moment."

She scoffed, "You're speaking of lust, not love."

He smiled. "Do you know how you keep me awake at night? Do you have any idea how long it's been since I've been able to sleep the night through without waking and thinking you'd left my bed?"

She shook her head at his admission and backed away, hedged toward the door. When she drew close enough she opened the door and fled.

Harrison didn't follow her. Within moments, she was back and standing in the doorway, her fists tightly clenched at her sides.

"Don't blame John. He was just following my orders." He inclined his head. "As you will."

"I detest you!" She ran from the library.

Harrison heaved a sigh just as Stanton stuck his head in the door. "I've told John to unhitch the horse and carriage, Laird."

"Thank you." Harrison lifted an eyebrow at his

coachman who lingered in the doorway. "Is there something else?"

The man was obviously uncomfortable about speaking. Harrison waited patiently until the older man finally said, "It 'pears this handfast doesn't agree with ye."

Harrison grunted, but said not a word, leaving his employee the opportunity to continue.

"Might I offer ye a bit of advice?"

"I'm listening," Harrison replied.

"Whatever yer differences, don't go to bed angry with each other, even if it means gettin' into a bloody brawl beforehand. It helps clear the air, ye know."

Harrison's relationship with Stanton had been a long, solid one, a loving one. The older man had been with the clan since before Harrison's birth. He loved Stanton, nearly as much as he'd loved his father.

"Explain something," Harrison said. "I've tried reasoning with her but she won't listen. I've apologized, but she refuses to accept. What else can I do to make her see the sense of things?"

"I'll not be askin' ye what ye squabbled about, but if ye have tried all that you say, it seems to me she might need a bit of coercing, ye understand?"

"Coercing?"

"Um-hum. The same kind the old Laird used with ye and Payton might work."

Harrison frowned. "I couldn't possibly strike Brianna."

"I'm not speakin' of beatin' her senseless. Just a few no-nonsense smacks on her rump with that fine paddle of your granddaddy's should make her see the right of things."

"I don't think so. It will likely make things worse between us."

The older man shrugged. "Then just threaten ye'll toss up her skirts. Maybe just a warnin' will do the trick."

"Perhaps," Harrison said thoughtfully, as Stanton left. Of course, he couldn't tell his coachman that he'd already threatened her aplenty, to no avail. He turned to the window once more and swore when he saw Brianna tugging on Challenger's reins as she led him from the stables. "My God! That blasted woman!" He charged across the room and out the door, all the while thinking she'd kill herself if she managed to get on Challenger's back. He ran down the hallway to the front door, wondering all the while how she'd managed to get him bridled since he rarely allowed anyone near him.

He saw Stanton heading for the kitchen and he shouted, "She's got Challenger!"

"What?" The older man's eyes widened as he rushed to the front door on Harrison's heels. "How in the world did she—"

"I have no idea! I've reconsidered your advice. Head her off if you can and I'll be along shortly." He swiveled on his heel and headed for the kitchen.

Stanton nodded. "Aye, now she'll soon be seein' the sense of things." Purposefully, Stanton headed out the front door as fast as his short bowed legs would carry him.

CHAPTER 11

*H*arrison's brow was sweat-slicked as he snatched the oval wood paddle down from the hook beside the stove. He tucked it inside his jacket's pocket. As he moved swiftly into the hallway, he met Grandmother Jean walking down the stairs, a troubled expression on her barely wrinkled face.

He stopped and assisted her down the last few steps, feeling a brittle smile play upon his lips. "Good afternoon, Grandmother. I'm sorry, but I cannot visit with you. I have a bit of an emergency to tend to."

She scolded, "I know what you are planning, Harrison James."

He sighed when he saw her eyes riveted on the handle protruding from his pocket. Then he prayed Stanton had stopped Brianna. "All right. Let's hear it then, but quickly."

"Brianna may likely hate you now, but believe me when I say time will heal her anger. Or, she may prove to be an exceptionally rational woman and decide you had the right to correct her behavior, and she'll forgive you."

"Believe me, Grandmother, I've reached my wit's end

and can't see any other way to handle her. She is, at this very moment, ready to ride Challenger into Edinburgh to go shopping, of all things! Hopefully Stanton has detained her."

"You know, the woman's used to keeping busy. She needs something to do to occupy her hands and her mind. I'll tell you now she wasn't going to the city to shop, but to find work."

Harrison gave his grandmother a disdainful look. "MacAulay ladies do not work. I've told her as much on several occasions."

Grandmother Jean shrugged. "Nevertheless, that's what she intends to do. I believe it would be to your advantage to find something to keep her occupied. And it had better be something worthwhile, or she'll know what you are about."

"I'll think of something," he growled.

"You know, we could always use another volunteer for our Women's Temperance Alliance, grandson."

He scowled at her over his shoulder. "Not a chance in hell."

Outside, Stanton was pleading with Brianna. Harrison was almost there when Brianna managed to escape Stanton's hold. She clumsily climbed on Challenger's back.

"Stop, Brianna!"

His shouting, unfortunately, startled Challenger. The stallion raced away and down the cobblestone drive, Brianna clinging fiercely to his back.

Stanton called, "John! Another horse. Quickly!"

Shortly the stableboytore outside with a big black horse. He shoved the reins at Harrison. Harrison flung himself onto Lucifer's back and Stanton handed him a quirt.

As he thundered down the road, Harrison prayed she'd hold on until he could reach her. He cursed himself for not anticipating her impetuous behavior. She'd been irrationally angry with him. In his mind's eye, he saw her falling from Challenger. Heard her screams as she landed on the hard-packed dirt road, followed by an awful silence. Imagined what his life would be like without her, and how his life would change without an heir. Up ahead he caught glimpses of brown and knew it was Brianna's coat. Within moments, he managed to catch up with her.

Brianna's face was pale with fright. Reaching over, Harrison grabbed at the dangling reins and missed. He cursed aloud as he fought to control the direction of his horse. He reached again. This time he managed to grasp the reins. He yanked them back with all his might. Challenger slowed. Eventually, he came to a halt. Harrison held the reins, breathing heavily as he stared at Brianna. She leaned forward against Challenger's neck, clinging to his mane as she gulped air.

"You could have broken your bloody neck!"

She'd buried her face in Challenger's lush mane. Her shoulders were shaking. Harrison heard her sob. He wanted to take her in his arms and comfort her. Then he saw one of her feet hanging free of the stirrup. He cursed again. How had she stayed on the horse?

Thank God, she was astride the animal. What would have happened if she'd been sitting a sidesaddle?

He shouted. "Damn, but your God was guarding you, woman! What in bloody hell we're you thinking, taking Challenger? You could have been killed if you'd fallen! And what about our bairn? You apparently have no feelings whatsoever for him or her, but I most certainly do!"

"You don't care a whit for me," she screamed. "'Tis only the bairn!"

Harrison scowled, but forced his voice to stay level. "Of course I care about our child, but I care for you equally as much. Now explain why you did such a foolhardy thing."

"Because I'm bored to death sitting day after day in your home with nothing to do! I need to be productive. I need to find something to do with my time, and you cannot stop me from securing a position in town. And don't you dare tell me again MacAulay ladies do not work! This MacAulay woman will! Do you understand?"

"Perfectly."

She raised her chin. "So, are you telling me you won't interfere in my finding work?"

"Hell, no!" he growled. He threw the quirt to the ground and dismounted. Staring up at her, hands on his hips, he said, "I'll warn every shopkeeper in Edinburgh not to hire you." His gaze flickered from her head to her toes. "Now, are you all right?"

"Yes, I believe so."

"Excellent."

Brianna watched his hand, following its movement until he reached into his pocket. She frowned. "What in the world is that?"

He pulled out the hefty piece of wood and held it up. "An old instrument of punishment. My father's preferred choice on his children's rears. Perhaps after a few well-placed taps from it, you'll think twice about leaping without looking first."

"Punishment for what? Fleeing your dominance?" she demanded.

He answered her question the only way he could. "I'm laird of the MacAulay clan. You will obey me," he said softly.

He truly had no choice but to discipline her. He wound his hands around her waist and hauled her down from Challenger's back. As soon as her feet touched the ground, she made a mad dash straight for the forest.

"Brianna, stop!"

She didn't, of course. Why in the world had he expected her to obey him this time?

He took a dozen running steps then stopped abruptly. He knew the woods. She didn't. If he were to hazard a guess, she'd likely come full circle and end up back on the road again. He ran to Challenger, vaulted onto his back and headed south. Off the road so that she wouldn't see him, he held Challenger still. Within moments, Brianna suddenly appeared no more than ten yards away. Challenger snorted a greeting. "Damn!" Harrison said.

Brianna whipped around and gasped when she saw him. Then she snatched up her skirts and ran down the road, away from him.

Harrison nudged Challenger into a trot until he caught up with her. Then he leaned down and caught her around the waist. She screamed into his ear, nearly deafening him as he lifted her up in front of him. It took all of his strength to manage Challenger and Brianna as she smashed him in the head and around the shoulders. He guided Challenger with knees, finally managing to control his headstrong wife by pulling her up and tossing her face down across his saddle.

"I hate you, you beast!" she cried.

He smacked her rump twice with his leather-covered palm before dismounting. Then he dragged her down from his horse, holding her hard against him. "No, you don't hate me." He retained his grip on her wrists, his voice grim as he took in her furious face and tear-filled eyes. "You just hate anyone having any sort of control over your behavior. You really must learn to control yourself, sweet." He lifted her into his arms and strode into the forest until he found a fallen tree trunk. There he took a seat and bent her over his knees.

"What about your behavior?" she shrieked. "You are far

from what I'd consider a paragon of gentlemanly manners!" She twisted and reached up, ready to claw his face.

He merely shrugged away her words as he fought off her hands. With her balanced over his knees, he hiked up first her coat, then her skirt and petticoats. The fabric ballooned over her head. The sight of her white silky drawers made him think of other things he'd rather do than beat her. He trapped her wrists in one hand and delved into his coat pocket for the paddle. He brought it forth at the same time she twisted and looked at him over her shoulder.

"Remember that I'm carrying your heir," she said anxiously.

He couldn't stop what he'd started. He'd lose all credibility in her eyes as head of his household if he did. "Don't worry," he said. "I plan on staying away from that sacred area." Gently, he rubbed her derriere. "It's this side that will hold my attention for the next several minutes."

"I'll never forgive you for this!" she raged.

"Over time you will." He growled, "My God, I thought I'd lost ye when ye stormed away on Challenger. Your independent streak has earned you a thrashing you won't soon forget."

Brianna gasped when the paddle landed squarely on her buttocks. A second sharp smack made her shriek. He raised his hand, ready to land a third when he swore and loosened his grip on her. Then he threw the paddle and watched it disappear into the woods. He pulled her up so she stood in front of him and cupped her chin. "You will obey me from now on. You will follow my orders explicitly. Do you understand?"

He caught the flash of anger in her eyes when she exclaimed, "If I feel what you ask of me is reasonable. I curse you and your damned clan. I'm an American. You cannot treat me this way."

"You are a MacAulay. Never doubt it. And while you are living under my roof, I'll treat you as I see fit."

She yanked his hand from her chin. "And I'm telling you I'll behave if I feel what you ask is fair." Then she planted a hand firmly in the center of his broad chest and shoved.

"Ahh!" he bellowed as he fell backwards and landed on his back, legs curled over the trunk.

She stood over him, her hands fisted on her hips. "Don't think a simple little kiss and apology will prompt me to forgive you, Harrison MacAulay. As soon as we arrive home, I want a room of my own. From this day forward, you may enjoy your own company."

Brianna glanced up when Harrison opened the door to the master bedchamber and strode inside. His lips thinned as he stood with his hands on his hips.

"What do you think you're doing, Brianna?"

She snatched up several dresses and headed for the door. Pausing beside him, she gave him a cool, long look. "Moving." Just as she reached the door, he grasped her elbow and swung her around.

He started pulling dresses from her arms but she held on tight. Between gritted teeth, she said, "I refuse to get into a tug-of-war, so let go!"

He released the fabric and she stumbled back. Reaching out, he caught her up before she could fall. "You're not leaving," he warned.

"Of course I'm not." She swung around and moved into the hallway.

She heard his heavy footsteps clomping along behind her. "By, God, Brianna. Where are you off to, then?"

"Grandmother Jean has generously offered to share her rooms with me."

She entered the room at the end of the hallway. As she turned to close it, Harrison boldly moved inside, giving her no choice but to back up. With a shrug, she made her way to the armoire.

"Didn't I say you couldn't have your own room?"

"You did, and I won't."

As she hung her clothing, her skin prickled at his closeness. "Won't what?" he asked.

She smiled fetchingly at him. "I won't have my own room. I'll be sharing with your grandmother?"

His face turned a mottled red. She glanced down and saw his hands fisted at his sides. She braced herself, ready to deal with his fury, when he said, in an amazingly calm voice, "And I say you will not."

"She most certainly will."

Harrison's grandmother, Jean, came out of the bathing room. She was clothed in a royal blue satin dressing gown. A matching turban covered her hair.

The elegant elderly woman purposefully approached Harrison, stopping directly in front of him. "Stop bullying the girl. I've allowed you to try and resolve your problems with your wife but you've botched the job. Your mother would turn over in her grave if she knew how abysmally you've treated Brianna."

"I've treated her no differently than father would have mother," he said disdainfully, meeting his grandmother eye to eye.

"Exactly! And that is the problem! How your poor mother ever came to terms with my son's despicable treatment of her is beyond me."

"Mother loved father," Harrison snapped.

Jean sighed. "Of course she did, but I also know she

raised you to be respectful of womanhood, unlike your father."

"I respect Brianna."

She took Harrison's arm and walked with him. "Then you'll do the right thing and fetch the rest of her clothing." She gave him a small shove through the door and slammed it shut, but not before Brianna caught the surprised look on his face. Jean swiveled to face Brianna, a satisfied smile on her lips.

Brianna giggled, then covered her lips with a hand. She slumped down on grandmother's bed and moved her hand to her heart. "I can't believe you managed to...well, manage him!"

"I've had years of experience, dear woman. Now, you really must find a way to manage him yourself. You do realize you staying here is temporary."

"Yes, of course. I just need time away from him." Brianna blushed at the twinkle in grandmother's eye.

"Won't you miss him beside you during the night?"

"Grandmother, really!"

Jean laughed. "Of course you will. You've been inseparable for weeks. Do you think the family is unaware of what you two are doing each evening when you leave the parlor before everyone else?"

"He is insatiable," Brianna whispered, her hands covering her hot cheeks.

"Certainly. He is after all, a man, and you are a beautiful woman." She smiled gently. "I believe my grandson has fallen in love."

Brianna shook her head. "No. He doesn't love me. He wants me because of what I can give him. His heir."

"True, but he could have taken up with another woman if that's all he wanted."

A small voice inside Brianna told her what Grandmother

Jean said made sense. "I can't share a bed with him any longer." She sighed. "There's no reason to since I believe I may be expecting his heir."

Jean shrugged. "Why deny yourself?"

"Grandmother!" Brianna was shocked.

"Stop being a prude," Jean chided. "It is rare for a woman to enjoy the sexual act. Why deny yourself the pleasure? My grandson has always been sought after by the ladies."

Brianna frowned. "According to Harrison, Payton was the charming one."

Jean smiled wistfully. "Oh, he's correct about that. Payton was a charming devil." She met Brianna's gaze and added, "But Harrison was the MacAulay heir. Never doubt he had more than his share of women."

Brianna didn't doubt it. Jean left the bedchamber and Brianna thought over her words. Why should she deny herself? She fought the battle with herself and was nearly on the verge of taking back everything she'd said to Harrison. She was ready to return to the master bedchamber when he stormed into the room and dumped an armful of clothing on the bed. He hardly looked at her. He turned on his heel, bypassing his valet, Wesley, whose arms were also full.

"Just dump it all on the bed. The ladies will put it away."

"Oh, but laird, maybe I should call on one of the maids..."

"Do so," Harrison said, reaching the door.

Brianna stepped forward, reached out to stop Harrison when he came to an abrupt halt. She pulled her hand back when he glanced at her over his shoulder. "Let me know when you are ready to be my wife again."

Wesley scuttled from the room.

"We never were married!" she shouted.

With two strides, he was beside her, his chest heaving.

"I've already explained to you about our handfasting. It's legal, so never doubt it. But, remember this. I made an offer for your hand in marriage and you declined."

She tilted her head back and met his angry gaze. Her eyes widened when she saw a glimpse of hurt there. No. Impossible. He didn't love her, and had only offered to marry her now that she carried his heir. Not only was it the law, but the dutiful thing to do.

"Just remember, *this* is what you'll be missing, here, in your cold, lonely bed."

She gasped when he captured her nape and swept her against him, planting his lips on hers. He ravished her mouth until she moaned and went limp in his arms. As quickly as he'd taken her, he let her go.

As she watched Harrison stalk from the room, Brianna had a feeling she'd just made the worst mistake in her life.

CHAPTER 12

March 1889

rianna's menses started shortly after she moved into Grandmother Jean's rooms. She dreaded telling Harrison, knowing he'd be disappointed. She was. Perhaps she was growing too old to have a child, she worried. But, the sooner she conceived and bore a child the sooner she could return to America. But she questioned herself; was that what she still wanted? To go home when more and more this place felt like her home? Unfortunately, she still hadn't found the nerve to tell him she wasn't pregnant.

He hadn't touched her since she'd left his bedchamber. Yet he appeared so calm, so unaffected while she was feeling agitated from the deprival of his warm body and attentions. But her pride kept getting in the way; he'd struck her, something no man had ever done. She couldn't allow him to do so again. She wasn't at all sure she could believe that he wouldn't beat her in the future, as he'd promised. But a little voice inside told her she couldn't go back on her word; she'd promised to give him his heir.

She sat sedately in the parlor, trying to enjoy her afternoon tea with the Grandmothers Jean and Mary, and Tess, who still hadn't returned home. But with each passing day, Brianna saw sadness in Tess's eyes. Brianna decided soon she would gently suggest that Tess return to her husband.

Thoughts of her own relationship with Harrison entered Brianna's mind. She decided she had far too much time on her hands, which meant too much time to think about herself.

"A penny for your thoughts, dear."

Brianna smiled at Grandmother Mary. "I'm afraid that's approximately what they're worth."

"What's wrong?" asked Grandmother Jean. "Are you still feeling ill?"

"Oh, I'm fine, thank you. It's just that with the children in school all day I have no idea what to do with myself."

"Don't let Harrison hear you say that, my girl. What are you thinking? Perhaps it's something I could help you with."

"I'd like to find some worthwhile work to do, but when I mentioned it to Harrison, he reminded me my job is to care for Winterhaven. I've learned the servants here are quite capable, and the place seems to run well with little interference from me."

"That it does," Jean replied. "Many of our servants have been here for years. What sort of work would you like to do?"

"Other than running my boarding house, I only held one other position in my life, clerking in a millinery shop. I enjoyed assisting the customers, and feel I was quite good at it. I appreciated the independence a weekly pay check gave me, even if most of it was spent moments after entering my pockets." She sighed. "And I'm lonely for adult companionship, truth be told."

"But you have had plenty of callers!" Tess protested.

"Yes, but we are strangers and one can only talk about family and the weather for so long. Am I being foolish, do you think?"

"I don't believe so. I've learned you are not a pampered woman," Jean said. "My grandson should thank his lucky stars to have found you. I am also of the firm belief idle hands are worthless hands. Perhaps you should find some useful work to do."

"Have you approached Harrison about this recently?" Mary asked.

Brianna laughed mirthlessly. "You must be joking! I hinted at the idea last week, for the third time in a few weeks, but he told me it wasn't open for discussion. MacAulay ladies do not work, he said. My job is taking care of his heir and Winterhaven, and that's all. Frankly, Grandmother Mary, I'm not the sort of woman to be coddled. I'm bored silly."

"I have an idea," said Jean.

Brianna's face lit up with excitement. "Yes? I'm listening!"

"Perhaps you would care to join us in our latest endeavors to save mankind."

"Oh, grandmother," Tess said, a smile on her lips. "You will provoke Harrison if you allow Brianna to participate in the movement."

Brianna sat up straight and stared, brows raised. "Oh, for truth, he will not be happy. Aside from that, it's a rather tall order, isn't it?"

"Yes, it certainly is, dear." Grandmother Jean moved her chair closer to Brianna and, in detail, explained her cause.

Harrison sat at a small table in his clinic, absently ate his beef stew as he stared out the window at the crowded street. Edinburgh was growing, becoming more populated every day, and his medical practice was growing along with it. Even though the city was inundated with doctors, he never failed to have less than twenty patients on any given day.

A fine black carriage caught his attention as it raced down Queen's Street. He recognized the crest, and the passengers. One was his grandmother and beside her was Brianna—or her twin—wearing her sapphire hat. Cursing, he slammed his cup into its saucer, rose from his chair and pressed his nose against the glass, just in time to see the carriage turn the next corner.

"Damn!" He snatched his coat off a hook. He shrugged it on and jammed his top hat on his head. As he stepped out of his office, he looked at his assistant. "Paul?"

The young man looked up from his work. "Yes, Doctor MacAulay?"

"I must leave but will return shortly."

Harrison found the carriage parked where he knew it would be, outside his Aunt Marianne's home. He loved his aunt, his mother's youngest sister, but she was much too independent for her own good. In his opinion, she required a man to keep her in check.

As a matter of fact, upon first meeting Brianna, he'd thought she behaved much like his aunt. Marianne was a very youthful thirty-five, just three years older than he, but she'd never married. On numerous occasions, she had told him that no man could give her anything that she couldn't supply for herself. She'd received plenty of offers of marriage, including a few from some prominent, wealthy, English lords, but she'd turned them all down. Of course, there was Marianne's long-time liaison with Alexander Ravens, Earl of Chisholm, a traditional highlander if ever there was one.

He reached his aunt's door and pounded on it. Marianne's stoic butler of many years opened the door. Before the man could utter a word, Harrison barked, "Is my aunt in residence?"

The older man raised his gray eyebrows. "She is, my lord. She has company at the moment."

"I am aware of that," Harrison muttered.

Brianna and Tess sat in Aunt Marianne's parlor listening to the stories his grandmothers and aunt told. At first she had difficulty believing the cruelty of some people, but the more she heard the more convinced she was she must help in some way.

"Well, I never heard such horrible things in all my life. Can you imagine that poor woman bearing another child to that drunken lout?" Grandmother Jean said. "How many does that make, Marianne? Three?"

"Four."

"Well, isn't it her duty to birth children for her husband?" Brianna cautiously inserted.

"Dear, you have no idea what poor Sally Fergussen has endured," said Marianne "Not every woman is lucky or wise enough to marry a gentleman who won't beat her. That awful man near broke her jaw last week, and all because he cannot control his drinking. Ask your husband, since he treated her."

Tess gasped, "The beast!"

"Broke her jaw?" Brianna asked, horrified.

Marianne explained further indignities the woman had suffered at the hands of her husband.

"I want to help, Aunt Marianne," Brianna said.

Tess said, "As well as I."

"Excellent," Marianne replied. "But what about Harrison?"

Brianna raised her brow. "What about him?"

"You know he's not terribly fond of the temperance alliance's activities," said Grandmother Jean.

"From what you've told me the alliance's activities are for good, humanitarian causes. He may object, but he cannot stop me from joining in." She turned to Marianne. "Excuse me. Could you direct me to your necessary room?"

"Of course, my dear!" Marianne led Brianna to the door, then opened it. "It's just down the hallway, first door on your right."

Brianna closed the door behind her. She'd taken one step when someone grabbed her elbow and spun her around. Her hand flew to her mouth, stifling her surprised gasp. Harrison was scowling down at her. He pressed her against the wall and raised a finger to his lips.

"What are you doing here?" she whispered.

"I might ask the same thing of you, wife. Why aren't you home where you belong?"

"Well! I never..."

"You've been listening to my aunt and grandmothers far too long," he said dryly. He pulled her away from the wall and dragged her down the hallway.

Her kid leather slippers couldn't find a foothold, and she protested, "I'm not ready to leave yet."

"You are through here." With an eloquent look, Harrison thanked Jansen for his efficiency as he accepted Brianna's cape and hat. He whisked the enveloping material around her shoulders and set her jaunty felt hat on her head. Jansen stood tall and straight beside the open door.

Just as they passed the butler, Harrison said, "My thanks, Jansen. Inform my aunt and grandmother I'll be escorting my wife home."

"Certainly, my lord."

"Harrison, have you lost your mind?" Brianna asked as he rushed her down the stairs. "How will I ever explain this to your aunt and grandmother?"

"I don't happen to feel that particular assemblage is a good influence on you."

Brianna widened her eyes. "Your grandmother and aunt aren't good for me?"

"They're all right, as long as they're apart, mind you. Put them together and they make a lethal combination. They're always searching for trouble. I won't have you associating with them."

"Then you will need to explain to them why you kidnapped me away from them then. Besides, you cannot dictate to me," she said, yanking her arm away. "You simply cannot. I've told you again and again that I need to find worthwhile work to do. I've been horribly lonely and at loose ends for weeks. And now that I've discovered your grandmother's cause, you tell me I can't participate. I say I will."

"Not useful, you say? You are useful to me. That's all that matters. I say you will not associate with my grandmothers and aunt," he said coolly. "You have no idea what they do when they go out on one of their crusades, and the results. I shudder at the memories."

"Of course I've no idea, since you precipitously yanked me out of the house before I could find out."

He came to an abrupt halt on the sidewalk. "I'll tell you then. Aunt Marianne, both my grandmothers, and several other women in the community march from house to house, trying to instill their beliefs on people, starting with relatives first. Certainly we are all aware there are men who drink more than they should, which may cause strife in the home, but it's their business."

"And I say thank God these women make it their business when terrible things happen to the wives and children of those men," Brianna said. "You must have heard what they said about poor Mrs. Fergussen, since you were listening outside the door."

He sighed. "Yes, I heard every blasted word."

"Did Sally Fergussen come to see you?"

"Yes."

"And you had no suspicions about her injuries?" she asked, astonished.

"Of course I did, but what could I do? When I asked if her husband had hurt her, she denied it. She said she'd fallen down the stairs when she stumbled over her cat."

"And you believed her?"

"Nothing else was forthcoming from the woman. Yes, I believed her. Now then, I will not discuss this further in the middle of the sidewalk where everyone can hear us. We'll stop by the clinic and I'll have Paul close for the day."

"And then?" she asked dubiously.

"Then you and I shall retire to my townhouse to discuss what you will do with your life that will make me happy."

She frowned. "I see. Not what will make me happy?"

"Of course. We'll meet half way, somehow."

"I'm delighted to hear you're willing to negotiate my life's direction," she said dryly. She walked sedately beside him. "It's not necessary for you to hold onto my arm quite so tight, Harrison. You'll leave bruises," she warned.

He immediately relaxed his grip. "Sorry."

"I do so admire your grandmothers' and aunt's strength

and independence, even though I hardly know them." She sighed. "And I do envy their freedom."

Harrison had no idea how to respond to that. Even after all these months together, she still thought about her damned independence. Wasn't she satisfied to be his wife?

They reached the clinic. Harrison opened the door and stuck his head inside. "Paul, close up any time. If there's an emergency I'll be at my townhome so tack a note on the door, would you?"

"Aye, good afternoon to ye, Doctor."

Harrison smiled at Brianna and tucked her arm through his. "Have you had your supper?"

"Marianne had rung for tea just before you arrived." She sent him a sidelong glance and walked beside him. "You owe me a meal."

"Would you care to try some authentic English dishes instead of Scots fare for a change?"

She nodded. "Sounds wonderful. Tomorrow, you will need to talk with your aunt and grandmother, you know."

"I suppose," he said vaguely. Then, he looked down at her as they walked, her arm tucked through his. "Are you really all that upset that I absconded you away from them?"

She shrugged. "I must admit I was intrigued by the works of their organization, but uncertain as to what I could do to help. I will find out shortly, I imagine. But at the moment, all I can say is I need food, and the necessary room."

Two short blocks later, they turned a corner. He glanced at her and grinned at the delightful look on her face as she took in the row of identical gray stone houses. They reached the one at the very end of the block and he opened the wrought-iron gate. After ushering her inside the townhome he watched her slowly make her way down the hallway. He followed her, his hands folded behind his back, grinning at her wondering expression.

He'd chosen well in furnishing his home away from home, with Aunt Marianne's advice. She'd convinced him that Turkish-style furnishings were all the rage now. When he wryly pointed out he was never one to follow fashion she said the furniture was also quite comfortable. That element convinced him to follow her advice.

Two enormous divans faced each other on either side of the hearth. Both were covered in velvet, one in bronze, the other in sapphire. They were long enough he could stretch out and relax after a long day's work. Brilliant colored pillows were scattered across the divans and on the floor beside them. Mellow, gold-toned oak tables stood beside the upholstered pieces for convenient placement of refreshments. On the tables were lamps with gold rope tassels hanging from their shades.

Brianna shrugged out of her cape and handed it to him. "This place is yours?"

"Yes." He took her cape and tossed it over the back of one divan.

"Why have you kept it a secret? And you've decorated it —well, it is rather unique, isn't it?"

"I keep the house for when I'm called into town in the middle of the night on a medical emergency, delivering a baby, for instance. Usually, I'm exhausted afterwards. Having this place nearby is convenient. Unique as in good or bad?"

She gave him a wide-eyed look. "I don't believe I've ever seen anything quite so beautiful. Wherever did you find such long divans?"

"Aunt Marianne stumbled upon them." He decided it wasn't necessary to explain they'd come from some far eastern harem.

He smiled. "Come view my bedchamber."

She looked at him suspiciously. "I'd like to see it, but you must behave, my lord."

"I'll be the perfect gentleman."

He waved his hand before him and Brianna moved up the flight of stairs, conscious of him close behind her. She reached the landing. Harrison stepped around her and opened a door. Her eyes widened at the sight of the enormous bed positioned against a far wall. Once again, brilliant colors were everywhere.

"Why haven't you brought me here before? This place is beautiful and quite intimate. It reveals an unknown side of you. I love it."

He grinned. "Is that a fact?"

She crossed the room and sat down on the bed. "It seems that you may be possessed of a very passionate nature.

"And how do you view Winterhaven?"

"Old, reverent, traditional. I prefer this place."

"I'm glad you like it." In a low voice, he added, "It's yours, as well. Come as often as you like, that is, until you're too uncomfortable riding in the carriage." He moved to her side. "Are you chilled? I could start a fire."

"No. I'm fine, but we need to talk."

"Ah." He smiled. "I've seen the way you watch me, Brianna. Day after day, even with my back turned, I feel you looking at me. Are you ready to return to my bed?"

She didn't reply but he saw her cheeks turn pink, saw her small nod.

"I thought as much," he said, satisfied. He'd patiently waited for her to make up her mind to return to him, knowing she would eventually. He wasn't blind, after all. He'd caught her admiring gaze often during the past four weeks, and he admitted to himself he was quite proud that he'd maintained control of the situation. He leaned over her, forcing her to recline flat upon the bed. "I suggest we go to bed now and talk later?"

She scrambled off the bed. "Talk first. It's important, but I do require the use of your necessary room."

Heaving a sigh, he slumped down on the bed. "Of course. He pointed a few feet away to a closed door. "The bathing room is there."

When she returned he asked, "So, what shall we talk about?"

"Something...well, something rather important. And I'm afraid you will be very disappointed."

He frowned and came to his feet. "Go on."

She met his gaze. "I'm not pregnant, Harrison."

His frown deepened. "You're not? For certain?"

"Yes. Absolutely. Unfortunately."

"Yes, most unfortunate. But, you were so certain..."

"I was. I believe I miscarried, thankfully very early."

Harrison raked a hand through his hair as he took in her news. It hit him hard. He felt as though he'd taken a blow to his stomach. Looking at her, he gauged her expression, saw the hurt in her eyes. Yes, she seemed as disappointed as he was, but then a slow smile formed on his lips. There was nothing they could do now but share a bed again. Having Brianna back in his arms meant everything to him. He decided it was a very real possibility he could truly learn to love this woman.

"I'm sorry, Harrison," she said softly.

"I'm running out of time, Brianna. We must a share a bed again, and bloody well soon."

"Yes. Immediately. But this doesn't change anything between us. You still believe I shouldn't find worthwhile work and I still believe I must. You still believe, as head of the MacAulay clan, that you must control me. But you can't, because I won't allow it."

"True, but as long as we keep what happens here separate from our disagreements, we'll both, in the end, get what we each require—my heir and your freedom to return to America."

She smiled faintly. "I'm glad you feel that way. Your words precisely express my sentiments. Now, then, I thought we could try out your bathing tub."

"The tub," he said, deadpanned.

"I noticed you have sumptuous tub in your bathing room."

Harrison swallowed the lump in his throat. "Let's relieve you of these clothes."

"Thank you," she said demurely.

He took her hand and pulled her toward him. He settled his hip against the bureau. Then he pulled her between his legs and carefully undid the row of tiny buttons down the front of her bodice. Her skin was creamy above the lace edge of her camisole. That such sweetness was his he found difficult to believe. He paused at a button level with her belly. Reaching down, he stroked the slight roundness, thinking sadly of their loss.

She gasped, "Your hands are cold as ice. Perhaps you should join me in a hot bath."

"You won't be able to stop me," he said. "But before I join you, I'm going to scrub every pore of your body."

"Oh, such an indulgence. You may try, sir, if you last that long," she said coyly, edging toward the bathing room.

He sent an amused scowl her way as he followed her. "I cannot believe you have the temerity to remind me of my dreadful weakness for you."

CHAPTER 13

*a*fter spending the night at the town home in Edinburgh, Harrison and Brianna returned to Winterhaven the following morning. They were, once again, on speaking terms. Brianna doubted it would last. She put the thought from her mind, smiling as she thought about Harrison's lovemaking last night. It had been perfect between them, and no words had been necessary. If only they could always be of like mind and feelings, but she knew that was impossible. Quite simply, she was too independent and he too domineering.

When he left her, she turned to more important business. Harrison's grandmothers had plans for her with their women's alliance. They had called another meeting for this very afternoon. Brianna sat in the parlor at Winterhaven, with Harrison's grandmothers and aunt, and several neighbors as they made plans.

"It's settled then. Brianna will enter McTavish's Tavern and confront Scotty Fergussen," said Mrs. Kennedy, Aunt Marianne's friend and neighbor. She turned to Brianna. "Do you understand what you must do?"

"I believe so," Brianna replied, tugging at the high collar on her shirtwaist. This first day of April was unseasonably warm, although the breeze from the Atlantic kept the temperature reasonably tolerable. "You know, it would make perfect sense for us to not only assist women who have been abused due to their husbands' excesses, but to counsel them about the sensibility of not having any more children," she added.

Aunt Marianne raised her eyebrows. "Why, Brianna, that is an amazingly progressive idea! We shall talk about this later, after we're through dealing with Sally's problems with her husband."

Sally implored, "But I love having children."

"Of course you do, dear, but perhaps you must first decide if you can afford to have any more," Grandmother Jean said practically. "I also favor further discussion on your ideas, Brianna."

"Yes, wonderful idea, Brianna," said Mrs. Kennedy. "Are we ready, ladies?"

Tess said, "Are you certain, Brianna? I'm willing to take your place."

Brianna smiled and took Tess's hands. "You are too well known in Edinburgh, sweet sister-in-law, but thank you."

"Onward!" The chorus of women's voices rose as they left the house. They rode in two carriages into Edinburgh, then marched down Queens Avenue, banners in hand and singing at the top of their lungs. Interested folks followed them. By the time they reached McTavish's Tavern, a fair sized crowd had gathered.

A cold, nervous feeling in the pit of Brianna's stomach caused her to wonder, not for the first time, what she'd gotten into. It pleased her to join the Women's Temperance in their cause to save mankind. She wasn't certain she was up to the task, but she couldn't disappoint these women.

The Women's Temperance Assembly had chosen her to confront Scotty Fergussen because she wasn't a notorious member yet. Her words, hopefully, should have more credibility than the other ladies'.

"We'll wait right here for ye. Now remember, coerce Scotty into leaving the tavern, then we'll deal with him."

Just before Brianna entered the building, Sally Fergussen stepped forward. "Scotty will be furious with me, Mrs. Kennedy. I've changed my mind. I can't go through with this!" she wailed.

"Now, Sally." Mrs. Kennedy took the woman by the shoulders and shook her lightly. "Nothing will change if we don't make him see reason. Next time he could kill ye."

She shook her head. "No, he wouldn't. But what we're planning to do will embarrass him and will only make things worse between us."

"Better worse than dead," Mrs. Kennedy declared. "If he doesn't change his ways ye must divorce him."

"But I don't want a divorce," Sally whined. "I love Scotty."

Brianna said gently, "Of course you do. You've told us up until recently he's treated you well. Something must be bothering him. If we can convince him to confide in someone, we'll be able to help solve your dilemma. That's why we are interceding, on your behalf, Sarah."

The woman visibly relaxed and nodded. "All right. I trust ye, Mrs. MacAulay."

Brianna straightened her spine and pushed through a set of swinging doors. She stopped just inside the door. Her eyes widened upon the number of men drinking at the bar, in the middle of the day! The room went dreadfully quiet. Before she lost her nerve, she approached the barkeep.

"I'm looking for Scotty Fergussen."

"You shouldn't be in here. Only men allowed," he replied brusquely, scowling at her.

Brianna looked pointedly at the women in various forms of dress and undress, then turned back to the barkeep.

"There are a number of ladies present."

"Them's women, not ladies. And—"

A throaty voice snarled from across the room, "Ye bastard, McTavish. Don't ye say it!"

A large breasted woman with wild red hair glared at the man.

"Just point him out to me and I'll leave as soon as I've finished my business," Brianna said.

The barkeep heaved a sigh and waved his hand toward the end of the bar. "That's him. The one with the black cap."

Tentatively, Brianna approached the huge man sitting upon a stool. His head was tucked down, chin bumping his chest. He appeared to be mumbling into his mug of ale and shaking his head.

"Mr. Fergussen?" Brianna stopped some distance away. When he didn't reply she cleared her throat and stepped closer. "Mr. Fergussen. I'd like a word with you, please."

The big man spun around on his stool. His handsome face split into a big foolish grin, and he looked her up and down. "Well, what do we have here?" He arched his brow at McTavish. "A new girl?"

McTavish growled, "This here's Laird MacAulay's wife, ye fool."

Brianna blushed because he'd recognized her. She guessed it wouldn't be long before Harrison learned of her escapade. She jumped, startled when Fergussen's voice boomed through the tavern. "I remember ye now! I remember seeing ye prancin' through town on the laird's arm!"

He seemed to have come to his senses and he peered suspiciously around the tavern then turned to her with a scowl. "And where might yer husband be?"

"That is none of your concern. Your wife is waiting outside to speak with you."

He raised his brows. "Sally's outside? Waitin' fer me, ye say?"

Brianna nodded.

Fergussen hauled himself off the stool and towered over her. "Why in the hell isn't she home, damn it?"

Brianna backed up a step. "She's enlisted the Women's Temperance Assembly to help you see the sense of things, Mr. Fergussen. Need I remind you she's your wife and you are responsible for her and your children?"

"Damned right she's me wife!" he exploded. "And it's no one's business but mine if I tip a pint or two after a hard day's work."

He stumbled across the floor and headed for the door with Brianna on his heels. He weaved in the doorway, his eyes bleary as he sought out his wife.

Sally stood on the walkway clutching the hands of two children, and two more stood behind her.

"Why aren't ye home, woman?" he bellowed.

"I'm not leaving until ye come home with me, Scotty."

Brianna nodded approvingly when she caught Sally's eye, admiring the woman's nerve in the face of her furious, inebriated husband.

He growled low, "I'll show ye where yer place is." He bounded off the step and Brianna stayed close behind him. She tugged on his arm just as he reached Sally.

"Mr. Fergussen, please. Just listen to what your wife has to say."

She gasped when he planted a palm in the middle of Sally's

chest and pushed. She fell to the ground, taking both children with her, and the two behind her managed to step back in time. The eldest Fergussen boy, who appeared to be about eight, pounced on his father. He pummeled him and screamed, "Don't ye do that, Da! No more hittin' Ma!" Fergussen stood there a moment, reeling in confusion in his drunken stupor. Finally, he gathered his wits and shoved his son away. The boy fell to the ground but immediately scrambled to his feet.

Sally cried, "No, Willie. Stop! I'm all right."

It was too late. The crowd of women yelling furiously at the blacksmith didn't do a bit of good. They formed a huddle around Sally, trying to protect her from her husband, but the man's attention was now focused on his son. The boy had his fists raised in a fighting stance, ready and waiting for his father to attack.

"Ye'll not be hittin' her again!" Willie shouted. "Ye won't!"

"Goddamn ye boy, get yer arse on home!"

Fergussen removed his wide, thick leather belt and swung it over his head. Brianna threw herself in front of Willie. The belt lashed her face, neck and chest as it came down. She screamed and clutched her face. Then she fell to her knees and huddled on the wet cobblestones.

Anger blinded Fergussen to all except his disobedient son. He swung the belt a second time. Brianna lurched up, intercepting the blow again. She trapped Willie protectively in her arms as she turned. The belt struck her back, knocking her to the ground once more, her pain-racked body wrapped around Willie.

All around her, the women were shouting and screaming. Eyes shut, Brianna held the sobbing boy in her arms. All sound faded as she retreated into the dark recesses of her mind where only pain dwelt. An eternity later, a loud snapping noise and a man's piercing howl of pain broke the silence.

She managed to sit up, raising Willie with her. The sound came again. She lifted her head, and her eyes widened in horror. Harrison towered over Scotty Fergussen, now on his knees in the dirt, blubbering. The man cowered under upraised arms as he tried to protect himself from Harrison's blows.

Brianna stared. Her husband snapped a long, wicked whip across Fergussen's back with stunning accuracy. Fergussen's guttural screams rent the air with each strike of the whip. Brianna saw four strips torn away from the man's shirt one after another, exposing bloody flesh. If she didn't stop Harrison, he'd kill the man. But she couldn't find the strength to stand up. She just sat there. The crowd murmured approval as the whip struck again, and again.

Brianna closed her eyes and covered her ears. But it didn't stop her from hearing Fergussen's bellowing cries over the noise of the crowd. She raised her head and saw a huge, fair-haired man, his arms wound around her husband's waist, pulling Harrison away from Fergussen.

"Thank God!" Tess exclaimed as she ran to Brianna and kneeled beside her in the road. With a grin, she said, "It's my husband."

Brianna watched the Herculean man calm her husband. Then the men turned and strode swiftly to Tess and Brianna. Tess scrambled to her feet and she faced her husband, a tentative, yet welcoming smile on her lips.

Harrison's strong arms lifted Brianna from her sprawled position. She looked up into his furious face, but she wasn't afraid.

"We're going home," he said as he walked down the street with her cradled against his chest.

Brianna shoved her palms against his chest. "What about Sally and her husband? I can't just leave her like this!"

"There's no need to worry," he crooned softly.

"We'll take care of things," Max said.

Brianna glanced at Max's serious expression, thinking that if he smiled he would be gloriously handsome. She was satisfied when she saw him slide his arm around Tess's waist. Tess appeared to welcome his closeness as she visibly relaxed.

Harrison's carriage was just a short distance away. Once they reached it, Stanton yanked open the door. Harrison lifted her inside and settled her onto the seat. She fully expected him to sit beside her, so she sat up, startled, when the door slammed shut.

Brianna stuck her head out the window. "If I'm leaving, you're coming with me! We need to talk."

Harrison leaned toward her, his face near hers in the window's opening. "We shall, later, after I've dealt with Fergussen. You do want to be sure Sally is safe, don't you?"

Biting her lip, she decided his words made perfect sense. "Then I shall see you at home, my lord."

"Home, Stanton!" Harrison bellowed.

The coach lurched away. Brianna fell back against the seat, shrieking at the pain in her back. She rolled to her side, too tired to think about her husband's anger; too tired to move. Eventually she fell into a light, troubled sleep. She roused and sat up when the carriage stopped and looked out the window at the lovely sight of Winterhaven. Stanton opened the door and gently assisted her from the coach and up the stairs to Harrison's chambers. She collapsed on the bed and Stanton fled.

"Oh, God, that hurts!" she exclaimed as she sat up again. The scratchy fabric of her shirtwaist was irritating so she unbuttoned it and pulled it off. Quickly, she unhooked and removed her skirts and yanked down her petticoats. Heaving a deep sigh, she rolled onto her side, managed to find a comfortable position and fell fast asleep.

She woke later to a sharp pain in her back, and the realization that someone was touching her.

"Stop!" she groaned. She started to rise from the bed.

"I know it hurts, dear, but I'm trying to help ye," Aunt Marianne said, pressing her down. "I'm applying a healing balm to your back and shoulders. Be still."

"Where is Harrison?"

"Still settling things in town."

She thought about the look on her husband's face as he'd carried her to their carriage. His thunderous expression she'd remember for a long while. "Is he very angry with me?"

"Oh, Brianna! He's terribly upset. I wouldn't say he's precisely angry with ye, but he certainly is furious with the assembly of ladies. He's banned ye from attending any more of our meetings. I don't blame him. Never had any one of us envisioned Scotty Fergussen turning on ye like that. Never."

"How long have I been sleeping?"

"Not long. There now, I'm through. Ye will be sore for a week or so, but ye'll mend. Ye will have to sleep on your side, dear."

"I'll manage," Brianna grimly replied.

The door crashed open.

Marianne rose from the bed. Brianna raised her head and looked over her shoulder. Her husband stood in the doorway, his clothes, hair and spectacles askew. There was no sign of the whip.

He leveled a hard look on his aunt. "Leave us," he growled.

"Now, Harrison, it wasn't Brianna's fault. We've told ye we had no idea the man would go berserk the way he did."

"Leave, Aunt Marianne!"

Marianne blanched, plucked up her skirts and moved toward the door.

"Harrison! How dare you speak to your aunt that way!" Brianna chided.

His silver eyes flashed before he turned to his aunt and bowed slightly. "My apologies. I'll speak to ye after I've settled things here. Meet me in the library." And then, as an afterthought, said, "Please."

After Marianne left, Brianna said, "All right, say what you will."

He didn't utter a word, but gently touched her back. Brianna felt self-conscious with her state of undress beneath the sheet. Just a pair of thin cotton drawers covered the lower half of her body, and a chemise on top. She stiffened when something soft brushed her neck and moisture dampened her skin. She looked sideways and discovered her husband sitting on the bed beside her, his dark head buried in the space between her nape and shoulder.

Frowning, she asked, "Harrison? What is it?"

She was stunned when he raised his head and stared at her. Tears sparkled in his eyes behind his spectacles. His eyelashes were spiky and wet.

"My God," he murmured. "I thought I was too late." He shuddered and wound an arm around her shoulder.

Brianna squirmed away from him and sat up.

"I'm very much afraid I shall be laid up for a while with my back. According to your auntie, it's quite torn up." She saw his face turn white. She took his hand and smiled. "I shall mend. Don't worry so. Tell me, is Sarah all right?"

"Fergussen escorted his wife and children home."

Brianna widened her eyes unbelievingly. "Oh, no! He'll hurt them. Scottie Fergussen should have been locked up!"

"He'll never beat them again. He's sworn off drinking and has promised never to enter a tavern."

"And you believe him?" she asked incredulously. "Heavens, you were beating the man. What else could he say to make you stop?"

"I believe him. Constable Murray, Max and I counseled him at the jailhouse. We sobered him up with coffee then forced him to tell us why he'd become a drunkard. He spilled his guts. By the time he finished, I understood his reasons."

Brianna blustered, "There's absolutely no excuse for a man to abuse women and children."

"Of course there isn't, but are you aware there are thirty-nine blacksmiths in Edinburgh?"

"No, I had no idea." She lifted her brow. "So, what does that have to do with Fergussen's penchant for drunkenness and violence?"

"Because of fierce competition he's been losing patrons. Drinking himself into a stupor was his way of coping with it. He couldn't tell his wife about his business failures."

"I've heard this all before," Brianna said with a sigh. "Men and their damnable pride."

Harrison took her hand and pecked her cheek. "Well, pride is a moot point now. He's accepted a job here at Winterhaven."

Brianna raised her brow. "Haven't we a blacksmith already?"

"Two, actually."

What a lovely man! She started smiling then caught herself when she thought about her own problems. She had to find a way to convince this dunderheaded man that becoming a permanent member of the Women's Alliance was a wonderful idea. There were so many ways she could help the poor, abused women of Edinburgh. She'd been frightened of Fergussen during his rage, but it had dissipated during the carriage ride home. She was confident and more determined than ever to continue her involvement in the women's alliance.

Brianna slept fitfully that night, after witnessing first hand Fergussen's abuse to his wife and son. She couldn't seem to find a comfortable position because of her pain. Even though she hadn't called out, Harrison heard her rustling about and spent the night at her bedside. She protested and told him to find his own bed. He ignored her and administered to her a dose of laudanum. She slept then, albeit fitfully.

She wakened later in the morning to the sounds of raised voices. Loud, booming bass tones mixed with shrill ones seemed to pierce her bedchamber floor. Her back and head throbbed with a dull ache. The arguing was aggravating the condition. She shoved her feet into her slippers, then shrugged into her robe. The shouting grew louder with each step she took as she made her way down the stairs. Standing outside the closed library door, she heard every word. Tess was in a high fury. Harrison's impatient voice burst forth time and again. The only calm voice was a low and gentle masculine tone she guessed was Max.

It was time to put an end to this. She opened the door and stepped inside. Tess paced the library, near a long row of windows. Harrison was leaning against the hearth, arms folded, a foreboding expression on his face. Max was seated with his arms draped over the arms of his chair, one leg crossed over his knee. There was that serious look on his face again.

Maximillian St. James, ninth Earl of Hardgrove's manly appearance was startling. His legs were long, his waist trim. The breath of his chest was wider than her husband's, which was amazing to Brianna. His wavy, white-blonde hair had been cut short, but the sideburns were long. He wore a full mustache, but no beard. His expression was serious, but was that a twinkle in his blue eyes? His tone was cool as he stated calmly, "It would take all the tea in China for me to take her back."

Harrison gave his brother-in-law a benign smile as he took a chair opposite him. "Which wouldn't matter in the least, since you are the most wealthy man in all of Great Britain. Come now, take Tess off my hands."

Just as Max opened his mouth to reply, Tess spoke. "Then why are you here?" She scoffed, "To have me arrested?"

She stood before him, her hands jammed on her hips, scowling. But Brianna saw the pain of rejection in her eyes, convinced that Tess did love her husband. But never had she seen two such mismatched people! Tess's fire-like temperament was a stark contrast to Max's cool, patrician manner. And she had to admit Max did seem more mature than Tess.

He raised cool blue eyes to her. "You know I wouldn't do such a thing, Tess. I'm here to tell you that you may have your annulment."

Brianna gasped. She looked at Tess who stared down at Max vacantly. Was that sadness she glimpsed in Max's eyes? Was it possible he didn't want to be separated from his wife? Tess's blank expression worried her so she bustled into the room. She wound her arm around Tess's shoulder and started leading her from the library. Harrison leaped from his chair. Max also rose and inclined his head to Brianna.

"What are you doing out of bed?" Harrison scolded.

"However would anyone be able to sleep with all the noise down here?" she replied. "Now, I suggest you two have your little discussion, without Tess's presence. Can you not see how you've upset her? Both of you," she added, glaring at Max. "When you are both going to behave in a gentlemanly fashion, you may speak with her. We'll be waiting in the parlor. And please, lower your voices." Quickly, she led Tess away. Once she closed the door, Tess collapsed against Brianna and sobbed.

"No annulment, Max," Harrison stated.

"Honestly, Harry, I don't relish the idea of getting shot again," Max snapped. He sank down lower in his chair.

Harrison had noticed the pronounced limp in his gait and hoped Max would heal well. Prayed his injury wasn't permanent. "Tess will be the perfect wife from now on. I give you my word."

"The perfect wife?" Max asked dryly. "I wait with baited breath to view this miracle. Imagine if you will, the position I found myself in.

Harrison shrugged. "You know how Tess used to spend time with the stable boys and my man, Carney. She could have learned from any one of them, I suppose. Just once more, Max. She understands this will be her last chance."

"No," Max said coldly. "You have no idea how close I came to taking a crop to her backside. Your sister behaves little better than a child, not a woman anywhere near ready for marriage. She needs to grow up."

"Come now. You knew you were marrying a girl rather

than a woman. Why in God's name didn't you take her in hand from the day of your marriage? Why didn't you take a switch to her?"

Max looked appalled. "I've never struck a woman in my life! There are other ways to deal with the fairer sex, Harry. Beating them isn't one of them."

"May I assume, since you are in this present deplorable state, you had no success with the ways you tried?"

"Unfortunately, you are correct." Max frowned. "And the thought of it is galling. You are probably right. I should have taken her over my knee."

Harrison glanced down at Max's injured leg and smiled ruefully. He admitted he wouldn't know how he would have reacted if Brianna had shot him.

"I must say I never expected her to be quite so inexperienced," said Max, his voice filled with irony.

Harrison took the chair opposite his friend and leveled a hard look on him. "Are you telling me you thought Tess wasn't an innocent before you married her?"

Coloring, Max gave Harrison a sheepish look and opened his mouth to reply.

Harrison warned, "Careful how you answer. You are speaking of my sister."

"Your sister. My wife. I admit she had me fooled for a while. Damn it, Harry, you know what a tempting little vixen she can be! The true test of her innocence came about on our wedding night, of course. I realized then she knew nothing at all about men, which made her even more attractive. I won't deny her innocence bolstered my ego."

"How did you determine she was innocent?"

Max stared at him fiercely. "How in blazes do you think?"

"Tess said the two of you hadn't had relations, but you're telling me otherwise?"

"Damn it all, I was stretching her a bit to see if she'd be able to take me." He shook his head. "I don't believe she can, Harry."

"Nonsense!" Harrison scoffed. "Women are anatomically made for men. Remember, an infant can squeeze through that small portal."

"Heaven save the world from virgin brides." Max rubbed his injured thigh then raised sad eyes to Harrison. "Why doesn't she want me?"

Harrison leaned forward, elbows on his knees. "I wouldn't be asking you to take her back if she didn't, now would I?"

"Of course you would," Max retorted. "I'm positively certain you spelled out Tess's "duty" quite firmly. Remember, Harry, we've been friends for years and I know you well."

"It seems I neglected my duty to her. It's my fault that she shot you."

"How so?"

"Do you recall my telling you how our Mother died while giving birth to Tess?"

Max nodded, an expectant look on his face.

"Well, it seems Tess has decided she's responsible for our mother's death."

"That's utterly ridiculous!"

"Of course it is, but not in Tess's mind. She told Brianna she's unwilling to perform her wifely duties because she's afraid of conceiving and dying in childbirth."

Max sighed. "My God, same as her mother, you mean." He looked at Harrison. "This changes things, doesn't it?"

"Take her back. She adores you. Allow her to prove it."

"Oh, I'll certainly allow her the opportunity," Max snapped. "Send her in then, and fetch me that crop you keep behind the door."

Harrison frowned. "Remember, now, you said you would go easy on her."

"Did I?" Max shrugged.

"You know," Harrison said, narrowing his eyes, "if I didn't know you as well as I do I'd say that was a threat."

"I must maintain authority in my household. Unfortunately, the servants back home know what happened. If I allow her to get off without any punishment I'll have a mutiny on my hands."

"You are right, of course."

"No more than five strokes."

Harrison nodded, grimacing at the thought of the thin crop blistering his sister's posterior, but she deserved the punishment.

Max's sudden burst of raucous laughter caught Harrison by surprise. He scowled at Max who slumped further down in his chair, grinning.

What in the world was so bloody funny? Harrison thought.

Max calmed. "Truthfully, the crop is for my protection. You know I'd never lay a hand on Tess." He reached out and took the crop from Harrison.

Harrison grinned and headed for the door. With his hand on the knob, he turned to Max. "When the time comes, don't give her a second to think about your intentions. The element of surprise may be to your advantage. And if words don't work, get her inebriated. She'll never know what happened to her. Then the deed will be done, and you may proceed to teach her passion without having to worry about causing her pain or discomfort."

He opened the door, went to parlor and found Tess sitting, crying on Brianna's shoulder still. He walked to her, took her hands and raised her to her feet. "Come, now, Max would like to speak to you."

CHAPTER 14

June 1889
Edinburgh, Scotland

The dreary spring rains during the past few months had turned Scotland's landscape to a rich emerald green. Harrison's concerns about Brianna's involvement in the temperance alliance lightened with the arrival of the summer sun. She seemed, however, to savor each moment of trouble she could find—accompanied by his grandmothers and aunt. After the incident with Scotty Fergussen, Harrison had been forced to intervene twice more, in other temperance activities, or he believed Brianna would have been hurt.

Tess had returned home with Max to England, after the two of them had formed a truce of sorts. Harrison was thankful for Tess's departure. She was one less female family member to worry about.

He'd risen an hour ago while Brianna was still abed. He

polished off his third cup of coffee, and read the entire newspaper but she still hadn't appeared. Last evening, as they climbed the stairs to their separate bedchambers, he'd told her he had something important to discuss with her in the morning. He decided she was avoiding him and the discussion. The doorbell caught his attention and he rose from his chair as his housekeeper answered the door. He heard light, rapid, determined footsteps just before Connie MacPhearson burst into the library.

"Thank God you're home, Harrison!"

Harrison lounged back against his desk. "Good morning to you, too, Connie. To what do I owe this visit?"

Connie tilted up her small chin. "We need to talk about something very important. Sit down."

He raised his brow. "You haven't changed a bit since I saw you last. What was it? Perhaps just three or four months ago, wasn't it?"

She gave him a skeptical look as she took the chair in front of his desk. "Is that a good thing?"

"Of course it is. You've always been beautiful. We grew up together. We have a fondness for each other."

"True, unfortunately, six months ago you put me in my place about how far that fondness should go, didn't you? Well, all it's done is lead me to another man."

Harrison sank into his chair. "Are you saying you and McKenna..."

"What about McKenna," she interrupted. "What has he told you?"

"Not much, I'm afraid. Has he proposed marriage?"

"Three times, thus far. I'm finding it more difficult each time to turn him down, as you bloody well should have guessed."

Harrison shrugged. "Then accept. You'll make him a very happy man, not to mention your slave forever."

She snorted. "Slave, hah! All the man can think about is the pitter-patter of feet in his house. He wants children for God's sake. Immediately."

"What man doesn't? Does that surprise you?"

"I suppose not," she grumbled, "but I don't think I'd be very good at it. Besides, I would want us to have a chance to get to know each other a little first."

"That's reasonable," he said. "So, why are you here on my doorstep?"

She stunned him with her next words.

"After we're married, I want a year with McKenna without conceiving. Help me, Harrison."

Harrison leaned forward and laced his fingers together. "Why an entire year? I should think within the first few months you should know him well enough."

"I'm not certain I love him."

"Of course you do. You wouldn't be thinking of marrying him if you didn't."

She shook her head. "No, you're wrong. I don't know if I can ever love a man as much as I love you."

"...if I can ever love a man as much as I love you."

In the hallway, Brianna froze at the sound of a woman's voice confessing her love for Harrison. She raised her hand to cover the cry that nearly slipped from her lips. She leaned back against the wall and listened, but the woman's voice had softened. Then she heard sobs and Harrison's soothing voice.

Maeve entered the foyer. Brianna raised her finger to her mouth. The older woman glanced at the partially closed library door with a shake of her head before she went away.

Maeve likely thought her horrible for eavesdropping, but

she couldn't seem to pull herself away from the wall. Laughter, both masculine and feminine, drifted into the hallway. For all she knew, they were carrying on a dalliance. What did she care? All she wanted was to go home and leave her arrogant, demanding husband.

She ran down the hallway and out the front door. As she sat down on the brick stoop, she wondered if any MacAulay woman had ever done so before. Her stomach churned, and not just because of the conversation, she'd overheard. She was pregnant—for certain this time. She planned on telling Harrison last evening, until he said he wanted to speak to her in the morning about something rather important. Likely, he'd guessed she was pregnant, just as he'd done the first time.

The door suddenly opened, nearly bumping her from the stoop. She gasped when a pair of hands hauled her to her feet. She found herself looking into her husband's surprised face.

"What in the world are you doing sitting out here on the steps, Brianna?"

"Waiting to speak with you, but you had company," she snapped. She glared at Harrison, then at Connie, who appeared about to laugh.

"Connie's leaving."

"Yes, and I can't thank you enough, Harrison," Connie said. She aimed at his mouth, but Harrison dodged it. She kissed his cheek instead and sighed.

"Let me know what happens with McKenna," Harrison told her.

"Oh, you'll be the first to hear, my lord," Connie replied, a dimpled smile on her lips. She turned to Brianna. "Nice to see you again, dear. Oh! When is the next women's temperance meeting?"

The question caught Brianna by surprise.

Before she could answer, Harrison said, "Bloody hell! Don't tell me my grandmothers have gotten to you too? I thought you had better sense than that!"

Connie's laughter filled the air. "We ladies must stick together. Besides, your grandmothers are very persuasive, and too delightful to ignore. Och, I'm late for home."

She rushed down the stairs and headed for her mount. A stableboy appeared and gave her a leg up. She rode off, her horse's hooves throwing dirt along the way.

Brianna envied the woman's competence in the saddle.

"You were looking for me, weren't you?" Harrison asked. He took her elbow and guided her into the house.

Brianna caught the knowing look in his eyes. "You knew I was listening at the door, didn't you?"

Harrison chuckled as he settled her into the chair in front of his desk. He leaned against it and folded his arm. "I caught a glimpse of those abominable black skirts as you passed by."

"Why was she here?" Brianna demanded. "You'd told me your business with her was finished."

"It is, but it's difficult to ignore one's neighbors. Besides, Connie and I have been friends for years."

"Friends," Brianna said, expressionlessly. "Don't you know the woman is in love with you?"

Harrison frowned. "Last year, for just a short while, but no longer." He cocked his head to the side. "If I didn't know better I'd say you cared. Do I hear a bit of jealousy in your voice?"

"Hardly! It's just that, well, I'm carrying your heir. So it's high time you put other women aside. At least while I'm expecting."

"For certain?" Harrison asked.

Brianna heard the surprise in his voice. Saw the hopeful expression on his face. Her cheeks turned hot under his very thorough gaze moving over her from head to toe. "Yes, truly. I've already been to the doctor."

"This is wonderful news, Brianna! How many months?"

"Just a month. It may be a bit premature for us to celebrate."

"Nonsense. How do you feel?" he asked gently.

"Horrible, which, I suppose, is a good thing. It's precisely how I felt with Harry and Jamie."

"That's good then."

"Oh? And why is that?" Why in the world would he want her to feel ill, she wondered.

"Because I highly doubt you'll be traipsing through town with the Women's Temperance Alliance while feeling horrible."

Brianna lifted her chin. "I will continue working for the good of all women until I have no choice but to seek my bed."

He tightened his jaw and clamped his teeth together. Then he gave a curt nod, and left the library.

Brianna was almost unable to believe he'd actually left without arguing. She thought he should know her better now. Just see if she would stay home and knit stockings for the duration of her pregnancy. She smiled. She'd show him.

A moment later, her smile slipped when she remembered the tight look on his face. He would try to find a way to stop her from pursuing her cause.

Let him try. She would not yield to him in this.

In August, Harrison proudly introduced his bride to Edinburgh society at his aunt Marianne's annual summer ball. Connie MacPhearson stood beside her brother,

Crawford, her head tilted to one side as she stared at Brianna dancing with Harrison.

"What makes her so sought after, I wonder?" she asked. Men had been lined up for the past hour waiting to dance with Brianna. Wryly, she noted how Harrison had deftly managed to snag his wife away from the next man in line.

"Yer claws are showing, Connie," Crawford MacPhearson reminded his sister. "Behave yourself."

"I imagine I must, since there are no eligible men beating a path my way," Connie said philosophically.

"We are exceedingly lucky to have secured an invitation to Marianne MacLeod's ball, considering the fiasco that occurred at the last one we attended."

"Which one?"

He gave his sister an incredible look. "How have ye forgotten already? I'm referring to the McReynolds ball last fall. Of course, I can't expect ye to recall a bloody thing, since ye made an absolute fool of yourself when ye became disgustingly inebriated. I suppose it's too much to ask ye to remember that ye spilled punch over half the guests, before I managed to hustle ye out of the place."

Connie gritted her teeth. "You know very well that I was trying to get over my feelings for Harrison. And thank you so much for reminding me. Now let's not belabor the point, shall we?"

Crawford took his sister in his arms and swung her onto the floor. She'd managed over the course of the years to pass up a number of eligible men's requests for her hand. Only Harrison MacAulay had appealed to her. Unfortunately, Harrison had merely thought of her as a sister, until last year.

One evening, Connie had filled Harrison's gullet with fine Scotch whisky while she listened with heartfelt sympathies to his woes. She woke in his bed the following morning and feigned shock and dismay. Harrison offered to court her, mostly from guilt, she knew. And he would have married her if she hadn't given into that tempting bastard, Raleigh McKenna. Harrison's barrister had pursued her relentlessly. She'd given the man one measly night, albeit a memorable one. When she learned Raleigh had confessed their liaison to Harrison, she could have killed him. With gentlemanly aplomb, Harrison had stepped aside, telling them they were meant for each other.

"You brought this upon yerself. I warned ye years ago to be careful or ye would ruin your chances for a good match."

She glared at him. "You just love informing me about how right you are about every little thing, don't you?" She wouldn't allow him to get the better of her. She'd learned her lesson and knew her limits. She smiled when she looked over her brother's shoulder and saw Raleigh McKenna as he entered the ballroom. *My, he looks incredibly handsome this evening.*

"Listen, dear sister, frankly, I'm tired of keeping ye company. It dampens my style, ye know."

She raised her brows. "What style would that be?"

Crawford's face colored and she immediately felt contrite. He'd never had much success with the ladies. Crawford stared off across the ballroom and she followed his gaze. Brianna was dancing with young Rory Cullen.

"Poor Brianna. She is far too tall for most of the men here," Connie said. "She does look a bit matronly now that she's expecting. One would think her further along than four months."

"She's a beautiful woman," was the only response from Crawford.

"No decent woman would ever wear red. Why would Harrison allow her to dress in that color?"

"I believe it's wine-colored."

He couldn't seem to get enough of looking at their neighbor. When the music ended, he escorted Connie to her chair. "I'll be back shortly."

"Where in the world are you off to now? You can't just leave me here unattended," she snapped.

"I'm fetching ye a glass of punch."

"I require something stronger if I'm to survive this boring evening. For instance, a scotch whisky would be nice." She saw Raleigh heading purposefully toward her and sent him a wide smile.

"One drink, Connie. No humiliating conduct this evening," Crawford said, piercing her with a dark look. "Ye will not make a fool of me again."

Crawford saw McKenna nearly upon her and gave a relieved sigh He'd be dancing attendance upon Connie. Which meant Crawford would have time to himself.

Swiveling on his heel, he headed for the refreshment tables. He poured half a glass of Scotch whisky and carried it back to Connie. McKenna stood behind her, waiting for her acknowledgement, apparently.

Crawford gave Connie her drink and made his way around the perimeter of the ballroom. Just once, he wanted to hold Brianna in his arms. Finally, his opportunity came when she slipped into a heavily draped alcove. He followed her and found her sitting on a cushioned seat, her head tilted against the backrest.

"Ye are a lovely sight, Mrs. MacAulay."

Her eyes snapped open. She gave him a wide-eyed look. He spread his legs in a wider stance. "Ye remember me?"

"Of course. You're Connie's brother."

"I passed the library and saw Harrison engrossed in a high stakes card game."

The deep, wide neckline of her velvet gown, edged in Brussels lace, framed her wonderfully naked bosom. Shortcapped sleeves showed off her slim, elegant arms. Even though he wanted nothing better than to slip his hand inside her bodice, Crawford managed to control his desire.

"Tired, my lady?"

"As a matter of fact, Mr. MacPhearson, I came here to find a moment of quiet. I'll thank you to leave."

He chuckled at her snooty tone. "I have no intentions of leaving now that I've discovered ye alone. Ye are quite one of the most fetching women I've ever met. Dance with me."

"I think not."

Leaning down, he traced the line of her jaw with a gloved hand. He grinned when she jerked away from him. "We'll stay here, if ye like. I can think of a number of things I'd rather do aside from dancing."

She snatched up her skirts, ready to flee, but he blocked her way. "Get out of my way!" she said, her voice low but strong.

He shook his head and moved forward a step.

She held her ground. He had to admire her courage. In this hidden place, he could certainly overcome her. His body felt hot as he saw her high breasts peeking out at him. He moved closer and ran one finger lightly from her wrist to her arm, then lightly touched the lace rimming her décolletage.

She slapped him hard across the cheek. "How dare you!"

Crawford's cheek stung. "I've been waiting all evening for yer guard dog to leave yer side, in between the constant flow of admirers begging a dance from ye."

He caught her in his arms. "If ye won't dance with me a kiss would suffice."

Just before his lips touched hers, she pulled free and kicked him in the shins, first one, then the other. "You measly little cur," she snarled. "Get your bloody hands off me!"

Crawford stumbled back in surprise. Surprise turned to anger then. "Why you little——"

She stalked toward him. "If you didn't already have that sniveling high-pitched voice, I'd make certain that you did before you left this place, MacPhearson. Make no mistake!"

Suddenly, the curtain opened and Connie stood in the opening. After a quick look at Brianna, she scowled at Crawford. "I suggest that if you value your life, you will leave immediately. Harrison has quit the gaming tables."

He swore as he slipped out between the curtains.

"Do you know what your husband would have done to my brother if he'd caught the two of you together?" Connie demanded.

Brianna swiped a tendril of hair back from her forehead and gave Connie a grateful smile. "I had no idea this would happen," she protested. "I certainly didn't encourage him to pursue me."

"Isn't it enough you have managed to snag the most eligible man in all of Scotland? What more do you want?"

"Your brother accosted me tonight. He would have done more if you hadn't arrived when you did."

Connie sighed. "He has difficulty with women. They don't seem to like him. It's his voice, of course. Now, then, I've something important to say to you. You've fallen in love with Harrison, haven't you?"

Brianna blushed and looked away, unable to meet Connie's eyes. Of course, she loved him, but she wouldn't admit it to this woman. Connie was, after all, a bit of an adversary.

"Even without speaking it aloud I can see that you do. I feel sorry for you. You see, Harrison will never love you, at least, not as much as you love him."

"You are wrong," Brianna replied. "He's told me he loves me."

Connie looked askance. "I know precisely how charming Laird Harrison MacAulay can be. You know that his primary reason for handfasting, and eventually marrying you is to beget an heir, don't you? But has he told you how he's lusted after you for years, since he learned of your marriage to his brother?"

Brianna frowned. "He said not a word to me about that." But Brianna couldn't deny his attraction for her. It would be a lie if she did. "We were traveling aboard the ship to Scotland when he told me about the conditions of his father's will. Earlier he'd informed me his primary reason for coming for me and my sons was duty—his promise to Payton to always care for us."

Connie smiled, somewhat grimly. "He planned on having you from the moment he learned of Payton's death. And believe me, once Harrison pursues something, he always wins."

Brianna shook her head in denial.

"Sad, but true," Connie continued. "It's unfortunate for you that Payton's death proved to be so timely for Harrison. From the moment he received word of his brother's death, he made plans to fetch you for himself. Traveling by sea was a risky venture for him, but he had something of great importance to gain by doing so."

"I've told you he said it was duty, nothing more. Once I've given him an heir I'll return home to America. He promised me this."

"Ah, yes, that damned, infernal MacAulay pride. I've no doubt that duty was a factor for fetching you." Gently, Connie added, "But it's true that he wanted you shortly after he received the picture of you and Payton after marrying, and most definitely after Payton's demise, so you may as well kiss America good-bye. He'll never release you. Now then, I'd better find Crawford before he gets himself into more trouble." She swept up her golden satin skirts.

"He's mine now," Brianna warned her.

Connie froze. "Yes, but I wonder for how long?"

Brianna's eyes filled with unshed tears as Connie left the alcove. She didn't know the woman well, and she had no reason to believe her. Connie had been in love with Harrison for years. Somehow, Brianna believed she hadn't been lying. Brianna faced the awful truth then. She was in love with the bloody man, yet she hated him for deceiving her, under the guise of fulfilling his duty toward family.

She heard Harrison's voice from the ballroom floor. More than ready to leave so she could question him, she rushed out of the alcove.

He smiled when she bumped into him, and took her hand. "So, this is where you have been hiding."

"I...I was just resting a bit."

Harrison's hands moved up her arms to her shoulders. "Why didn't you tell me you were exhausted? I've been ready to leave for quite some time. You have no idea how difficult this evening has been for me."

Difficult? Brianna frowned. "How so?"

"Watching you dance with every man here."

Brianna felt heat creep into her cheeks at his words. She looked away, unwilling to meet his eyes. She knew she'd find unequivocal desire there. She trembled, knowing there was nothing for her to do but bide her time. Yet, a small voice inside her niggled at her conscience. Why not just give in and stay in Edinburgh? What did she really have in America anyway? But his lies made her furious. They must have honesty between them, for she refused to live with another worthless male—ironically another MacAulay!

Once she was alone in her bed, she'd think of a workable plan to leave him. She must leave, for she could not trust him. She would never forgive him for deceiving her.

The butler retrieved their wraps. Harrison donned his coat then helped Brianna with her midnight-velvet cape, buttoning it up to her chin. He caught her by surprise when he swept her into his arms. Before she could think about protesting, he carried her outside to his carriage.

He settled her onto the seat, then vaulted inside and sat beside her. The carriage lurched forward and Brianna fell back. Harrison pulled her against him, but she stiffened and held her clenched fists in her lap. She blinked away her tears in the darkness as she wondered how she would deal with his betrayal.

At home, Harrison escorted Brianna into the house. Faithful Maeve stood by, arms outstretched and scolding. "Ye should have found yer bed hours ago, m'lady."

"You didn't need to wait up for us, Maeve," Harrison said.

"Och, I couldn't sleep knowing Mrs. MacAulay's out all hours of the night." The small gray-haired woman scowled at Harrison. "It isn't good for her or the babe!"

"Ah, Maeve, Brianna was the belle of the ball. We couldn't deprive the gentlemen of her charms too early," he said. He noticed the dark shadows beneath Brianna's downcast eyes. Guilt set in. He took her hand and brushed it with his lips. "Good night, sweet. Maeve is right. I can see you're exhausted. I'll be up shortly." He headed for the library but paused when Brianna spoke.

"I won't be seeking my bed until we've talked."

Harrison studied her a moment, then waved his hand toward the library. She swept past him and sat down on the chair in front of his desk.

"Would you like a cup of tea?"

She shook her head. Harrison sat down and stared at

her, waiting for her to begin. When she didn't speak, he asked, "Did you enjoy yourself this evening?"

"Yes, I did."

"I worry about you, Brianna."

She stared at him. "You do?" At his nod she added, "There's no need to."

"You danced nearly every dance this evening." He smiled. "I was afraid you would drop my heir on the floor, before it was time for him to make an appearance."

"Your heir," she said softly. "Yes, we certainly can't have anything happen to him, now can we?"

Harrison heard bitterness in her tone and his smile slipped. "Let's stop this verbal fencing, shall we? Ye are obviously upset about something."

"Why did you lie to me about your reasons for wanting me to come to Scotland?"

His eyes widened and for a moment, she saw astonishment there. He concealed it and asked, "What makes you think I lied?"

"Why must you always reply to my question with a question? One would think you were an attorney and not a physician, for heaven's sake!"

"I wasn't aware I did that."

She nodded. "You do. Each time I pose a question you have no desire to answer. I...I heard things this evening that lead me to believe you haven't been completely honest with me."

Harrison frowned. "Who, may I ask, provided you these revelations?"

"Constance MacPhearson."

Harrison sprang from his chair to pace the floor. "That interfering little...She had no reason to tell ye anything." He whirled away and stared into the fire. Something struck his back. He turned in time to catch his furious wife in his arms.

"She was telling the truth, wasn't she? You've lied from the very beginning, haven't you?" she shouted, pummeling his chest. "It wasn't just duty that prompted you to come for me! You required an heir, so that was your main reason for coming for me, wasn't it?"

He managed to restrain her. "Stop it or you will hurt yourself." Then, slipping a hand behind her head, he pulled her close, pressing her forehead into his chest. "Hush, now."

She continued striking him, wherever she could. After the second slap to one cheek he pressed her against his body, entrapped her arms against her sides. Still, she squirmed until he growled, "Will you listen to my explanation now?"

Brianna gave his chest another impotent thump with her fist. "Give me one good reason why I should believe anything you say."

"Did it never occur to you that Connie could have been exaggerating? Or lying outright?"

She pulled out of his arms and sent him a baleful look. "Then why won't you deny what she said?"

"I did what needed to be done," he said flatly. "I did the only thing I could do to save my clan—your clan now."

"My God, there are thousands of women in this world, and any one of them would have willingly given you an heir. Why me?"

"I fell in... suffice it to say I had my reasons."

"What reasons?"

"Have it your way. I came for you because you were perfect for my needs." Harrison knew his words had sounded cool and distant. How was he to convince her that he cared for her? Loved her enough to reveal his true feelings? Once he'd worn his heart on his sleeve and had paid the price for it. Not again.

"So duty had nothing to do with it?"

"Of course duty played a large part in my decision. And

I had promised Payton I'd come for you if anything happened. I explained all of this before."

Her voice shook when she asked, "A large part? I don't believe so. Here's what mattered most to you, my lord. I birthed sons for your brother. If I could give him two I could certainly give the Clan MacAulay patriarch one." She lifted her chin and met his eyes. "That is the primary reason you came for me, isn't it?"

He stared at her, but didn't reply.

"Answer me!"

"Lower your voice," he ordered as he sank to the divan.

After a long moment's silence, he met her eyes. "All right. The truth. As soon as I received the wire informing me of Payton's death, I was determined to marry you, my primary purpose to beget an heir. But, my duty to care for you and your sons was never a question, even if we hadn't handfasted. I would have cared for you, Harry and Jamie. Brianna, my feelings have changed for you since we met."

"How have they changed?"

"You know that I care for you deeply, Brianna." *Tell her you love her!*

"Perhaps you do, my lord, but how can I trust you? All you've done is tell tales from the day we met."

"Haven't I given you everything I have to give since you came to Scotland?"

"Every creature comfort, for certain. But life is more than those material things. You forced me to give up my boarding house business and leave my home, but those were the least of your crimes. You took something away from me that I cherished—freedom to live my life as I chose to live it.

"Now, if you'll excuse me, I will be occupied over the next several hours packing my bags." She swung away from the window and went to the door.

Harrison cursed under his breath. He caught her in a

gentle hold. "You can't leave. You're having my child and our laws dictate we must marry. I won't allow you to leave me. After you've birthed my son I know you will feel differently."

"I'm not staying and you will not stop me," she said, and squirmed out of his hold. "And I won't abide by your Scots laws."

He shoved his fingers through his hair. "You're too far along to endure the journey."

There came a knock on the door and Harrison called out, "Yes!"

The door opened and Wesley stuck his head inside. "The master chamber is ready for ye and yer lady, laird." He took a quick look at Brianna and muttered, his cheeks reddening, "Mary's laying out yer night things."

"Thank you, Wesley," Brianna said. "Please tell Mary she needn't wait up for me."

"Oh! Aye, m'lady." He looked at Harrison.

"Seek your bed, Wesley."

Wesley slipped out the door and quietly shut it behind him.

Harrison looked down at Brianna. "You're not leaving."

She opened the door, but paused at his words.

"For your safety, I cannot allow you to travel across the ocean while you are pregnant. And we must marry before the babe's born. Whether you agree with the law or not. After the babe's born we'll get a divorce, then you may leave, but not until then." He braced himself for her answer, hoping she'd be reasonable. The more he learned to know Brianna the less he wanted to dominate her.

Brianna stared at him and his heart ached at the tears he saw in her eyes. "I can see that you do care for me, and your reasoning is sound. You are right. I can't travel now, but as soon as the babe is born, I will for certain leave you."

Harrison stood in the doorway and watched her flee up the stairs. He groaned and closed his eyes. How could he convince her to stay with him? He must convince her to marry him. He'd thought up the lie, telling her she must now marry him legally, but obviously, that meant nothing to Brianna. No MacAulay heir had ever been born a bastard. His heir wasn't going to be the first.

CHAPTER 15

A month later, Harrison still hadn't managed to make peace with Brianna. He'd tried to woo her with evenings out to the theater and opera, and had frankly been surprised when she agreed to attend. He loved watching her expressive face and her joy as she watched the performances. She'd told him she especially appreciated William Shakespeare's The Taming of The Shrew—likely because she saw a resemblance to their relationship.

He proposed marriage to her once, and had slid the betrothal ring off her finger and replaced it with his mother's wedding ring on her finger—a ring worn by every MacAulay chief's bride for over three hundred years. She had immediately pulled it off and slammed it into his palm.

He'd tried browbeating her but was met with icy regard. From the day they met, he'd known she was strong-willed, but invincible? Lord, what would it take to make her change her mind about marrying him?

His last patient of the day had just left. As Harrison removed his stethoscope, there was a knock on the door.

"Paul! Tell whomever it is they'll need to return in the morning. Unless it's an emergency."

As he shrugged into his coat, he heard muttered voices from the front of the clinic, then the sound of the outer door closing. He picked up his medical bag and moved to the doorway. Paul stood in the anteroom, holding a letter in his hands.

"What is it?"

The younger man looked up. "The constable said it's a summons."

Harrison took the letter and sat down behind his desk.

"He said ye should open it right away and that ye must respond within a week's time," his assistant said. "Have ye further need of me?"

"No, thank you, Paul," Harrison muttered. He carefully pealed the sealing wax off the envelope and slid out the document. Then he read it from beginning to end.

"Well, Raleigh?" asked Harrison the next morning, after his solicitor had read the summons through.

"I won't deny you have problems, my friend, but they aren't insurmountable." Raleigh McKenna sat behind Harrison's desk and leaned back in his chair.

"Good." Harrison took the chair across from him. "Now, if you could be more specific, I'd appreciate it. How shall I respond? This summons is requesting my appearance before a magistrate for a meeting with Brianna and her solicitor, one Jasper Hawkins."

"First off, I'd like you to tell me why in God's name you haven't opened a bank account for your handfasted wife, as I suggested months ago?"

Harrison's face heated under his solicitor's accusation. "I meant to, but in the end decided against it."

"Why?"

"I believed at the time she would have taken the money to purchase tickets to return to America."

Raleigh growled, "You are treating your wife like another of your possessions, which is unfortunate. Setting up an allowance for her would have been a sign of good faith and trust on your part. I've also heard rumor that you have been holding her prisoner on Skye for the past four weeks. Is it true?"

"What! Who told that bald-faced lie? Brianna traveled with my grandmother to her home on the Isle of Skye. It was purely her choice, and she only stayed a short while."

"You call a month a short while?"

"It was three weeks. I admit I rather firmly insisted Brianna stay longer to visit with Grandmother. After another week passed, I couldn't hold such a tight rein on her any longer so I fetched her home. But I've worried ever since that she would try and return to America."

"I understand, but did it never occur to you to look into the laws? If you had, you would have learned you have Scots law on your side with regards to your unborn heir. I advise you to rid yourself of your autocratic attitude. It won't do you a bit of good when we appear before the magistrate."

"So, then, how do you advise me to respond to this summons?"

"Forgive me, Harry, but before I give you my reply I must first ask you some rather private questions. It's important I know where we stand before we continue."

"Ask away," Harrison said, folding his arms across his chest. "I've nothing to hide."

Raleigh nodded. "Good." He leaned forward, elbows on the desk and frowned at the paper. Finally, he looked at Harrison. "First things first. She's demanding dissolution of your handfast due to the fact you've been untruthful with her from the moment you met her at the train station in America."

"I wasn't aware telling falsehoods to one's wife was a crime," Harrison retorted.

"I'm not denying you had good cause to be less than honorable, to lie, because of your father's will, but I encourage you not to add another one on top of it by denying it, or making excuses about the fact you had indeed lied."

Harrison sighed. "All right, I admit it. But will I have the opportunity to defend my position?"

"Certainly." Raleigh pierced Harrison with a level look. "Have you ever beaten your wife?"

"Damn it, man, don't be ridiculous!"

Raleigh raised his brow. "Think again. Think hard about events over the past several months before you reply."

"Does...does she say I did?"

"There is brief mention of an incident. Did you or did you not strike your wife with that damned, infernal paddle hanging on your kitchen wall?"

Harrison scowled at his feet. "Two swats on the derriere, that's all."

"Did you believe you had good cause?"

"Yes!" Harrison leaned forward. "And she'd better not have lied about the fact."

Raleigh went on to read aloud the events of that memorable day as Brianna had recited them. Harrison agreed with her telling, even as a small smile appeared on his lips.

Raleigh scowled. "I can't see one humorous thing about the event, Harrison."

A huge grin split Harrison's face, but slipped when Raleigh added, "I'll inform you now old Magistrate Phillips Rothaway won't find any of this amusing."

Harrison groaned. "With the way my luck's running, it doesn't surprise me that Rothaway is the justice."

"Which may be to your advantage." Raleigh arched one eyebrow and smiled. "Since he happened to be your father's best friend, and your godfather, I believe you haven't much to worry about. We certainly know how Rothaway hounded you to marry over the past several years, completely supporting your father's wishes. I also believe Rothaway will agree that you were within your rights to physically chastise your wife on that particular occasion. Did I hear it occurred in some forest just down the road from Winterhaven?"

Harrison narrowed his gaze on Raleigh's mocking expression and nodded curtly.

Raleigh continued, "You had been concerned for her safety and had acted accordingly, as you would have with any one of your dependents. That you would not tolerate impetuous behavior, with the possibility of disastrous consequences, was your right. Would you say that about sums up things?"

"Precisely." Harrison sighed. "So, she doesn't want to be married to me."

"No, she doesn't, and she has every intention of returning to America with her children."

"Damn it, Raleigh. She cannot leave me. Would she take monetary compensation, and agree to stay?"

"She hasn't asked for so much as a farthing, which frankly amazes me."

Harrison smiled. "Not surprising at all. Even before my brother all but abandoned her, Brianna's been working to support herself and her sons by taking boarders into her home."

"Damn, but the woman does put up a good case for her independence. And, if her story is true regarding Payton's desertion, that could go against you, but I doubt it."

"And why is that?"

"Two MacAulay men taking advantage of her could very well hurt your chances of keeping her here in Scotland, which don't appear good in the first place, with one exception."

"And that is?" Harrison inquired.

"Luckily she is carrying your heir. Until the child is born, she must remain on Scotland's soil. After she gives birth, you won't be able to prevent her from leaving with her elder sons, but she won't be able to take your heir."

"Look, Raleigh, I love her, damn it. And what about Payton's will? He wanted his sons raised in Scotland."

Raleigh shook his head. "Doesn't matter. Brianna and her sons are American citizens and are entitled to the protection of their home country, as you are well aware. They have the right to return whenever they like." He arched one eyebrow. "Have you told her you love her?"

"No, but she knows I do," Harrison muttered.

"So, when were you planning on revealing this rather vital piece of information?"

Harrison swore under his breath. "I will, eventually. You know how difficult it is for me to express myself about something like this. As I said, Brianna knows I love her. Hell, I can barely keep my hands off her."

"Not good enough," said Raleigh. "Women count on words, not mere actions where love is concerned. Unfortunately, it's too late to tell her now. She won't believe you. Your heir is your lucky charm. In the end, you know she won't leave her babe behind, no matter how much she dislikes you."

Two weeks after receiving the summons, Harrison and Brianna sat in Magistrate Rothaway's chambers and listened to the elderly man clarify things.

"Mrs. MacAulay, ye have the right to leave Scotland with yer sons, Harry and Jamie, but only after you've given birth to the MacAulay heir. Then, the child will remain here in Scotland, with his father."

"Please, your honor," Brianna's attorney protested.

"Not another word will I hear from ye, Jasper Hawkins," Rothaway warned, glaring at the man from beneath gray, bushy eyebrows. "How dare ye try and fleece this woman! I'm informing ye now that ye will not receive so much as a pound from her in payment."

"But—"

"Not another word!"

The magistrate turned to Brianna. "Now then, Hawkins was unjustified in leading ye on to believe yer case was a strong one, and I extend my heartfelt sympathies and apologies. Nevertheless, the law is the law." He glanced at Harrison. "I believe we've all agreed and have established that the one domestic corporal incident that occurred some months ago was deemed necessary. Is that correct?"

Harrison nodded and leaned forward, relieved to see Brianna give a slight nod. He sank back in his chair, but shot forward when Brianna asked, "May I speak, your honor?"

"Of course, my dear."

Harrison groaned inside at Rothaway's benign response.

Between tears, Brianna said, "Doesn't it matter that Laird MacAulay deceived me from the beginning? That he tricked me into handfasting with him. That he'd planned from the very start, from the moment he'd heard about my husband's death to coerce me into giving him his heir?"

As Harrison listened to her sobbing, guilt prompted him

to want to promise her anything if she'd only stop crying. Raleigh nudged Harrison, a warning to keep silent.

"Mrs. MacAulay, I intend addressing that very issue with yer husband momentarily."

"Oh, but we're not married," she said quickly.

Rothaway scowled. "Ye're handfasted aren't you?" At her slight nod he continued, "Good. Then I encourage ye now to go home and think on how the lives of yer sons will change if ye returned to America. Think how ye will be denying them the love of family. I also extend my condolences to ye fer yer first husband's deplorable behavior, and this one's deceit." He nodded toward Harrison. "Think long and hard before ye come to a decision, but know this; ye will not be leaving Scotland with the MacAulay heir, not without his father's consent. Do ye understand?"

Brianna nodded as she sniffled back her tears. As she came to her feet, she wobbled. Harrison quickly reached out a hand to steady her, but she stumbled away from him.

He swore then and there to do everything in his power to make her stay, to make things right between them. To do everything he could do to make her happy. Hopefully she would learn to love him. His gaze followed her as she moved to the door. Raleigh stepped around Harrison and opened the door for her. Harrison scowled when Raleigh leaned down and whispered in her ear. Brianna met Raleigh's eyes, nodded, and left the chambers.

After first reprimanding, then dismissing Brianna's solicitor, Magistrate Rothaway turned a jaundiced eye on Harrison. Never before had he been subjected to such a look from anyone. No one would have dared. But he deemed it wise to hold his tongue and take his punishment.

"My God, what was going through yer head when you planned this?" Rothaway barked. Before Harrison could think of a reply, the man turned to Raleigh. "And I'd better not find out ye had a hand in this!"

"He knew nothing of my plans, sir," Harrison said.

Raleigh had, in fact, been stunned when Harrison explained how he planned on fetching his sister-in-law himself, knowing well his inability to cope with sea travel. Besides, in this day and age, that sort of job would have been turned over to servants. Harrison had known he couldn't afford to have one of his retainers ruin his chances in gaining Brianna's cooperation. He'd had no choice but to fetch her himself.

"There isn't a single, viable excuse for the foul manner in which ye treated that poor woman. None! Ye should have found another way of handling the affair. An honorable way."

Harrison flinched at that last remark. "I plan on working hard to make things right between us. If it takes me the rest of my life, I will."

The chair creaked when Rothaway sank back in his chair. "Yes, well, it very well may take ye that long, but meanwhile I intend to mete out justice. I do not enjoy doing this, ye being my godson and all, but I cannot allow ye to leave unscathed."

Harrison remained silent and braced himself for his sentence.

"I'm ordering ye to pay yer wife a sum of eight-hundred pounds per month, in an account in her name only, and two-hundred pounds a month to each of her sons. Ye will also perform one year of medical service to the Edinburgh community, free of charge, not a pound will ye receive until then. Ye will also make good on yer promise to provide her with her own home, and..." He glanced down at a document on his desk. "Oh, yes, a carriage for her use and ponies for the boys." He looked up at Harrison. "Do ye remember agreeing to these items?"

Harrison sighed and nodded. "Yes, but the stipulation was that she birth my heir first."

"That's all changed now," the magistrate said briskly. "Ye'll give them to her immediately. Do ye understand?"

"Yes," Harrison replied as anger burned inside him. She was his handfasted wife and should remain with him at Winterhaven. A house of her own? Ridiculous! He wanted nothing better than to argue with Rothaway but knew it was unwise. He also knew the man wasn't finished with him yet.

Harrison braced himself for what he believed would be the cruelest punishment, since he didn't feel the aforementioned discipline to be too terrible a hardship, with the exception of Brianna not living beneath his roof.

"Unfortunately, that blasted lawyer of hers told her it wasn't a law that she marry ye now that she's carryin' your bairn—not a good thing ye did, son, fibbing like that."

"I know. I shouldn't have done that, sir."

"So now what ye'll do is return home and convince the woman that ye love her, and that ye desire to marry her before the babe is born."

Harrison nodded. "I've been trying to, with no luck, thus far."

"She is an extraordinary woman," Rothaway continued, "Convince her that ye are an equally extraordinary man."

Rothaway rose and Harrison and Raleigh followed suit. Harrison caught the twinkling in his godfather's eyes and grinned.

"Good day to ye both and good luck." Rothaway stood behind his desk, his eyes leveled on Harrison. "Oh, and one more thing. Get rid of that damned paddle. There are other more civilized and delightful ways, I might add, to handling an ornery woman."

"I've already done so," Harrison assured him.

Brianna entered Winterhaven through the double doors Stanton held open for her. She was sad and furious. It wasn't that she hated Scotland, or that she particularly missed America. What she did miss was her freedom to come and go as she pleased. If she could have that, she would be quite content to stay in Scotland.

Magistrate Rothaway had made a valid point with regards to her sons' welfare. She wouldn't feel right about taking them away from their only family of whom they'd grown attached. But she also knew she couldn't continue to live under the same roof with Harrison, no matter how much she loved the jackass. She sighed, deciding even after all his lies she loved him. At the same time, she detested her weakness for him.

She handed her coat to the maid and entered the parlor. There she found Harrison's grandmothers having tea.

"Ah, you're back!" Jean exclaimed. "So, what did Magistrate Rothaway have to say?"

"Well, it went as I thought it would; Harrison has won this particular battle." She looked up when her sons ran into the parlor and came to a screeching halt in front of her.

"Yes! Uncle Harry won!" Harry shouted.

The women gasped.

Brianna inquired sharply. "Where ever did you hear that kind of talk, Harry?"

Harry blushed and muttered, "No one."

"Don't you lie to me, Harry MacAulay! I won't stand for it."

"Joel Culliver, MacPhearson's stableboy told us."

Brianna's eyes widened. "And where the devil would he have heard the news so quickly when I just arrived home?"

Harry shrugged. "Don't know. May we go for a ride? We're done with chores and homework."

Brianna sighed. "All right, but be back in an hour for dinner."

The boys ran from the parlor and Brianna looked at Jean. "How could news travel so quickly?"

"You'd be amazed, my girl. Is it true?"

"Yes." Brianna's lower lip quivered. "It's all true, I'm afraid. I've lost, and he's won. And tell me now, is that anything new?" She looked at Jean. "Your grandson is a very clever man."

"I'm happy, dear," Harrison's grandmother Jean replied. "I've never wanted to see you leave, but I do not want you deprived of your own happiness, either. What will you do?"

"I'm not certain. I do know that I can't stay here."

Grandmother Mary chose that moment to enter the parlor and had overheard her words. "Well, of course you must stay here! Where else would you live?"

"I don't know," Brianna said.

"I must admit I've heard of rather modern couples living apart," Grandmother Mary said.

Brianna gave Mary a thoughtful look. "In separate homes, you say?"

Mary nodded. Her words reminded Brianna of Harrison's long ago made promises.

"Do sit down," Mary said. "All that pacing reminds me too much of my grandson."

Brianna plunked down on one end of the divan and bit her lip thoughtfully.

"Look who's arrived," Jean said dryly. Rising, the grandmothers left the parlor.

Brianna glanced up and gasped. Harrison stood in the

doorway. She narrowed her eyes and lifted her chin, daring him to make so much as one gloating remark.

He crossed the room and sank down beside her. He slipped an arm across the back and tweaked one of her curls that had loosened from her upswept hair.

Brianna couldn't believe the audacity of the man, after all that had occurred this day. "Remove your hand," she snapped, stiffening her spine.

He released her and said, "I'm not sorry you'll be staying, Brianna. I need you. You may not believe me, but it's the truth. I've never truly needed anyone before in my life. Until you."

"What makes you think I'm staying?"

"Because you've no choice, not until you've delivered my heir. Besides, I think you'll be thoroughly delighted with Magistrate Rothaway's words and punishment he issued me after your departure."

"I cannot imagine what punishment, if any, he gave you."

"You'll not live here any longer to start." He frowned. "You'll have a house and carriage of your own, and the boys may take their ponies. You should begin packing tomorrow."

"Well, that *is* initially what you'd promised me, but how this can happen quickly is beyond me. Building a house takes time."

"I've a cottage on my land that will be yours. It was the first house my parents lived in after they married. Great-grandfather built it. I think you'll be more than satisfied with it."

Brianna clapped her hands and a small smile crossed her lips. "Well, that is some wonderful news."

"Yes, isn't it?" he replied.

She heard the irony in his voice and decided not to waste

time. He could change his mind. "I must start packing," she said quickly and rose from the sofa.

Harrison scowled and sank lower into the cushions as she moved to the parlor door. She slowed then, stopped and turned to him with a brilliant smile.

"Thank you, Harrison. I'm happy that you are living up to our bargain. It means so much to me, especially in view of the untruths you've told me thus far."

"Yes, well if it were up to me you wouldn't be leaving this house. If you'll recall our agreement you were not to receive the house until after you birthed my heir."

She lifted her chin and gave him a disdainful look. "And you wouldn't be obliged to provide them now if you hadn't forced my hand in this, my lord. You brought it all upon yourself and have no one else to blame."

He coolly watched her leave the parlor, then he rose and paced the floor, muttering, "Damn, damn, damn!" He wasn't used to losing. Now, without her living with him, he'd have even more difficulty convincing her to marry him.

CHAPTER 16

November 1889

In early autumn, Brianna and her sons moved into the cottage Harrison's great-grandfather had built. There were four bedchambers above a spacious parlor and kitchen, and even a tiny bathing room. Harrison hired a crew of workers to thoroughly clean and renovate the house. Then he moved the few pieces of furniture shipped over from her home in America into the cottage, and took her shopping for new items before settling her into the house.

Brianna seemed pleased that the kitchen was suitably equipped with a newer model stove. She insisted she'd be doing her own cooking. Harrison insisted she have a housekeeper and a nanny to assist her after the birth. She reluctantly agreed, likely because she'd been in a euphoric mood ever since he'd told her she could have her own house.

Once she moved into her new home, he found himself stopping by each day when he was through at the clinic. He felt comfortable in the old house. It was quaint, charming and clean.

With the swift passing of time, he was growing uneasy about his heir being born before they married. He set out, with unmitigated determination, to win her over. He was attentive to the boys, taking them riding several times over the next months. Each time he arrived, he brought her a gift, something beautiful, unique and expensive—a cameo brooch, a finely beaded fan, a pair of white silk gloves. While she protested each time he brought the gifts, he could see she was delighted. But he also knew he couldn't buy Brianna's love.

The first snow fell early in November, and a thick blanket already covered the ground. The weather wasn't a deterrent to Harrison when he left Winterhaven and traveled easily down the snow-covered road to the cottage in a bright red sleigh. The sleigh was another gift for Brianna. She had invited him to celebrate Thanksgiving, an American holiday, with her and the boys. She'd also invited his grandmothers but they politely declined, as they would be hosting a dinner for all of the other relatives that lived around and at Winterhaven.

The Clydesdale came to a stop at his command, and he threw off the heavy woolen blanket and leaped from the sleigh. He pulled out an enormous burlap bag and hauled it over his shoulder. Shouts came from behind him. He whirled around, balancing the bag, as Harry and Jamie barreled into him.

"Slow down!" he said, chuckling as he widened his stance to keep from keeling over. He gave them a mock scowl when he noticed they were in their shirtsleeves. "Are you two daft? Where are your coats?"

"We've come to help, Uncle Harry!" Jamie shouted.

"Then you'll dress for the outdoors."

They sped inside the cottage and returned in seconds, coats on, halting abruptly beside the sleigh. "Where did you get it, Uncle?" Harry asked his voice filled with awe.

"It's brand new—a present for your mother."

Harry looked at his uncle, then at the burlap bag over his shoulder. "Do you need help?"

Harrison grinned and waved his arm in front of him. "Not with this precious cargo. I'll bring up the rear. After I unload this we'll come out for the rest."

Brianna stood in the hallway. "Happy Thanksgiving, my lord."

He grinned and said huskily, "A happy one to you as well, Brianna." She was a lovely sight to behold. Her elaborate, upswept hairstyle was very becoming on her. Her skirt was green and black—the MacAulay plaid. His chest swelled with pride. Yes, she was a MacAulay, and she could deny it until it snowed in July, but it wouldn't change the fact.

She'd tied a shawl over a crisp white shirtwaist. Even though the neckline was modest, and long, full sleeves covered her arms, she was the most sensual woman he'd ever seen. Lord, he wanted her. He enjoyed the heightened color on her cheeks and found he couldn't take his eyes off her.

"What have you there?" she asked.

"Yes, what is it?" Harry asked. He stepped nearer, Jamie beside him.

Harrison just grinned as he set the bag down carefully on the floor and untied the knotted strings. The bag fell open. Brianna gasped in delight at the sight of an exquisite baby carriage. It was a sleeper carriage, made of wicker and built on a spring frame, which would make for a comfortable ride.

Brianna leaned over and gently touched a tall wheel with many spokes, then she lifted the heavy paper tag hanging from the wheel. "Go Cart Sleeper from Sears Roebuck and Company." Her voice trembled. When she finally straightened and looked up at him, he saw the tears welling in her eyes.

"I'd wanted one for the boys but never seemed to manage to secure the money. I'll never be able to pay you back for this, Harrison."

He shrugged. "No need to. It's a gift for my first child. I remembered seeing them in the catalog in your home." He waved his hand at it. "It's a wonderful invention, don't you think?"

"Yes, it is," she said.

He caught the shy smile on her lips, saw how her eyes positively radiated happiness, tears and all. He grinned and looked at the boys. "How would you like to unload the gifts I brought for you?"

"You bet!" Jamie shouted. He ran out the door, with Harry right behind him.

"You spoil them," she said, bending to lift the carriage from the bag.

Harrison intervened, "I'll do it. Don't want you hurting yourself." He lifted the carriage and set it on the floor.

Brianna grasped the handle and pushed the carriage down the foyer.

He watched her, seeing how she'd grown quite rounded with his child. Damn, but he had to convince her to marry him soon! There was only one way that he could do so. He must confess his love to her and not mince words about it. She would have to know that he meant every word.

He knew now that he did love her. With each passing day that she didn't live with him at Winterhaven, he realized it more and more. But could she forget and forgive his past lies?

He knew precisely what to say to make her believe him.

Tonight, after their Thanksgiving supper, he vowed to speak with her; vowed to convince her of his love, beg her to marry him and set a date to do so quickly.

"It moves so smoothly." She smiled. "I cannot thank you enough. This was a most thoughtful gift, my lord."

"More thoughtful than the brooch?"

"Absolutely."

"And the fan and gloves?"

"No comparison."

He quirked an eyebrow and folded his arms across his chest. "You are an easy wench to please, Brianna MacAulay."

She smirked. "Hum, you are just realizing that, are you?"

He stared at her for the longest time and saw the truth in her words.

"Come," she said, "it's time to eat."

Harry and Jamie came running into the cottage, shouting gleefully.

"Oh, ma!" Jamie said reverently, "You gotta see what Uncle brought us!"

"Yes, ma. Come outside right now," Harry ordered and grabbed her hand.

She looked back at Harrison as Harry pulled her out the door, a curious expression on her face. "What, outdone yourself again, my lord? You do realize Thanksgiving isn't taken literally as far as giving gifts—we do that at Christmas time."

"I couldn't wait until Christmas," he said with a laugh.

He followed them outside and paused in the portal, leaned against the doorjamb as he enjoyed the scene playing out before him.

Two bicycles, one red and the other royal blue sparkled in the brilliant sunlit day. Harry sat atop the seat on the taller bike, the red one, balancing it with one foot on the ground. He looked at Harrison. "Can I try and ride it?"

Harrison shrugged. "Sure, if you can find a clean road with no snow on it." He took Brianna's hand and followed the boys around to the back of the cottage. There they found a piece of road where the sun had melted the snow.

Harrison caught the pleased look on Brianna's face as she clapped her hands and gave them encouragement in their attempts to learn to ride. Then she clutched his arm. "Oh, my! They're going to fall!"

With a chuckle, he caught her around her burgeoning waist and held her in front of him, tucking her head beneath his chin. "Of course they will—again and again, until they finally learn how to balance. They'll be fine! Stop fussing."

He felt her stiffen in his arms and sighed when she slipped out of them.

"After supper we need to talk, Brianna."

"Do we?" she asked, giving him a sidewise look.

"Yes! And don't play coy with me. You know that I mean for you to marry me."

Her eyes widened. "You do? I thought you'd have given up the idea by now."

"Never," he said boldly. He turned on his heel and walked around to the front of the cottage.

Brianna sighed as she watched her boys achieve some success on the bikes. They'd been disappointed leaving their ponies at Winterhaven, but it was for the best. There was no stable here for them so they rode whenever they visited the grandmothers at Winterhaven. Why was she hesitant to hear Harrison out, she wondered? She wanted to marry him, but could she trust him? Would he tell more untruths in his efforts to gain her consent to marry? What else could he possibly say that he hadn't already said? She'd hear him out, then make up her mind, although in her heart it had been made up for a long while. She loved him and wanted to marry him, but she couldn't allow him to control her.

His giving her the house made her want to believe he was changing his archaic attitudes regarding women, but she knew Magistrate Rothaway had ordered him to keep his promises to her. She didn't want him to change just so she'd marry him, but because he loved her enough to allow her to be independent. If they married, she'd continue her activities in the women's temperance alliance with his aunt and grandmothers.

More importantly, when all was said in done, she had no desire for her child to be born a bastard.

Harry and Jamie joined her and she walked with them to the front of the house. They leaned the bikes against the house and followed her inside. She was surprised to find Harrison had already removed the turkey from the oven. He was grinning as he held a large fork and carving knife in his hand. Her heart somersaulted at that look, and she had a difficult time concentrating on his words.

Standing at the kitchen counter, he asked, "Were you going to feed an army with this bird?" He looked around and added, "Where are the help I hired for you?"

"Home, with their families, where they belong on a holiday." She looked at the turkey and chuckled. "You wouldn't believe the dishes one can make with leftover turkey."

Harry piped in. "Yes! Turkey sandwiches, turkey pies, turkey soup..."

"I understand," Harrison said dryly. He sliced the turkey and placed the pieces on a platter while Brianna placed bowls of cornbread dressing, buttered squash, green beans and hot, buttered crusty rolls on the dining room table. Off on the sideboard two pumpkin pies sat, waiting to be eaten.

Harrison cleared his throat when Harry and Jamie sat in their chairs. They looked at him, confused, until he nodded at Brianna. They scrambled from their chairs and waited behind them until Brianna settled into her chair.

Bowls of steaming hot food were passed around the table until everyone had heaped their plates. Serious eating and little conversation took place until finally, sometime later, Harry leaned back in his chair and groaned. "I'm too full to eat any more!"

Brianna stared at his plate and at his hands rubbing his tummy. "You've eaten too much." She glanced at Harrison's empty plate. "As I recall you had as full a plate as your uncle."

Harry said, "I wanna be big like Uncle Harrison some day."

She pointed her fork at his plate. "Keep eating like that and you will be." She laughed but stopped at the look on Harrison's face as he stared at her.

Heat seeped into her cheeks when she saw his gaze flicker down to her breasts then rise to her face again. The hot, penetrating look in his eyes made her shiver. His look said more than words ever could. He wanted her. Could she blame him? It had been several months since they'd shared a bed.

"Think so, Uncle Harrison?" Harry asked.

It took Harrison a while to reply, but at last, he removed his gaze from Brianna and focused on her elder son. "Yes, I believe you will. You've a good start."

Admiration crossed Harry's face at his uncle's words. Then he turned to his mother. "May we ride our bikes?"

Brianna checked the pin watch on her bodice. "It's

already four o'clock, so just fifteen minutes is all the time you'll have. It'll be dark soon."

"All right!" Jamie said. Both boys jumped from their seats. Harry said, "May we be excused, Ma?"

"Certainly." Brianna smiled as they ran from the kitchen.

"I need to speak with you about something."

Brianna reluctantly turned and looked at Harrison. She bit her lower lip. "We won't have much time since the boys will be returning shortly."

"It's now or after they are abed this evening."

"I've dishes to do first."

"Well, then, I shall stay and keep you company until you're through."

She rose from her chair with a sigh. "No, we'll talk first."

Harrison followed her into the parlor. It wasn't going to be easy talking to her he could see. He'd noticed her quick response about his staying after the boys went to bed. She was avoiding him, and she had every right to. Damn, but he'd been a fool to yank her from her home the way he'd done. He'd pay for it the rest of his life if he couldn't convince her to marry him.

She took a seat on the divan and asked, "How are your grandmothers?"

"Fine, fine," he said absently, as he took a seat just across from her, in a large, comfortable chair. "They miss you."

"They may visit any time they like."

He met her eyes and Brianna's cheeks heated beneath his intent, censorious look. "You know very well they would not do that."

"Why not?" she asked, perplexed.

"Because of their loyalty to me, even though I've mentioned to them on several occasions I wouldn't be offended if they visited."

"I'm sorry," she murmured and looked away.

He sighed. "I'm the one who should be apologizing."

She looked at him, surprised.

He leaned forward and took her hands in his. Then he raised his gaze to hers. "I'm asking you, with all my heart, to marry me."

Tears pooled in her eyes.

He groaned and added, "But, I'm very much afraid what I have to say will permanently damage my chances for that happening. I love you, Brianna."

Her mouth gaped as she pulled her hands from his. "Pardon me?"

"You heard me the first time," he said in an ironic tone. "I said I love you. I've loved you for quite some time."

She clasped her hands, looked down at her lap but said not another word.

Frowning, he leaned forward. He was close enough that he reached out and smoothed his palms over her dress, across her knees. "Brianna?"

She looked up quickly and he groaned at the tears in her eyes. "It seems I've waited forever to hear you say those words to me."

"Damn it, woman," he said, taking her hands in his, "this had better mean you're staying."

"I've wanted to stay here in Scotland for a long time."

He growled, "Then why in bloody blazes were you so stubborn? Why did you insist upon leaving me and moving into this cottage?"

"Pride, for the most part. I couldn't allow you to dictate to me, as you were prone to doing."

He sighed. "I'm sorry. Being the heir of the clan has prompted me to be rather overbearing at times."

She rolled her eyes.

His broad smile slipped as he released her hands and

continued, "I've a confession to make, and I owe you another apology."

She looked at him in confusion. "You've fulfilled your promises to me by giving me my own home, that fine carriage and horses, and the ponies for my sons."

"Yes, but not without a bit of coercion from Rothaway. Will you listen to me?"

"Of course."

"Good." Straightening up, he raked an unsteady hand through his hair. "I lied to you, by omission, Brianna. Payton's desire to have his sons raised within the MacAulay clan was his dearest wish. You know that. But, no law could have legally bound you to that will."

"But, you said—"

"I'd told you that by law you were required to move to Scotland when in fact, that wasn't the case at all. Remember how you'd wanted to pay your solicitor a call?" At her nod, he added, "But when we stopped by his office we were told he'd be gone a while. He left because I'd bought his silence. I paid him to not let you know the truth; because you are an American citizen, my brother's will was null and void. You could have stayed in your home, and no will or law could have forced you to leave."

"Another deception? But why?" she asked, her voice trembling.

"I won't mince words with you. I'd wanted you for a long time, and when I traveled to America I had every intention of making you mine, and not just because of duty, and because I required an heir."

"But we were strangers!"

"Yes, but it doesn't change the fact I wanted you from the moment I first viewed your portrait."

She frowned. "You haven't one of me."

"Yes, I have." He reached inside his jacket pocket and

pulled out a tiny oval gilt frame. "Payton sent me this shortly after you married."

Brianna took the frame and stared at the wedding portrait of her and Payton. Then she looked up and whispered, "It's impossible to fall in love with someone from a portrait!"

He gave her a sad smile. "Ah, but you're wrong. I dreamed about you for ten long years. Thoughts of you filled my every waking moment, and my dreams at night. You've no idea how much I hated my brother for finding you first and taking you to wife when you should have been mine. Yes, I planned on having you, even before receiving the letter informing me of Payton's death."

He grimaced. "Not terribly honorable of me, I know, and you, of all people, know how much I prize that trait. If Payton hadn't died, I'd actually devised a plan to steal you from him. I'd always had difficulty competing with my brother for the fairer sex, but I planned on winning this time."

Brianna gawked at him.

"I know you may find this difficult to believe, but my younger brother, affable fellow that he was, managed to snatch up every woman with whom I'd shown the least bit interest. Women adored his fair, innocent, blue-eyed looks. I, on the other hand, was the arrogant, dark clan chief. Women were frightened of me."

She laughed.

He scowled and straightened in his chair. "This isn't humorous, Brianna. I'm baring my soul to you."

She offered him a gentle smile. "You are, by far, the most loyal and dutiful of men. I must admit I was a bit intimidated by you at first, mostly because you towered over me, which in itself, is quite unusual since I'm a well, rather tall and larger than most women."

He nodded and stared pointedly at her abdomen. "And growing larger by the moment." He raised his gaze to her. "I won't allow my child to be born a bastard, Brianna." He frowned when she didn't reply. Then he leaned forward and brushed her lips, taking her hands in his. "Will you marry me, and make me the happiest man on earth?"

Her lips trembled as she tried to speak. When tears spilled down her cheeks, he groaned. Was it possible that she would turn down his offer? If she did, could he blame her?

"I need time to think, Harrison."

His eyes darkened. "I'm a man of my word. I've confessed my love for you. Don't you believe me?"

She nodded. "I do believe you love me. But, I'm not certain I can trust you, Harrison. It's difficult dealing with all of the untruths you've told. I remember once you said you truly enjoyed a challenge, and that you always play to win. Are you truly in love with me? Or perhaps I am merely that —a fine challenge. If I did consent to marriage, would you be satisfied with me forever?"

"You've my word of honor, Brianna. I will never tell you another falsehood. In all honesty, you were a challenge at first, but not anymore."

"Please!" She leapt to her feet and crossed the parlor. As she stared out the window she said, "I need time to think about everything that's occurred since the day we met. I will let you know my decision soon."

"I've admitted my love for you," he said softly. "I've apologized. I've kept my word by giving you a house, even though you belong with me at Winterhaven. What more do you want?"

She faced him and said, "I don't know. I do know that I'm not ready to make a commitment to you now. I said I need time to think, and I will not be rushed into making a decision. Stop pressing me!"

"I haven't paid enough for my crimes, is that it?" He stepped back and made a small bow. "I will honor your wishes and cease to bother you with my presence. Until you've come to your decision. But I do have the right to see my nephews. Henceforth, I'll send Stanton over for the boys and visit with them at Winterhaven." He turned and headed for the doorway.

"You have no desire to see me?" Brianna asked, clearly shocked.

He whirled around just as he reached the door. "Of course I do! But it's too difficult for me to continue doing so, knowing that you are uncertain about your feelings for me. Until you can trust me, forgive my past lies, and consent to be my wife, I don't believe we should see each other."

"And, if I decide not to marry you, what then, my lord?"

It took him a long while to answer. He leaned his forehead against the cold wooden door. Finally, he pulled away and looked at her over his shoulder. "I pray you do not come to that decision, because I don't believe I'll be able to live without you."

Her hand rose to her breast and she gasped, "Don't say that!"

He gave her a wry smile. "Sorry for the melodramatics. It was a momentary lapse. If you decide marriage between us isn't possible, then you will, of course, return to America."

Jamie chose that moment to poke his head out the door. "We're back, Ma!"

Harrison inclined his head and bowed formally. "I await your decision, Madam."

CHAPTER 17

December 1889

The howling winds off the sea kept the temperature frigid in Edinburgh. Brianna longed to sit outside on her porch swing, but she knew it wouldn't be possible for several months. Two weeks after Harrison had made his declaration of love to her, she had come to a decision to marry him. She'd been able to look past his lies and realized she loved him dearly. She prayed, with the passing of time, his untruths would fade and her trust in him would grow. She also knew she must marry him quickly since their child was due in late February.

Now she needed to speak with him. Each time she'd visited Winterhaven in the past few weeks, he'd been absent. His family was always delighted to see her and the boys, but they were also evasive about Harrison's whereabouts. Today, however, she'd managed to corner Grandmother Mary, who'd never think to tell a lie.

"Why is Harrison avoiding me?"

Mary stuttered and turned fiery red. "Oh! My-my dear! He isn't. You must understand he's very hurt by your indecision." Mary stuttered and turned fiery red.

Brianna leaned forward and clasped Mary's hands. "Please, you must tell me where he is. I stopped by his clinic today and John said he'd left for the day. Is he here?"

Hope gleamed in Mary's eyes. "Have you decided to take him up on his offer of marriage?"

"Yes."

"To tell him ye love him?" Mary hopefully inquired.

Brianna blushed, a faint smile on her lips as she nodded.

Mary grinned. "He left three days ago for the Isle of Skye. He said he needed to get away and think things through."

"Then it appears I will be taking a trip to Skye," Brianna replied. "Will you be able to manage the children without me? I'm not certain how long I'll be gone."

"Of course, dear. Heavens! I raised six children on Skye with little household intervention. Taking care of those darling great-grandsons of mine will be just like old times."

"Thank you, Mary." Brianna rose and swiftly headed for the door.

"Wait, Brianna!"

Brianna paused. "Yes?"

"I don't think it's wise for you to travel such a distance in your condition. Harrison would not advise it."

Brianna grinned. "I'm very healthy. Now, don't worry about me. I'll be careful."

The rest of the day, she spent gathering her things, and setting a schedule for the boys for Grandmother Mary to follow. She packed enough clothes for a few days, while she dreamed about spending time with Harrison—making love and convincing him of her love for him.

By the time Stanton took to the road in Harrison's sturdy carriage, Brianna was exhausted. Wryly, she glanced down at her protruding tummy, which had amazingly seemed to grow rounder overnight. Here she was, a pregnant femme fatale planning to seduce her handfasted husband. She shook her head and decided she'd left her brains at home in the cookie jar.

Harrison hadn't taken a carriage, but had strapped his pack of clothing on the back of Challenger, along with a few food supplies, and other necessities. Initially, he'd planned on not breathing a word to anyone about his destination. He'd grown depressed over the few weeks since he'd last seen Brianna. He decided a respite from Edinburgh would help him stop thinking about her. But he couldn't afford the luxury of not reporting his whereabouts, because of his responsibility to the clan.

The weather had turned cold and damp since his arrival at Skye a few days ago. As he walked along the snowy cliffs, he pondered his dilemma while the wind tugged and pulled at his heavy tweed coat. Lord, he missed Brianna, and he wondered how in the world he'd possibly live the rest of his life without her, if she decided not to marry him.

He snatched up a rock and hurled it over the cliff, watching until it disappeared from sight. The more rocks he threw, the angrier he became. She was an ungrateful little witch. Hadn't he given her everything she'd asked for?

Raleigh had told him he was daft—that he should continue to press her to marry him. Harrison had learned when dealing with Brianna, applying pressure would be the wrong tactic. He'd had no business deceiving her, even though saving the MacAulay estates had been paramount.

In hindsight, he realized he hadn't been thinking straight. He could have married any number of eligible women here at home, but he'd wanted only Brianna.

When he'd first seen Brianna's portrait, he'd been caught by something haunting in her lovely face. As the years passed, his medical practice grew and his responsibilities to his clan increased, yet he'd been unable to forget his brother's wife. He'd wanted her, with a gut-deep hunger that would not be satiated, no matter how many women he bedded.

None was Brianna.

Then Payton died. His brother, whom he loved, but who had always been a wastrel, a ne'er-do-well. And Brianna was free.

From the moment he learned of his brother's death, he'd had only one thought—to make Brianna his wife. To have her bear his heir.

To have her in his bed.

Ruefully he thought about her penchant for freedom, her desire to live in America and raise her sons on her own. He still couldn't understand it. She had no living relatives in America, and he knew she communicated with only one friend in Wisconsin. Here, in Scotland, she had a large family who loved her and wanted her to stay.

He reached down for another rock and hurled it over the cliff. Harrison faced the reality once and for all. Brianna might, in the end, reject his proposal.

Brianna ached from head to toe after the long journey through the highlands, though her carriage had been built for comfort. As she slowly headed up the walk to Grandmother Mary's cottage, she rubbed her sore backside.

She ambled through the rooms but found no sign of Harrison. When a knock sounded on the door, she turned to find Stanton sticking his head inside.

"He's here, m'lady. I'll find him for ye. He's likely walkin' the cliffs. He's always enjoyed it, ye know?"

Brianna smiled. "I'll go. I'd like to surprise him."

Stanton grinned. "Sure and he'll be likin' that, he will." He frowned and swept a cursory glance over her body. "Now ye be careful, ye hear?"

"I will."

She was dressed for traveling, not climbing over rocks and hills, yet, she didn't want to take the time to unpack and change her clothing. A piece of gray cloth stuck out from behind the closed doors of the armoire. It was Harrison's gray coat. The sleeves were so long they swallowed up her hands. The skirt came to her ankles. She shrugged and decided it would have to do. Winding her arms around her middle, she breathed deeply of Harrison's scent.

Her fashionable leather shoes pinched her toes as she headed for the cliffs in the distance, but that didn't stop her from running across the boggy lawn. She saw movement from the corner of one eye. Harrison was doing precisely what Stanton had said—hurling rocks over the cliffs and into the water. He'd removed his jacket. Brianna watched him for a moment, mesmerized by the rippling muscles in his shoulders.

The closer she drew to him, the more her steps lagged. She stopped several paces behind him, frowning when she finally understood the words he was shouting. Curse words, spoken in rage. Or frustration? She opened her mouth to call to him then closed it again.

She must have made a sound though, for he froze, arm in mid-air, ready to hurl another rock into the sea. Turning slowly, he lowered his hand and fixed his eyes on her. He mouthed her name.

Brianna lifted her chin and smiled. "Well, then. Are you going to stand there and stare, or are you going to welcome me as a good husband should?"

Harrison threw back his head and squeezed his eyes shut. Brianna saw his lips moving but couldn't hear his words. He lowered his head then and pierced her with a level look as he strode toward her. She met him halfway. Then he swept her into his arms and twirled her in a circle until she was dizzy. He stopped abruptly and lowered her to the ground. He released her, only to reach inside the opening of the voluminous coat and clasp her hips in his hands. "Wife," he murmured, pulling her against his pelvis.

"Husband," she whispered. She wound her arms around his waist and held on tight. He lowered his head and kissed her fiercely. She relaxed against his strong body. Oh, she'd missed it so much, his body and his touch. When he eventually released her and raised his head, he was grinning foolishly.

"Christmas," he said. "We'll marry that day, in two weeks' time." He frowned. "I'm afraid it will have to be immediate family only, Brianna. In your condition, well..."

She chuckled. "It's all right! A small, intimate wedding would be lovely."

Harrison scowled then and held her hands away from her body. "I can't believe, in your condition, you traveled all this way. What were you thinking of? Something could have happened to you or to our baby."

Grinning, she said, "Do you know this is the first time you've referred to our child as our baby and not your heir? I think there's a chance things may work out fine between us, my lord."

Growling, he swept her up into his arms. "Don't do

anything so foolish again. Otherwise, I'll regret having thrown away my grandfather's paddle!"

She just laughed as he held her in his arms. When his kisses grew more intimate, she stiffened her arms and pressed her palms against his chest.

He released her and she stood before him, scowling.

"What's wrong?" he asked.

"We've more to discuss before we allow ourselves to be frivolous."

"Frivolous? Hmm, I don't believe I've ever heard making love defined quite that way."

She paced across the snow, first in one direction, then the other. Eventually, she turned to him and said, "I know you are exceedingly proud of yourself at this moment, but I beg you to stop and think about my feelings. I will be just shy of twenty-eight when this child is born, and I haven't done a blasted thing with my life yet!"

"Well," Harrison began then cleared his throat. "I would say that birthing three children is certainly doing something with one's life. What more could you possibly want?"

"Before we discuss my wants and desires for the future, I'd like to discuss something else first, Harrison. I truly have no desire to have more children." She looked at him, considering. "Perhaps I won't need to ask Dr. Benson's advice. After all, since you are a physician, I assume you must have some idea how to prevent conception."

Harrison stared down at her. "You are not serious."

"I most certainly am. I can't very well pursue my goals for the future if I keep getting pregnant, can I?"

Brianna could see he really didn't want to have this conversation. He confirmed it when he suggested, "Why don't I make us some tea?"

She started walking back to the cottage. "I'll make the

tea while you find yourself that drink you seem to desperately need at the moment," she said dryly.

Inside the cottage, Harrison poured himself two fingers of Scotch whisky, then sat down at the table across from her. "Being a wife and mother to our children should be work enough for any woman, but I want you to be happy, sweetheart."

"I don't want any more children, Harrison," she said firmly.

Sinking back in his chair, he evaluated his own feelings on the matter. In his and most men's minds, it was a woman's responsibility to breed children, until nature prevented them from doing so. Yet, to answer Brianna's earlier question regarding conception, he did know of ways to prevent pregnancy. He'd aided countless women in the matter; from prostitutes to lords' wives, but with their husband's consent, of course.

Brianna's feelings about pregnancy and birth weren't all that unusual. As much as he would enjoy having more children, he decided three would do. He prayed she'd give him the son he required, and then he'd be quite content with one son and his nephews.

"I'll adjust to the idea of having only three children. Eventually. I admit I am worried that the child you are carrying is a girl. We'll lose all the MacAulay holdings if this is the case."

With a nod Brianna said, "No need to worry." She cupped her hands around her abdomen. "This child is a son. I can feel it."

"But how can you be sure?"

She shrugged. "Intuition, I suppose. I admit I will be surprised if this is a girl."

He clasped her hands and smiled. "So, what else do you want from life, Brianna?"

She squeezed his hands. "I know you're not fond of your grandmothers' and aunt's involvement in the temperance movement, but it greatly interests me. And, I believe I have something to contribute. Providing education for women regarding the use of contraceptives would be beneficial. Yes, that would be a worthwhile thing to do. Oh, my! The Lord above is likely fuming at this very moment at my words. He'll forgive me, don't you think?" she asked worriedly.

Harrison grinned. "I can't say about your God, Brianna, but you've done your duty as a good wife should."

"Then I shall count on you to educate me in the matter. I'd also like you to provide medical services for women in need. Once I learn about contraception, I'd like to hold classes, if you will, to educate women about their choices."

"That is a wonderful idea. Although I will caution you that you will not find some of the husbands particularly happy with the information you will be providing their wives. Things could turn quite ugly."

"What if these men believed the information was coming from you?"

"Now, wait just a minute. You mean to place my hide in the line of fire, then?" he retorted. "This is your vocation, wife, not mine."

"But you agree that we shouldn't have more children."

"Yes, but that's our choice, and has nothing to do with other men and women."

"So, you won't help me?"

Harrison sighed. "I'm not saying that at all. We've made our decision, together, as a husband and wife should. I believe that others should come to their decision in the same manner. It can't just be a woman's decision."

"In some instances it may need to be," she said abruptly.

"A few, perhaps. The important thing is that we educate

husbands along with their wives, which I've done over the past several years, on a limited basis."

Brianna's eyes widened. "Truly?"

He came to his feet. "Yes. I'll inform you not another physician in all of Edinburgh would even consider doing such a heinous thing. I believe in contraception, Brianna. I grew tired of finding more and more homeless children on the streets with no one to care for them."

Brianna stood and wrapped her arms around his waist. "Oh, but this is wonderful." She tilted her head back and grinned.

"One thing more," he said, tapping her nose gently. "I draw the line at aborting fetuses. I will not kill, Brianna. I save lives, not end them."

"I understand and completely agree." She stepped back. "When may I begin my education? How long do you think it will be before I'm qualified to teach others?"

He grinned, took her hand and pulled her down the hallway. "We may begin right this moment, wife," he softly replied.

She followed him, running to keep up with his long strides. "Wonderful! But you have no study materials here, have you? And why would we study in the bedchamber?"

Pulling her in behind him he shut and locked the bedchamber door then eased her into his arms. Holding her close, he kissed her until she went limp. Then she wound her arms around his neck. He smiled, satisfied with the languid expression on her face.

"We don't need books and manuals. You see this is precisely where all necessary instruction in this delicate matter begins and ends. And since we don't have to worry about pregnancy at the moment with you already breeding, it's the perfect time for me to demonstrate how to not get pregnant."

Brianna frowned. "Without any books?"

"Not one," he said his grin widening.

Harrison drew his independent American wife into his arms, lowered her to the bed, eager and willing to teach her everything she would ever need to know about the subject.

Much later, as Harrison walked the cliffs, his arms around Brianna, he stilled when she said, "I'd like to go home, Harrison."

He shoved up his spectacles and tried swallowing the lump in his throat. "Home?" he asked with uncertainty. Not America again!

"To Winterhaven."

He narrowed his eyes on her dimpled smile. "You little vixen," he murmured, reaching for her. She had known perfectly well her request would cause him worry. She laughed merrily, and ran back to the cottage. He darted after her.

CHAPTER 18

*T*he next day they traveled back to Winterhaven. The journey was torturous for Brianna. It was late afternoon when they arrived home. Her body ached from head to toe. The gnawing pain in her stomach was definitely worrisome. She didn't say a word to Harrison, though. There was no sense both of them worrying, at least not until she determined whether she was in early labor or not. She was excited to birth this baby, yet she had an awful feeling, as well. Nearly two months early, the baby, if born now, might not survive.

Harrison set her down on the edge of the bed in one of the guestrooms. "This will do until after you've delivered."

Brianna looked up at him from her position, tears welling in her eyes. Why was he being so cool all of a sudden? They'd laughed and talked the entire trip home. Now it seemed as though he wanted to rid himself of her. "But, don't you want me in your room?"

He stalked to the door, opened it and paused. He stared at her and she knew what was wrong. His words confirmed his expression. "I don't want to take any chances with your health this far along in the pregnancy." He raked his hair back with unsteady fingers, his gaze lingering on hers. "Don't you understand how much I want you with me? I should never have made love to you last evening. This far along, well, anything could happen. We just can't take that chance. I'll bring a tray up with your supper."

"Wait!" she called, not willing to end the conversation. He hadn't, though. She laid back on the bed, deep in thought. She smiled as she thought about last evening and their lovemaking. Her smile slipped when she realized how guilty he'd feel if she were in labor.

Night had fallen, and with it came more snow. She slept the afternoon away, and then, true to his word, Harrison had a meal delivered to her room. She ate sparingly of the boiled potatoes and roasted chicken. Setting the tray aside, she stared out the window at the falling snowflakes. Her eyes started closing so she lay down on her bed and fell asleep.

She wakened some time later when a sharp pain knifed through her stomach. Her hands encircled her distended abdomen. She sat in the rocker, waiting for another pain. Soon she found she needed to concentrate on her breathing. Babies were unpredictable as to when they decided to arrive. Even though it was early, it was time. She called out, "Harrison! Come quickly!"

As she paced the floor, the sound of pounding feet on the stairs calmed her. She needed Harrison. Oh, my Lord! He was going to be so disappointed they hadn't married yet. The door opened and slammed against the wall just as another pain caused her to groan. There was something wrong. The pains were coming one right after the other. She couldn't lose this baby! This labor was different from Harry and Jamie. Her pains were coming too fast, and too hard.

Harrison rushed into the room just as she grasped the bedpost.

In two long strides, he arrived at her side. He wound his arms around her and held her against him. "Brianna? It's time?"

"Yes!" she whispered harshly, her fingers digging into his shoulders. "You'd better send for Dr. Benson, immediately." She gritted her teeth and clenched her fists against the pain.

"Relax," he said soothingly. He settled her on the bed beside him and ignored her request.

"I'm trying. Oh, Harrison, I'm worried." Tears flooded her eyes. "It's too soon."

Grandmother Mary stuck her head inside the room. Harry and Jamie's heads appeared below her in the doorway's opening.

Brianna met Mary's surprised look. "Please, send for Dr. Benson or I'm afraid this baby will be born on his head."

Grandmother Mary gave Harrison a worried look. "It's rather soon, isn't it?"

Harrison nodded. "It could be. You won't need to call for Dr. Benson. Just fetch my bag, and bring boiling water."

"Certainly! Come boys. Yer mother and uncle will be busy for a bit. We don't want to disturb them. In due time ye'll have a new brother or sister."

With an arm around Brianna's waist Harrison stood and raised her up with him. "Let's walk a bit, shall we?"

She glared up at him as he started guiding her around the room. She clutched her stomach. "You must be joking! Do I look like I'm in any sort of condition to move about? I just want to lie down," she groaned.

"You will, in due time." He frowned. "Didn't your doctor in America tell you to stay on your feet and walk as long as possible? Until you couldn't bear the pain any longer?"

Brianna's eyes widened. "Why, no. He tucked me into bed with instructions to lie still until it was time to push."

She frowned. "As I recall I was very feeble at the pushing. I was so exhausted."

"How long were your labors?"

"Only six hours or so, a bit longer with Harry. Oh! And I remember being very sick from the laudanum."

"Laudanum!" he shouted. "What was the man thinking?" Harrison growled. "What sort of doctor was he? And where was Payton through all of this?"

"Why, up north cutting down trees," she said.

"No woman about to deliver a baby should be given drugs, especially not laudanum, unless there was a need for surgery. It's no wonder you couldn't push. You won't have that problem this time."

Another pain overtook her and she paused and breathed in and out slowly, as he directed. Oh, but it was wonderful having Harrison with her, she thought as she commenced pacing the floor. She held onto his shirt and he held her up with a strong arm around her waist.

Grandmother Mary returned with his bag and the boiling water.

Brianna walked for another hour, until she finally collapsed on the bed. He bent to pull her to her feet when she stiffened her arms and leaned back. "I can't take another step, Harrison!" She gasped, curled her knees to her chest and rolled to her side. "Oh, the baby is coming!"

He started unbuttoning her bodice. She grasped his hands and shook her head as heat seeped into her cheeks. She knew she must look as bad as she felt. Even last evening, when he'd made love to her, she'd insisted he extinguish the lamp.

"You will be more comfortable in your night dress. Besides, all these infernal skirts and petticoats you women insist upon wearing only get in the way."

She saw the sense of that so she allowed him to help her

out of her layers of clothing and into a soft white gown. Harrison moved to the end of the bed and said, "Lift your knees and spread your legs, sweetheart. I'm going to wash up, then examine you."

She stayed on her side and kept her legs clamped together. "That is precisely how I got into this condition in the first place. Just leave me alone," she groaned.

He moved around the bed, leaned over her and gently stroked her hair off her forehead. "Look at me, Brianna."

She met his gaze and saw the love in his eyes. "Do you trust me? Do you believe I'll not allow any harm to come to you or to our child?"

She stared into his eyes for the longest time before replying, "Yes, of course I do."

"Then let me help you."

She nodded, swiped at her tears and said, "Never again, my lord. This is the last baby I'll be having."

She lay on her back and watched him remove his coat and tie, draping them over the back of a chair. He washed his hands and dried them on a cloth. Then he sat down beside her and rolled up the sleeves of his fine linen shirt. His medically trained gaze roamed her body, assessing her condition.

"You'd better change that fine shirt or it'll be ruined," she warned him.

"This shirt is of no consequence to me. Now be a good girl and allow me to examine you."

A pain came again. Her eyes widened and she groaned, "Oh, I have to push!" She dug her heels into the bedclothes and arched her back, gasping for breath.

"Relax. Breath slow, easy breaths," he encouraged her, rubbing her stomach.

After the pain subsided, she scowled and said, "I'm trying, but it's not easy."

"I know you are. Believe me. I'd do anything to be the one in that bed taking that pain for you. I can't believe this is happening." He grinned. "It seems I've waited a lifetime to be a father." He sighed. "Unfortunately, it's too bad we hadn't married first."

She clutched his hand and smiled through the pain. "Oh, but we have, darling. In our hearts and minds, we are legally wed. Now, examine me and let me know if you can see our child." She raised her legs and spread them wide, her gaze focused on his handsome face.

Instead of moving to the foot of the bed, he stayed at her side, and leaned over her to press one large palm on her lower stomach. His other hand he moved to her core where he inserted two fingers inside her channel. With the other hand, he pressed down on her stomach.

Brianna slammed her eyes shut as another pain came. "My God, that hurts!" she gasped, trying to evade his fingers.

"I'm sorry," he said, easing his fingers from her. "I know it does, but it won't be long now. I felt the baby's head. It's right there, Brianna."

Tears filled her eyes. "It hurts something awful, Harrison! Where is the laudanum?"

He rose and moved to the end of the bed. He took a seat on the ottoman, which placed him in a perfect position to deliver a baby. Brianna only realized now that someone had removed the bed's foot rail.

"You don't need medicine, Brianna. It's time to push with all your might."

Brianna heard his excited tone and smiled through the pains as she pushed half a dozen times and her baby slid into the welcoming hands of his father. Cameron Frasier MacAulay, the seventh Laird MacAulay was born, big and healthy and squalling at the top of his lungs.

A euphoric, relieved feeling overwhelmed Brianna. She smiled at the baby Harrison held as he examined him. Then she looked in to her husband's white-faced, stunned expression and she laughed outright. Her eyes misted over when he gave her a boyish grin and sat down beside her with the baby cradled in one big hand. Until her dying day, Brianna would always remember the reverent look on his face as he stared at his son. Laying the child across her stomach, he returned to the end of the bed and finished tending to her needs.

"He's beautiful, Brianna," he murmured, as he put the afterbirth into a bowl his grandmother had provided.

"He's too young to protest now, but I do believe he'd strongly object to being called beautiful as he grows older."

Harrison's tender smile tugged at her heart. She stilled when he returned to her side and settled his lips on hers. As he moved back, he said, "Thank you, Brianna."

He looked at his son again and Brianna swallowed the lump in her throat. "He's the longest of my sons at birth, I'll give him that, and it appears he may be the heaviest, as well." She frowned. "Which makes me believe that I hadn't lost the baby when I first thought I was pregnant. But I did bleed. I don't understand it at all."

"Sometimes it happens that way," he said softly, his eyes on the baby. "I was large at birth."

The baby squirmed, then screamed and flailed his arms and legs. Harrison quickly handed him to Brianna. "I believe he's searching for something I am not equipped to provide," he said dryly.

Brianna set him to her breast and she blushed at Harrison's overt interest.

"You do that so..."

"So?"

"Efficiently."

She grinned. "I've had a lot of practice, even though it's been well over eight years. You know, Harrison, you amaze me."

He raised his brow. "Do I?"

"Yes. You remained steadfast and self-assured throughout your son's birth. You were a veritable rock throughout the entire process."

He gave her a wry smile. "You wouldn't think that if you knew how many babies I've assisted into the world."

"Yes, but it's quite different when it's your child being born, wouldn't you say?"

"I'll admit to a bit of apprehension, sweet. If I appeared as strong as a rock, you were as steady as the Cuillin Mountains. Not in size, but in strength of will and heart. I owe you greatly, Brianna, for the rest of my life."

"Yes, I believe you do, my lord." She grinned suggestively. "Most definitely."

"I love you, Brianna MacAulay," he murmured. He lowered his head, ready to take her upturned lips when the door opened. They broke apart just when Harry peeked inside.

"Is he here yet?"

They laughed and Harrison said, "Come meet your new brother."

EPILOGUE

Christmas Day 1889
Winterhaven Manor

*B*rianna grasped the bedpost as her maid tightened the strings on a lightly boned corset. Once Jeanne tied the bow, Brianna faced the full-length mirror.

"That's tight enough. The dress should fit well, yet allow me enough room to breathe, I think."

Jeanne stepped forward with the wedding gown draped over her arm. She tossed it over Brianna's head. Brianna was lost amidst yards of satin and lace when she heard the door burst open.

"Wesley can't get this blasted stud fastened," said Harrison. "I've tried but my fingers are too large. Could you help...stop!"

Brianna poked her head out of the neckline and met Harrison's scowling face in the mirror. He hadn't tucked his crisp white shirt into his kilt yet. She admired his dark furred chest visible in the shirt's gaping opening.

He moved up behind her, undid Jeanne's work, and tossed the corset to the floor. Brianna took a deep breath and silently admitted to being grateful he'd removed the torture device.

He leveled his eyes on her. "You are still mending, Brianna. No corsets yet, if ever."

Brianna smiled when he pulled her against his chest and stared at their reflection in the mirror. She asked saucily, "How would you like to stay and assist me into the gown?"

He gave a curt nod and turned to her maid. "We won't need you, Jeanne."

Jeanne's face turned pink as she curtsied and left the bedchamber.

Harrison turned to Brianna and guided her arms into the long sleeves. He pulled the dress over her breasts, smoothed it down around her waist and hips then buttoned the first of several tiny satin-covered buttons running down her spine. When he reached her waistline, he paused.

"Ah, I see why you needed the stays," he said. "Let's get you into it, again, although I hate the damned things."

When he finished he stepped back and looked at her in the mirror. Brianna stared at her reflection, dismayed to find the front of the dress was tight across her bosom and the waistline snug, even with the stays.

She shook her head. "This won't do, Harrison. And it's such a lovely gown," she wailed. "You must lace me up tighter."

"You look beautiful, sweetheart," he murmured, then lowered his head and nibbled on one earlobe. "I am enamored of your curves, wife," he murmured.

"It was a wise idea you had, getting married here at

Winterhaven. Still, I'll be so embarrassed I won't be able to take a step down the stairs."

"I'll carry you, sweetheart."

She laughed. "Hardly! As you well know, I'm not a petite woman. I dare say you won't be able to lift even one limb."

He raised his brow. "Are you doubting my masculine prowess?"

She smiled at him sweetly. "I'd *never* doubt that."

Harrison laughed heartily, then took her in his arms and drew her tight against him, blessing her with a bruising kiss. He raised his head. "I'll leave you to finish your toilette, unless you would like me to stay?"

"No, thank you. But wait. I believe you came looking for assistance. Give me the stud."

He dug into his pocket, pulled out the black pearl fastener.

Brianna fastened it, saying, "Luckily, fashion dictates only one."

"Yes, luckily," he said softly. He made to claim her lips but she stepped back, pressed her palms against his chest.

The door suddenly burst open and Harry tumbled in. "Come on, Ma and Uncle, everyone's downstairs waiting for you!"

"We're almost ready," Brianna replied.

Jamie came scampering into the room and rammed into Harry's back. Before either adult could react, they started wrestling on the bed until the covers hung off one edge.

Harrison shouted, "Boys! Haven't I told you before that there'll be no roughhousing on the beds? Now make it up the way you found it," he ordered.

The boys hurriedly followed his orders. They made up the bed, albeit not perfectly.

Harry asked, "Is it done right, Uncle?"

"Perfectly," Harrison replied with a smile. "Now go to the library and work on your studies until we are ready."

"Yes sir," they said in unison, and fled the room.

Brianna sighed. "They listen to you. More importantly, they obey you."

"Now that I'm their father, I'll correct them in their errors, and you may continue to be their gentle, loving mother."

She liked that idea. It would be nice not to nag at them about their responsibilities. That's precisely what she'd been forced to do in the past. Harrison merely spoke a few words and they immediately complied with his requests. She smiled at him and placed her palms against his chest. Tilting her head back, she met his gaze and saw the heated look in his silver eyes.

"You know, you shouldn't have instructed them in those ridiculous tussling moves if you didn't want them behaving like undisciplined little urchins."

His face split into a wide grin. "It's called wrestling and Highlanders have been enjoying the sport for years." He stepped back and held her hands in his, as he looked her over from head to toe. "You make a beautiful bride, and I'd like nothing better than to ravish you at the moment," he said softly.

"You are quite ravishing yourself, my lord. I especially like the skirt."

He gave a raucous laugh. "What? Is that envy I hear in your voice?"

"Hardly!" She looked at his knees. "Unfortunately, women aren't allowed to expose that part of their anatomy, or much of any other portion for that matter. You have no idea how my knees compare with yours."

"If you will recall, I've seen your knees on occasion. Now

would be the perfect time to see how yours do measure against mine."

She squeaked and skipped away from him, but wasn't quick enough. He hauled her down across the foot of the bed and shoved up her gown. Her full skirts blossomed around her waist. She pressed the mass down when it threatened to engulf her face.

"Harrison, you are mad! You're going to crease my gown before the wedding, now stop it this instant."

He shoved up one leg of her fine silk drawers and exposed her knee.

"Stop!" She shouted when he found the ticklish spot there behind her knee, setting her into wild, uncontrollable laughter.

The pins in her hair came loose. She reached up to secure one when he launched into another attack, his deft fingers going for her armpits. The merriment ended and they both turned at the insistent rapping at the door.

Harrison placed a finger to his lips and called out, "Yes?"

"Laird?" Stanton asked. "Everyone is waitin' for the two of ye. Now stop that tusslin' and come along! The Priest's been here half an hour already."

Brianna grinned at Harrison. "See? Didn't I say the proper word was tussling?"

"No, not tussling, but tusslin'," Harrison replied. "Ye see ye must drop the last..."

She squirmed out from under his heavy body with a laugh and jumped off the bed. "If you have any intentions of marrying and making an honest woman of me we'd better get down to business. After all, we don't want society saying Cam is a bastard child, now do we?"

He lurched off the bed. "Don't suggest such a horrid thing." He straightened his spectacles, ran a shaky hand through his hair, and departed.

After their wedding Mass and exchanged vows in the library. Harrison's Aunt Marianne had planned a lavish celebration for them in the ballroom. She'd invited far more guests than either Brianna or Harrison had wanted, or expected. Brianna received many requests for dances. Harrison was thoroughly disgusted when half the night passed and he still hadn't danced with his wife. He knew precisely when she'd reached the end of her endurance, so he guided her into the library late in the evening.

"But I can't just leave our guests," she protested. "It wouldn't be polite."

"You've celebrated enough for five weddings," he informed her. "Now stay here and rest while I encourage our guests to leave. I'll return shortly."

Brianna stood in the center of the library, her hands on her hips. "I should be the last one to leave our reception, not the first."

He pointed at a large velvet chair. "You, my lady, are exhausted. Now sit down before you fall down on your pretty...just sit."

"You are impossible," she exclaimed. "You know how I detest your controlling ways. I won't stand for it."

"What do ye plan to do?" He leaned a shoulder against the door and folded his arms.

She knew then there was no arguing with the headstrong man. She lifted her chin. "I'll rest for five minutes, no more, then return to the last of our guests as a good hostess should."

He merely shrugged. "You will do what you need to do, I suppose." Then he left and closed the door behind him.

Brianna wondered at his seemingly casual tone, but sat on the edge of the chair. She closed her eyes and rested, listening to the ticking of the clock. After a few moments, she stood, shook out her skirts and made her way to the door. She tried turning the knob, but it wouldn't.

She frowned. "What in the world?" After a few more tries she stared at the knob, realizing he'd locked her in.

"Damn you, Harrison MacAulay!" She slammed the heel of her hand against the door and shouted again. The orchestra was still playing so she knew it was unlikely anyone heard her.

Furious, she threw herself into her chair. A blazing fire crackled on the hearth, and the heat made her feel warm and drowsy. There was nothing for her to do but rest. She gazed into the fire until she couldn't keep her eyes open any longer. She turned sideways and laid her head down upon the chair's arm.

An hour later, Harrison found his bride curled up like a small kitten in the deep velvet chair. He'd grown impatient for their guests to leave, finally venting his frustration on the last few, who luckily happened to be good friends. They'd laughed and slapped him on the back, obviously in their cups. As he'd ushered them to the door, he'd taken their lewd remarks in good stride, knowing they would pay the price for their over-indulgence the next morning.

It had been a merry celebration, one people would remember years later.

Harrison stood over his bride, noting the fine sheet of perspiration on her upper lip. He couldn't resist stroking the bottom of one prettily arched, silken foot. He grinned when she squeezed her toes together in her sleep. She must be exhausted, he decided as he continued the light, stroking movement. He knew she was ticklish

He gradually slid his hand up the back of her calf, delighted to discover she'd removed her undergarments. His fingers travelled farther up her leg, across the incredibly soft back of her thigh. He stopped when she jerked in her sleep. He continued on his journey, reaching the top of her limb and moved inward. His hand reached the apex of her legs, and went on to her woman's center, where he proceeded to stroke her ever so gently.

She writhed, her eyes closed, and gasped at his touch. Her breathing quickened. Within an embarrassingly short time, she stiffened and uttered a small shriek when she found her release.

Harrison felt his own burgeoning arousal, felt his control slipping when she opened her eyes and gave him a drowsy smile.

Everyone's gone?" She sounded breathless.

He nodded. Without a word, he plucked her up easily in his arms and strode to the door. Heat spread up his neck and over his face as he flung open the door and took the stairs two at a time.

"Darling? I'm too heavy for you! Your face is red."

His answer was a short grunt. He reached the top of the stairs, strode down the hallway to their bedchamber. With a growl, he fairly dropped her in the center of the bed. "Don't move."

Quickly he lit the lamps, so that the room held a soft, golden glow. When Brianna started to sit upright, he stopped her with a sharp, "I told you not to move." He stripped the end of the kilt off his shoulder. He tore off his shirt and tossed it in the general direction of a chair across the room. His hands reached down to remove his kilt, but he paused when the shape beneath it caught his eye—evidence of the effect his wife had on him.

He whipped the pleated wool from his loins, and heard Brianna's gasp. Then he was with her, his hands on her corseted waist. "Turn over," he commanded. When she did, he quickly unbuttoned the dress, in his impatience tearing one button free. As it hit the floor with a tiny ping, he stripped the bodice from her and tore the corset laces open.

"Harrison, stop!" she cried, when he rolled her onto her back. "My gown...you're ruining it!"

"I'll buy you another," he said, his mouth dry. His eager hands unwound her from the yards of silk and tulle. Her skin gleamed like precious gold. Tossing the skirt and petticoats aside, he ran his hands along the length of her legs, feeling her heat. She was fire, she was satin, she was all things beautiful and exciting.

She was his wife.

"I love you, wife of mine," he said. Then he drew her into his arms, where she belonged.

THE END

Don't miss out on your next favorite book!

Join the Satin Romance mailing list
www.satinromance.com/mail.html

THANK YOU FOR READING

Did you enjoy this book?

We invite you to leave a review at your favorite book site, such as Goodreads, Amazon, Barnes & Noble, etc.

DID YOU KNOW THAT LEAVING A REVIEW...

- Helps other readers find books they may enjoy.
- Gives you a chance to let your voice be heard.
- Gives authors recognition for their hard work.
- Doesn't have to be long. A sentence or two about why you liked the book will do.

ABOUT THE AUTHOR

Nancy Schumacher is the owner-publisher of Melange Books, LLC, writing under the pseudonyms, Nancy Pirri and Natasha Perry. Nancy started writing nineteen years ago while raising four children. She is a member of Romance Writers of America. She is also one of the founders of the Minnesota RWA chapter, Northern Lights Writers (NLW).

She has written five full-length novels, and many stories included in anthologies with Melange Books, LLC.

www.nancypirri.com

facebook.com/NancyPirriAuthor

ALSO BY NANCY PIRRI

Montana Women

Katie and the Marshal

Annie and the Outlaw

Janie and the Judge

Laura and the Railroad Baron

The Montana Women Boxset (Books 1-4)

Contemporary Romance

Bait Shop Blue

All I Ever Wanted

I Wish You Love, a Spicy Romance Anthology

Make Me Behave (An Anthology) with Tara Fox Hall

Western Romance

Rugged Edges

Historical Romance

The MacAulay Bride

The Duke and the Lady Sleuth

A Husband For Christmas

Featured in the following anthologies:

Western Ways

Food and Romance Go Together, Vol. 2

Writing erotica as Natasha Perry

Ruined Hearts

Maid of His Heart